PRAISE FOR CHRIS WOODING

THE HAUNTING OF ALAIZABEL CRAY

"one of the most intelligent novels ~~published~~ ... in recent years ... brea..."

"enormously inventive ... and suspense than a ... missed" *... Telegraph*

"shiveringly exciting" *The Times*

STORM THIEF

"[a] powerful blend of thriller, science fiction and fantasy" *TES*

"all the compelling paranoia of a fever-based fantasy" *Books For Keeps*

"dizzying imaginative detail with action-adventure ... for kids who find fiction second-best to Playstation games, Wooding is ideal" *The Times*

POISON

"breathlessly exciting" *Guardian*

"thrilling" *TES*

"Wooding's explosive visual imagination knows no bounds" *The Times*

C333776202

CHRIS WOODING

VELOCITY

Scholastic Children's Books
An imprint of Scholastic Ltd
Euston House, 24 Eversholt Street,
London, NW1 1DB, UK
Registered office: Westfield Road, Southam, Warwickshire, CV47 0RA
SCHOLASTIC and associated logos are trademarks and/
or registered trademarks of Scholastic Inc.

First published in the UK by Scholastic Ltd, 2015

Text copyright © Chris Wooding, 2015

The right of Chris Wooding to be identified as the
author of this work has been asserted by him.

ISBN 978 1407 12429 2

A CIP catalogue record for this book
is available from the British Library.

Printed by CPI Group (UK) Ltd, Croydon, CR0 4YY
Papers used by Scholastic Children's Books are made
from wood grown in sustainable forests.

1 3 5 7 9 10 8 6 4 2

This is a work of fiction. Names, characters, places, incidents and dialogues are
products of the author's imagination or are used fictitiously. Any resemblance to
actual people, living or dead, events or locales is entirely coincidental.

www.scholastic.co.uk

CHRIS WOODING

VELOCITY

SCHOLASTIC

01

Over the line, into the final lap, ambushed by the rough raw howl of the crowd. The bleachers were a dusty smear, faces lost in blurred chaos, gone in a moment. Then there was only the race.

Cassica slid up through the gears as they sped along the straight, chasing down second place. Her eyes were calm, mind all angles as she drifted across the track to find the line into the next corner. She was never so still as when she was racing. Only in the driving seat did she know exactly where she was.

Shiara, strapped in the seat beside her, had her eyes on the dash. Needles quivered behind grimy windows; counters rolled with numbers. Everything was moving there, everything alive, reporting from the hot heart of the car. Her car, built with her own hands. Maisie was a mongrel of so many parts that nobody could tell which had come from what. Nobody but Shiara.

The leaders jockeyed for position beneath the low red glare of a poisoned sun, tyres billowing parched and powdered earth. Ahead, the track swerved left, lost behind a rock outcrop the colour of rust. They took the corner and were gone.

"Wreck ahead, right side," Shiara called over the noise of the engine. "Trim your line."

Cassica's face was unreadable behind her goggles and the dirty bandana that covered her mouth and nose. Likely she needed no reminder; Shiara reminded her anyway. It would only take one little slip to finish them.

Cassica decelerated hard, dropping down gears as they hit the corner. The track lifted beneath them and tipped out of sight. They took the rise just slow enough to keep all four wheels on the dirt, then plunged down the other side.

Lying half off the side of the track was the ruin of a Jackrabbit, tail buckled after it almost backflipped coming off that rise with turbos firing. The driver and his tech were safe, having scrambled clear, but the car remained as an obstacle to the unwary.

Cassica slipped past it without a glance. Shiara spared a moment to check her mirrors and saw the car behind them cresting the rise, too far to the right. They'd forgotten about the wreck. The driver's attempt to correct their course as they skidded down the slope was desperate but doomed. The car clipped the wreck, fishtailed, and went into a bouncing roll, shedding fenders, wheels and engine panels as it flipped and leaped, until it was consumed in a cloud of red dust.

"Scratch the Desert Wolf in camo paint," said Shiara flatly.

The track dived and swooped through the cracked hardpan of the badlands, now dipping into a dry gully, now rising to show them the wide, shattered plain all around. Eerie guardians overlooked them, ancient stones worn by the wind into shapes watchful and menacing.

Five laps in, Cassica knew the course by now. She knew the corners where she could shave off half a second, where to ease off the speed and where to hit the gas. But the racers ahead of her knew those things too, and she couldn't gain ground.

"What've you got?" she demanded of Shiara.

Shiara was studying the miniature route map stuck to the dash, a squiggle of lines without detail. Ahead, the track split, one way obviously shorter than the other. They'd learned on previous laps that the shorter way was packed with obstacles and the longer route was smoother. One was better for vehicles made for quick turns, the other for speed merchants.

As ever with these unofficial boondock circuits, there was a trick to the track. A cut-through, not marked on the map. Shiara, sharp-eyed, had spotted it before anyone else had. It allowed them to take the shorter route but switch off it before they hit the worst of the obstacles, saving them precious seconds. They'd made a lot of ground that way before the others caught on.

Shiara brushed away a whipping frond of milk-white hair that had escaped her helmet, her brow furious with concentration as she tried to calculate a better route. "Left," she said at last, defeated. "Take the cut-through."

Cassica shot her a frustrated glance. She needed something better, a way to claw back the advantage and get ahead of the competition. Shiara had nothing to give her.

The track divided, split by a tall wedge of rock. The two cars ahead took the left route. In the lead was Guyden Cross, a local kid, slight and well-mannered with a rich daddy who had bought him that C9 Quantum he drove. His car was faster than theirs, low and flat and built for speed, dirty cream with dark red flanks and spoilers. Pushing him from behind was Ren Tubbock in a scarred black Terrorizer, its tail bristling with exhausts. Tubbock was a Mohawked thug and drove like a bully, but the Terrorizer's wide axle and superior suspension won him a fraction of a second every corner he took.

Maisie, built on a shoestring, couldn't compete on

specs. So that just left them with skill and smarts to win it.

Pillars of scrap crowded the track ahead of them, decayed girders driven into the ground, a forest of metal with earth walls to either side. Cross and Tubbock darted in, swerving and sliding, throwing up dirt. Cassica followed, slamming the wheel left and right, riding the skids as metal columns flashed past her with a thump of air. Then Cross pulled hard right, driving towards the wall, and disappeared behind a bulge of rock. Tubbock went next and Cassica after, rounding the obstruction. Beyond, hidden, a narrow fissure drew them in.

Hot wind, exhaust fumes and stinging dust blew over them. The bellow of the engines became a low threatening roar. Maisie rattled and shook; Shiara hung on to her roll cage. Stone shouldered in close. Just a tap on their flanks and they'd never reach the light at the end.

It was a matter of moments, but they stretched like snakes.

Then they were out, bursting into the bruised light of the morning, skidding hard and shedding rubber as Maisie's wheels scrabbled for grip. They tore away with open track ahead of them, and they hadn't made an inch on their opponents.

"Give me something!" Cassica snapped.

Shiara didn't need telling. Up ahead was a short run along a dry riverbed. They were down

5

on turbo fuel, just enough for one good burst in the final straight. Maisie's settings were already at optimum; no wriggle room there. Opportunities for improvement looked slim. They'd have to rely on their opponents making mistakes, and that was a bad situation to be in.

They took the curve leading down to the riverbed: a smooth-sided trench, its surface crazed with cracks. The terrain favoured Cross's faster car; he'd gain time on them. Tubbock's Terrorizer was at least as fast as Maisie was. The other racers were so far in the dust that Shiara couldn't find them in her mirror.

Third place, then. But that wouldn't be good enough. Not for Cassica, anyway.

In the distance, another route peeled off left, rising away from the riverbed. The first of three exits. Cassica traced it with her eye, following the hump of land until it split, a knife-slash gap in the track through which the mad sun glowered.

"No," said Shiara, following her gaze. "Can't do it. Maisie ain't fast enough."

"We can win it if we make that jump. We'll get ahead of them."

"Can't do it."

"Says you. Nobody's tried."

"She ain't capable. Wishin' won't make it otherwise."

Cassica stared ahead resentfully as the exit neared.

Shiara turned her attention back to the dash, the matter settled.

Then Cassica slammed the wheel to the left, throwing Shiara against her belts, and Maisie slewed out of the riverbed and up the exit ramp.

Shiara turned to Cassica in horror and alarm. But Cassica's eyes were hard behind her goggles, and Shiara knew that look. No sense in argument, no question of pulling out. She was decided.

"Make it happen," said Cassica.

Shiara set herself to it. Angle of ramp, length of approach, distance to jump, all unknown. Nobody had tried it because nobody wanted to risk it. Maybe it was easier than it looked, maybe harder. Some track designers had a sadistic streak, and the crowd liked a crash. You never knew till you went for it.

But get it wrong, and you'd like as not cripple yourself. If you came out breathing at all.

She searched her mind for solutions as they hurtled up the incline into the sun. Heart thumping, face burning, it was hard to keep thoughts in her head. She calculated trajectory and weight, theories flashing through her mind, discarding ideas, reworking them. The readouts on the dash gave her everything but an answer.

The jump rushed towards them. Instinct made the choice for her. She twisted a dial, hit a switch. Everything to the turbos, all at once, one huge compressed burst of speed. Probably they'd blow the engine or backflip Maisie and land her on her roof, but either was better than falling short.

"Turbos, on my go," she said.

Cassica's thumb shifted to hover over the red button on the wheel grip. The lip of the jump charged at them, close enough now so Shiara could guess at the angle. She delayed another split second to compensate, then:

"Now."

The word was barely formed before Cassica pressed down with her thumb. Maisie's turbos detonated with a sound like sudden thunder. The G-force shoved them back in their seats. Maisie hit the jump and the world tipped upwards, and in that weightless moment Shiara had the cold clear thought that this sky might be the last she ever saw. Then the ground slammed into them from below, jarring her tailbone to teeth. Cassica wrestled with the wheel like she was holding down a sand-croc as they swung wildly this way and that. Maisie's tyres bit, and they powered down the ridge, back into the race.

Cassica whooped with joy. Shiara, less joyous than relieved, worked frantically at the dash to calm the engine before Maisie could chew herself up.

They slid back on to the track, reaching the final straight a full three seconds ahead of Cross's Quantum. Cross hit his turbos, but the fastest car in the world couldn't have closed that gap in time. Maisie crossed the line comfortably ahead of her rivals, at which point something shrieked and snapped inside her, and her engine boomed and died.

Cassica steered off to one side. Maisie was belching black smoke from her exhausts as they freewheeled to a halt in front of the bleachers.

They emerged from the cockpit with the din of the crowd in their ears. Shiara threw off her headgear and hurried round to check the car, her first concern for Maisie. Cassica removed her goggles and bandana, shook out her hair as she pulled off her helmet, raised a fist to the crowd in triumph.

Standing unmasked, the differences between them were obvious in a way they weren't before. Cassica was slender, dark, fierce in victory; Shiara shorter, rounder, the pink of blood beneath her skin an angry contrast to the startling white of her hair and lashes.

Shiara fussed about Maisie, grabbing gingerly at the scorching-hot engine panel, eager to know the damage. She paid no mind to the crowd or the other racers passing the finish line; she just wanted to fix things. It was only when she felt Cassica's hand on her arm that she turned away from the car, and saw her friend smiling at her, face lit up with a look like the raptures of the faithful.

"Hoy," she said. "Take a turn, why don'tcha?" And she motioned towards the bleachers, lined with people cheering and clapping.

At first, Shiara didn't understand what she meant,

dazed as she was with adrenaline. Only when Cassica slung an arm round her and the crowd's cheers redoubled did she understand.

"We did it," said Cassica. "Both of us."

Shiara raised her hand slowly, the crowd yelled and hollered, and it was only then it occurred to her they'd won.

02

The sun beat down on Coppermouth, on corrugated iron roofs and rusty wrecks hiding hood-deep in yard weeds. Doghawks hung in the air, tatty shadows searching the scrub fields where saltgrass and catcher plants grew, hoping for the sight of a lizard or a cat. Up on the ridge were fields of solar panels, dust-streaked faces turned like daisies to the light.

The heart of the town was down by the water, where the Copper River met Division Lake and a proud old metal bridge spanned the milky-brown waters of the estuary. There you could see the ghost of the town as it had been: the closed-down docks that had serviced tugs and tankers; the faded boulevard and dry gardens where passengers once walked, fresh off a barge from upstream; the shuttered stores on the main street, shabby with neglect.

The life of the town was by the highway now. Auto

shops, gun dealers, supply stops for passing traffic on their way to and from the Rust Bowl. Prospectors, freedom nuts, desperate settlers; biker gangs, bandits and sometimes Howlers out of the waste.

The streets of Coppermouth were never busy, but today they were quieter than usual. The townsfolk were elsewhere. Today was a celebration.

Meat sizzled and spat, quivering in the heat haze that hovered over the huge blackened grill. Blane DuCal stood over the carnage, booming with laughter like some diabolical master torturer, his eyes made void by his shades. He was big-bellied, thick-armed and shaven-headed; a thin blond beard and moustache straggled down to touch his chest.

Children hovered nearby, watching the piles of meat grow higher on the warming plate. Goat, snake, sand-croc and even a chicken or two; rarely did they see such bounty. Other children, more patient or more easily distracted, ran riot among the long linoleum-covered tables. Some pretended to be daring adventurers in the Blight Lands, battling with iron monsters from the old days. Others pranced and sang into imaginary mics, aping their heroes from *Celestial Hour*, stopping only to pester their parents for plastic cups of sparkling fazz. "Ain't it all a bit much?" Shiara asked, eyeing the bunting strung overhead, the same bunting they used for Pacifica Day and Restoration Day and every other time the town gathered up on the Point to cut loose and make merry.

Cassica returned the wave of a shy little girl who was watching them from behind a table. "Town's throwing us a party and you're complaining," she said with a wry smile.

Shiara looked over at Blane, who was swatting away undisciplined hands trying to filch flesh from the warming tray. "Just don't feel right, Daddy closing the shop on our account. Ain't like we can afford all this, neither."

"So a few scavs don't get their axle grease. Who cares?" said Cassica. "Look at 'em! First time in for ever, Coppermouth's got something to shout about." She slung one arm round Shiara's shoulder and threw the other out expansively, as if to invite in the world. "Us!"

Shiara tutted in mock disapproval. Coppermouth wasn't the kind of place where you boasted. People took you down a peg for that. Cassica gave her a grin to show she was only half serious, then she slipped away and headed over towards Card.

Shiara felt a faint sense of abandonment, as she always did when Cassica left her for someone else. It had been that way since she could remember: so normal, she barely noticed it any more. Wherever Cassica was, that was where it was happening. Her restless energy was addictive. When she departed it was like a light had burned out somewhere nearby.

Shiara wandered back towards her daddy, awkwardly fielding congratulations as she went. Half the town had come to the cookout. There was greasy-haired Edison Rip, selling hooch to the grown-ups from a barrel in his cart. There was scrawny Nana Mee, surrounded by her brood of daughters, sitting in her wheelchair like it was a throne. There was Johns Weston and his idiot brother Cled, who didn't do much else but laugh since he got a brain bug as a babbit, but was well liked for all that.

And there was a stranger, a man she didn't know, which was something unusual in Coppermouth. He was narrow-shouldered, with slicked-back hair, and he wore a suit even in the heat. There was a drink in his hand and he was laughing with Bonzy Brice as if they'd known each other for ever, but she noticed he scanned the crowd constantly, his mind on things other than Bonzy's dirty jokes.

Janny Thump swept her up in a surprising and unwelcome hug. The woman had never given her the time of day before, but suddenly she was all smiles. It made Shiara momentarily angry. Did Janny think she couldn't tell the difference between people who were genuinely happy for her and people who just wanted to share a glory they had no part of? She managed a passable thank you and pulled herself free, but by the time she had, she'd lost sight of the stranger.

"Here she is!" said Blane, enfolding her in one massive arm. "My little socket jockey!"

She felt a flood of pleasure at that. His affection was given easily, but his approval had to be fought for. Shiara was the last of five, and there'd never been much time for the youngest with Patten running amok and three other brothers before her. There was even less after Cassica's mom died and the family took her in. Most of Shiara's childhood had been spent quietly attempting to impress her daddy, who usually had his hands too full to notice.

Most of her brothers were gone now, dead or moved away, only Creek still hanging about the auto shop these days. But habits learned in childhood set fast: it was her daddy's good opinion she valued over all others.

"Can I salvage the camshaft out of that old Jakeley you've got up on bricks?" she asked. "I need to patch up Maisie."

"That old thing?" he roared, flipping another slab of goat meat. "I've got a consignment in new from HawkerCorp. Take one of them instead."

"Alright, I will," she replied with a smile, because that was what she'd hoped he'd say. Blane's generosity depended on his mood. Getting something out of him was a matter of tactics and timing, like racing.

"Did a good job out there. Keepin' enough back to take on that jump." He shook his head. "How'd you ever work out the ratios? Fuel weight, tyre wear, engine stress. Couldn't keep it all in my head. You've got a gift, Shiara. You do."

"Thanks, Daddy," she said. She let him carry on believing they'd planned the jump from the start. Safer that way. He didn't know Cassica like she did.

She looked out over the road that ran past the Point, to where an enormous billboard presided over the cookout, displaying a poster bleached by years of sun. It had been there since she could remember, familiar as family: that handsome, attractively lined face, the wicked smile that promised sass and seduction, the dewed bottle raised to the town below. GOODBYE TO THE DRY, said the shoutline. RUTTERBY LAKEYNE DRINKS FAZZ!

There wasn't a kid in Coppermouth didn't know that face intimately: his crafted hair, skin without a mark, teeth white and even. No one knew anyone with a face like that. His perfection made him otherworldly. A Celestial, come down from Olympus to grace them with one simple message: that Rutterby LaKeyne drinks fazz, and you should too.

Someone should probably tell him he needn't bother any more, thought Shiara. Since the processing plant packed in, it was easier to get fazz than drinking water, and cheaper too. You could drop iodine tablets in a bucket from the tap, or boil it, but nobody liked the taste and the shops kept running out. Pretty much everyone who wasn't drinking coffee or alcohol drank fazz, and when they got sick of one flavour, they just switched to another.

*

"Great drive, Cass! You killed it!"

Benno gave her a double thumbs up as he passed, and she raised a hand in thanks, elbows resting on the old metal safety barrier that ran round the edge of the Point. Beyond, a cliff fell away to the river. The harbour was visible down there, only fishing boats in dock since it all silted up and killed the town. Past that lay the glittering immensity of the lake, big as the horizon, so huge it never seemed to end. Usually Cassica loved looking out there, loved how limitless it was. But Card was being funny again – funny weird, not the other kind – and it was getting on her nerves. She heard him sigh in pointed irritation as Benno headed off.

"What?" she demanded.

He ignored her, preferring to sulk. Everyone was having a fine time but Card, which was pretty much typical. He only got away with it because he made sulking look so good.

Somewhere nearby, she heard a terrible hacking cough, ringing out over the crowd. A little chill went through her. Mrs K had the dust lung bad. It wouldn't be long for her. The sound spoiled Cassica's mood further, made her want to pick a fight.

"You weren't there this morning," she said.

He sensed the accusation and bristled. "I had to patrol for jackwolves, didn't I?"

"You knew I was racing. You could've swapped shift."

"Oh, right. And I gotta tell my boss every time you go for a drive?"

Purposely missing the point. She rolled her eyes. "Forget it."

"Yeah, let's," he said with a faint sneer. He eyed her over; she was still slouched against the barrier. "Stop doing that," he told her.

"Doing what?"

"The barrier'll give way."

Cassica stared at him incredulously. "It's been here longer than I've been alive."

"Yeah, so it's old, and it'll break if you lean on it like that. You wanna go over the cliff?"

Cassica shoved herself off the barrier, turned round and kicked it hard with the sole of her foot. It didn't budge. Point proven, she glared at him challengingly and then stalked away. He didn't follow.

Sometimes she wondered why she wasted her time with him at all. The truth was, she couldn't help it. It was his face, his hair, the smell and feel of him. Most of all it was the knowledge that he wanted her as badly as she wanted him. They bickered and fought a lot, but he was sweet sometimes and irresistible always. Even when he was being an ass she wanted to jump him – more than when he wasn't, in fact – but she wouldn't give him the satisfaction. That would be letting him win, and a boy that fine was too accustomed to winning already.

A bunch of the younger girls roped her in to show her their dance routine. They'd set themselves up in front of a battered plastic audiodeck and were blasting out songs from a hit parade of Celestials. She perched on a table and watched as they pranced and posed to a Lissy Malp number, and at the end she applauded gravely to show she was serious about how good they were. The girls, delighted, ran off to find somebody else to impress.

By the time the dance was done, her anger at Card was forgotten. She was always quick to argue, quick to forget. She sought out Shiara, finding her at the grill with Blane.

As she headed over, the rude, throaty clatter of engines caught her attention.

They came up the road from the highway, following the music and the crowd. Four of them, bikes darkened with dirt and hung with totems that spoke of Howler lands. There was a wildness to them, a swagger that set them apart from the kind of folk who'd settle in a dead town like Coppermouth. Everyone sensed it, and the joy was sucked from the crowd and replaced with wary fear. They carried holstered shotguns on their bikes. These were not predictable sorts. They could be trouble, if they had a mind. The kind of trouble that left bodies in its wake.

The first of them put out his kickstand, rested his bike and swung his leg over. There were pistols at his waist, a knife in a leather sheath on his forearm. He seemed a man held together with tattoos and scars, a warrior risen from the asphalt to loot and burn.

"Who is it runs the auto shop back there on the highway?" he called in a voice made smoky by drink.

Blane laid the meat down with a sizzle on the grill and put aside the tongs. "That'd be me," he called back, and turned around to face the man.

"We're in need of seein' to," the biker said.

"Shop's closed," Blane replied. "Won't open till the morrow."

The biker chewed his lip. "We need seein' to now."

"They can see to you in Southtown. Two hours on the highway. You head off now, you'll be there before they shut up."

The biker appeared to consider that, but he wasn't moving and nobody was fooled.

"This here cookout's for my daughters," said Blane. "One mine by natural means, the other I'm guardian of. They won the Jessen Plains race just this mornin'." It was an appeal, to their good nature and their love of speed. Move on. We don't want any trouble here. Nobody has to lose face.

The biker's gaze found Shiara. Cassica joined them by the grill, half out of solidarity and half for protection.

"That so?" said the biker. His eyes lingered on Cassica for an uncomfortably long moment, then flicked back to Blane. "Tell you what," he said. "We gonna go back to the shop, and if there ain't no one there to sell us what we want for fair coin, we'll just break in and take it. And more besides. How's that?"

Shiara's heart sank as she watched her daddy face off against the biker, his big fist clenching and releasing as he searched for a way to come out of this with some pride intact. There wasn't much worse than being made another man's servant, except if it was done where others could see. But even if the men of Coppermouth had had their guns, there'd only be one outcome here. Too many kids and women nearby to be otherwise.

"Why don't you see to the grill?" Blane told Shiara. "Make sure everyone gets a piece?"

"I'll come with you," she said. "You'll need more hands."

"Me and Creek can handle it," he said. "It's your day. You stay."

He walked away from her, calling for her brother. His shoulders were slumped in shame as he went to do the biker's bidding. She watched him go, anger making blooms on her pale cheeks and forehead.

In other towns, there were squads of Justices that saw to law and order. Men paid to defend decent folk so they couldn't be bullied this way. But there was no Justice in Coppermouth; not any more.

It always began with bare feet on floorboards. Soft steps creeping. Her little girl's nightie flapped around her shins, covered in moons and shooting stars fast and numerous as wishes. She knew the spots where the wood would groan. Don't wake Momma. Momma needs her rest.

The corridor was a shadowed throat, dark with the dawn. She dared to raise her head and look. The door at the end pulled away as she approached, air treacly with dread in the way of dreams. She didn't want to see what was behind it, but she was carried forward by her feet.

Don't wake Momma. But she had to check. The little girl had been up every few hours in those last days, when Momma couldn't so much as raise herself from her pillow to take soup. Sometimes the little girl slept too long, taken by exhaustion, and she'd wake in a panic, afraid that her lack of vigilance had caused her momma's end.

Hand on the door, she pushed. The hinges were silent in her dream.

Momma's room had the smell of death to it. The grey first light of day pressed against the windowpane. She didn't look at the bed; first she went round the room, touched light fingers to the old wooden chair, the dresser scattered with powders and creams, the curtains gone musty since Momma stopped washing them. It was a ritual, a superstition. If she did everything just right, maybe Momma wouldn't die.

Finally she turned to the bed. Momma had yellowed and turned witchlike of late, and it frightened the little girl. Her nose was a sinewed fin in her face, her chin gone loose, neck scrawny. Momma dragged in a breath as if with chains and hooks; it tumbled and clattered out of her. Then something tripped in her chest and she began to cough, that horrible raling cough, bad enough heard through the door but unbearable up close. In the dream, each cough threw out a thin cloud of red dust, and when Momma settled again there was a haze of it hanging over her.

She was wrapped in blankets, tucked up to the collarbone. The little girl reached for the edge of the coverlet, fearing to see what was beneath. She peeled back a layer and looked.

A thin frail arm, a clawlike hand lay exposed. But what looked like skin was not; as she peered close, she saw that the tips of Momma's fingers were worn away, and there was powder on the bedspread beneath. Suddenly she knew, with a kick of cold terror, that her mother was all turned to dust, and that the slightest disturbance would cause her to crumble. She should never have lifted the coverlet, never looked beneath.

If she could only lay it back with enough care, then all might be well again. But no matter how she tried, the result was always the same in her dream. Momma came apart, puffing out from beneath the coverlet in soft clouds, her face caving like a broken sandcastle. The little girl backed away tearfully as the room filled with red dust, and the stinging in her eyes drove her awake.

Cassica stared at the ceiling and let the sadness take her: a profound, aching sense of loss, beginning low in her belly and spreading to her chest. Cool tears slipped down her face. She knew it was better not to fight it, so she focused on the grain of the wood in the planks above her, the feel of the rough-spun wool blanket against her skin, all the things of the here and now; and she waited for it to pass.

Pink sunlight warmed the room. It was simple and small, two beds with a chest and dresser between. Shiara was a hump in the other bed, her blanket pulled over her head, curled up in the stuffy dark.

Shiara's breath came in heavy sighs. Cassica listened, and it comforted her. She didn't like it when she couldn't hear her friend breathing.

Shiara didn't come to breakfast. She wanted to work on Maisie before the shop opened. Cassica found her afterwards, oily fingers deep in Maisie's guts, and delivered a tray set with coffee, flour biscuits and a bowl of goat gravy.

"You know how your mom is," said Cassica.

Shiara wiped off her hands on her overalls, dunked a biscuit in the gravy and crunched it absently, still staring at the tangle of pipes and cables before her. A radio played in the cool shady depths of the auto shop, hidden somewhere among the quiet vehicles waiting for attention.

"How is she?" Cassica asked. She stood well back; she'd catch hell if she got oil on her waitress uniform.

"Well, the piston rings are shot, so are the bearings, we pretty much trashed the turbo system and there's a crack in one of the cylinders. Plus the camshaft I'm getting off Daddy." She took another bite of her biscuit. "Gonna cost us everything we won in that last race to fix her."

"You want me to go easier on her next time?"

Shiara gave her a look. Cassica grinned. As if she would.

There was a violent clatter as the security shutters were rolled back, casting sunlight across the interior. Shiara's brother Creek sloped into view, dusting his hands.

Cassica checked the clock in mock disbelief. "Is that who I think it is? Opening up, no less?"

Shiara frowned. "Daddy had words last night."

They watched him as he mooched his way over to the office. Creek was lean like dried meat, face set in a permanent scowl, mouth puckered and nose scattered with freckles. There was a dullness about him, like just talking to you made him weary. He had no love for his daddy's business and made no secret of it, preferring the lonely wild places where he could hunt.

But he'd get the shop when Blane gave it up, by dint of age and because their customers wouldn't trust a female mechanic. It went down easier if they saw a man in charge, even if it was a girl doing the work. Creek would be the face of the place, Shiara the talent.

It ate at her from time to time, but Shiara wasn't the kind of person to rail against things she couldn't change. All the arguments in the world wouldn't stop their customers driving on to Southtown where the staff better suited their expectations. Daddy knew she was the better mechanic. That was what counted.

"Qualifier for the Widowmaker tonight," said Cassica, tapping her fingers against her thigh. She'd been still too long, and was restless.

"Gonna listen on the radio. Reckon you can catch it at the diner?"

"Gonna try," said Cassica. "Speaking of which, I better get. Have a good one."

"You too."

"Y'know, we should go in for one of those qualifiers," Cassica tossed over her shoulder as she left. "Blane could join the guild, be our official manager."

"Yuh. Just need to win another fifty of them races and we might just scratch the entrance fee!" Shiara called.

Cassica's laughter trailed after her, out into the fierce light of the new day.

A solitary fan beat the air in Gauge's Diner; the other hadn't worked in a while. Slat windows cut the sun into strips, and a damp close heat hung in the air. Outside lay a stony forecourt, and past that, the highway. A doghawk hunched on a rusted water tower, licking its underwing, worrying at feathers with its teeth.

The only diners here were a scav family, on their way up to the Rust Bowl to pick over the wasteland for pieces of the war no one else had found yet. They had a resigned look to them; they knew their chances, but knew no better way. Cassica doled out their plates with extra perkiness to compensate.

"Spicy snake stew for you, tuber chips, there's your pigeon burger, and you had eggs, cornbread and grits.

Honeyed locusts to start and a bottle of original fazz for the table. Now can I get you anything else? No? Enjoy your meal."

Gauge watched them with half an eye from behind the counter, a suspicious ogre lurking in the gloom. The scavs didn't look like they could afford to eat this way too often, and someone had skipped out on a bill yesterday. But Cassica reckoned they were alright, just a poor family spending big on a morale-boosting last feast before they headed into hardship. There'd be no diners in the Rust Bowl.

She carried her tray back into the kitchen, where the rest of the staff were watching a crackling television set on top of a fridge. It was showing the build-up to a qualifier, one of a series of elimination events that culminated in the Widowmaker, the pinnacle of the Maximum Racing season and the most hotly contested rally in the world. Cassica settled herself back in her spot on the worktop as the camera panned across a sleek black car, its silver exhaust pipes and alloys gleaming, logos plastered over its flanks, spoilers and fins.

"Who's driving *that*?" she asked enviously. She struggled to hear the commentator; the audio was barely more than a hiss.

The camera cut to the driver, drawing a loud whoop from Beesha, the only other female in the room. The boy in the frame was a study in sullen beauty, black hair raked across his brow, lips pursed in a pout, one ear heavy with rings. KYREN BANE, read the caption.

"I would take a piece o' him!" Beesha announced, slapping the counter.

The cooks laughed. "That pretty thing? Boy'd spend longer in the bathroom than you would!"

"Boy could have his *own* bathroom if he came out lookin' like that every mornin'." Beesha cackled happily at the thought.

"Hoy! Cassica's in love!" crowed the busboy, and Cassica, too late, realized what had been written all over her face. The boy was like a statue from the old times, like something legendary. For just a moment, she'd been awestruck.

"Well, she ain't blind!" Beesha cried, and everyone laughed. Then the television switched to a race, footage from last season, and their attention was snared. The waitress gave Cassica a sidelong wink. Cassica kept quiet, feeling lucky to escape a ribbing, thankful to Beesha for deflecting it.

Cassica recognized the footage; she'd seen it a dozen times. It was a moment that had drawn a collective gasp from the world, as relentless nice guy Chabley Pott – people's favourite and tipped to win – went out on the first day of the Widowmaker.

The scene was hellish. A burned land crawling with lava; infernal peaks; ash-black skies that flickered with lightning. Devil's Basin.

The shifting earth and scalding geysers had

already claimed two racers by the time Lady Scorpion caught up with Pott. She snuck in under cover of the fire and smoke, while Pott and his tech were busy negotiating a tricky series of ridges. By the time they saw her, she was already on them. Out of the black she came, a dirt-streaked mass of armour, engines howling.

Pott should have tried to outrun her in his agile Pioneer, but perhaps he feared the lava more than he feared the Lady, and he tried to evade instead. This way and that he skidded and swung, hoping to dodge her stinger, knowing she only had one shot at him. But Lady Scorpion picked her moment and nailed him, cool as you please.

The hovercams zoomed in hard as a metal spear fired from Lady Scorpion's roof-mounted cannon and sliced through the air, a long cable uncoiling behind it. It punched into the Pioneer's fuel tank, a thousand volts surged invisibly down the cable, and Pott and his tech disappeared in a blast of flame and twisted metal.

The cooks and busboy cheered; Beesha held her cheeks in horror. Lady Scorpion drove on, the cable detaching and falling away. The blazing shell of the Pioneer rolled to a halt behind her.

"Gotta love that Lady!" one of the cooks cried. The hovercams moved in close. Through the smoke and fire, you could see glimpses of the blackened bodies inside. Cassica couldn't look away.

That was how it was on the Maximum Racing circuit. Not like the backwater races she and Shiara competed in. Official races had Wreckers, drivers whose only purpose was to take out the other participants. In the Outer Leagues you'd face no-name psychos whom the general public had never heard of, but the top racers in the Core League competed against famously deadly Wreckers like Lady Scorpion. The stakes were higher, but so was the glory.

Cassica stared at Chabley Pott's burning body. *She wouldn't have got me*, she thought. *I'd have beat her.* And she wished for the day when she'd be able to prove it.

The door to the kitchen burst open and Gauge loomed. "Hoy! Anyone doin' any work in this joint? Got a group on table three gonna turn cannibal if we don't feed 'em soon!"

Night was almost upon Coppermouth as Cassica headed home. She took the path of the old aqueduct, which ran parallel to the highway but not too close. Many times she'd been warned about walking the highway on her own. Easy for someone to pull up and snatch you. They'd all heard the stories.

Most nights Gauge drove Cassica and Beesha home, out of concern for their safety, but tonight he had a date with Con Witler and he needed to brush up. Cassica didn't mind. The day had left her in a pensive mood, and she fancied the walk. Ever since they won that race, there had been something up with her, some unresolved feeling that had yet to make itself known. Strange that she'd had the dream again that morning. She hadn't had it for a year, and she'd thought it gone for ever.

The rhythm of her steps lulled her, and her mind soon drifted to breezy fantasies about Kyren Bane. He'd won the race with ease – more than a pretty face, then – and that meant they'd be seeing more of him. Maybe he'd make it to Olympus. He had the look of a Celestial; he'd fit right in.

To her left, the land reared up, a great ridge dark against the purple dusk. Above, stars, like someone had spray-painted the sky with light. Some of them moved steadily, restless orbital weapons left over from the Omniwar, dead death machines that once had destroyed whole cities with lances of fire from space.

At times like this, with the light behind it, you could see the dust blowing off the ridge. Dust from the Rust Bowl, seeded with microscopic metal-eating nanobots that corroded everything they settled on. It got into your lungs, killed some, weakened others and left the rest unscathed for reasons no one really understood. Just part of life's lottery in Coppertown. Shiara accepted that, as she accepted many things Cassica couldn't. But Cassica couldn't bear to feel so helpless.

When the time came, she cut back to the highway.

The town and the lake lay on the other side. As she approached, she spotted a convoy coming, and waited at the roadside to let it pass. She stood with toes almost touching the tarmac, closer than she ought to, the way she liked it. She wanted to feel the speed, the shove of air as they went by.

The bikes passed first, flak-jacketed men with shotguns on their backs flashing across her field of view. An instant later came the cars, windscreens hidden behind mesh grilles. Then the armoured trucks, three of them, punching past her, hard enough to make her stagger. A horn blared, a warning or a greeting, and she laughed at the noise, delighted by the chaos.

Their tail lights dwindled, the turbulence calming in their wake. Cassica brushed the hair from her face and watched them until they were out of sight. She dearly wished she could go with them, away from here, away to the cities and green places and distant lands. Away from the slow creep of days and the same unchanging faces.

She was too fast for this town; it couldn't keep her. Winning that race, she'd shown them that. And yet nothing was different the day after. Escape seemed as far from her as ever.

She dreamed of racing, but a dream was all it was. Shiara worked miracles, but they'd never have the money to build a car quick enough to compete. They'd never find a manager or a sponsor out here, where government barely held and civilization only existed by the will of good people.

A shadow touched her heart, and she wondered where she'd be in twenty years, if Coppermouth kept her. Those the dust lung didn't get were got by the drink, like Shiara's brother Patten. He was someone who couldn't be confined, like Cassica was, and it drove him crazy in the end.

She crossed the highway and followed it on the other side. The town twinkled to her right, becoming beautiful as night hid it. By the time she saw the auto shop, her mood had lifted a little. She'd lost her parents but gained a family. In Shiara, she'd found the kind of friend most people only wished they had. Coppermouth would never excite her, but it would care for her, as it cared for all its people. This town had its troubles, and there wasn't much by way of luxury to go around, but they had a roof over their heads and food in their bellies, and they got to race every once in a while. All in all, there were worse places, worse outcomes for a life.

The lights were on over the auto shop. Melly would have dinner on the table and they'd be eating without her; Blane was particular about his mealtimes, and the walk had made her late. It didn't matter. Melly always saved her a plate.

The rattle of keys announced her arrival as she worked her way through the locks on the reinforced side door. She sprang up the stairs two at a time –

she never could just walk up steps, it seemed so ponderous – and found her way to the kitchen, drawn by the smell of stew.

She was aware of a silence ahead, but Shiara's kin weren't big talkers, so she put it down to nothing much. It was only when she came to the doorway that she stopped. Every face turned to her: Blane, Melly, Creek, Shiara and the stranger at the table. They'd been waiting anxiously, she realized with a thrill of dread. Waiting for her.

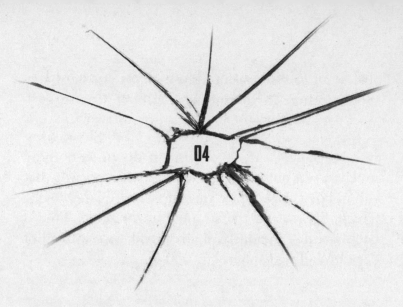

04

The stranger's suit was new: pin-clean, stiff-shouldered and one size too big. He was long-bodied and thin of frame; his shirt stuck to him where a little pot belly pressed against it. His hair was black, receding in a widow's peak, slicked back along his skull. Sweat glistened on his brow, and it gave him a sheen, a slippery look. A hard man to lay a hand on.

He stood as Cassica entered, extended his hand. "Miss Cassica Hayle, I reckon. My name's Harlan Massini. It's an honour to meet you."

It took Cassica a second to realize he wasn't mocking her, and to remember her manners. She shook his hand uncertainly; it was surprisingly dry. "Well, likewise," she said.

"You ought to sit down," said Blane, and Cassica did so. Harlan settled himself after.

Melly started fixing Cassica a plate from the pots

of stew and tuber mash on the table. It was her habit to take refuge in routine when she was perturbed. Most days Melly was a jolly, bustling sort, plump and warm, plain and clucky. But some days you'd catch her staring into nowhere as if shocked by the grief the world could dole out, stunned by the memory of the children she'd lost. Those days, she was like an automaton.

There was an atmosphere in the room. Melly's kitchen was usually a place of ease, made warm by the memory of meals from the flaking stove and conversations round that scratched old wooden table. But the presence of Harlan made it otherwise. No longer was it their domain, no longer a place of safety. Just by being here, he was taking it from them and making it his.

"Quite a race you drove yesterday, Miss Cassica," he said in a lazy coastal drawl. "You and Miss Shiara. It's been longaday since I saw daring and invention like that. To overcome the limitations of your vehicle, to outrace opponents in superior cars ... that's the mark of champions."

"Mr Massini is a racing manager," said Melly quietly, as she put Cassica's plate in front of her.

Cassica was no longer interested in food. Her stomach flipped as she realized that this stranger wasn't here to deliver terrible news, but possibly, just possibly, the opposite.

"Indeed I am," said Harlan. "Racers are my game

these days, but I got my start in entertainment. Perhaps you've heard of Liandra Kesey?"

Creek coughed into his stew in surprise and looked up from his food for the first time since Cassica had arrived. Even Creek, who paid little attention to Celestials, had heard of Liandra Kesey. She was a diva, an icon, her image and influence so pervasive that Cassica had long become sick of her. Her songs were played endlessly; her picture was everywhere, inescapable. Her opinions were eagerly received and recycled by a generation of young girls; by wearing this dress or that she could kill or cause a craze.

"You manage Liandra Kesey?" Cassica asked.

"Managed," said Harlan, brief regret creasing his eyes. "It's a manager's fate, you see. I found her when she was nobody. I took her to the top. But, up there – " he pointed skyward and lifted his gaze "– there's no place for me. I make Celestials; I don't desire to be one. My place is here on Earth, finding people like you. My calling, if you will." He picked up his spoon. "This is a wonderful meal, Mrs DuCal. Delicious," he said, though he hadn't tasted it yet.

"Why don't you speak plain, Harlan?" said Blane. "Tell Cassica what you told us."

"Plain-speaking folks, that's what I like about a town like Coppermouth," Harlan said with a wide smile. He turned to Cassica. "I came here with a proposition, that's all. I'd like to be your manager."

Cassica had guessed that was coming the moment

she learned of his trade, but it still rocked her to hear it.

"Twenty-five per cent," said Shiara, ever practical, bringing her down to the ground. "That's what he wants."

"Yes, and not a cent up front, not a cent of risk on your part," Harlan cut in smoothly. "I only take a cut of the money you make, so you can be sure my every waking hour will be dedicated to making you that money! And seventy-five per cent of something is a whole heap better than a hundred per cent of nothing, am I right?" He didn't wait for agreement. "Now, what I'll give you first and foremost is my endorsement. I'm sure you know you can't be registered for an official Maximum Racing event without a guild-accredited manager. After that, what you get is the benefit of my extensive experience, contacts built up over many years in the field. I'll open doors for you that you can't open yourself. I'll introduce you to the people you need to meet. Not to mention the considerable financial capital I'll be investing in order to get you to the big leagues. *That's* how much faith I've got in you. I know talent when I see it, and I see that you two have it in spades!"

Cassica was wearing a dazed smile. Shiara seemed less taken by his speech. "Maisie's shot," she said.

"Who?"

"Our car," said Shiara. "She needs repairin'."

"Maisie!" Harlan cried. "That's darling! What a name!"

"It sounded classic," Shiara said, with a shrug.

"Can you fix her?" Harlan asked.

"She can fix anything," said Cassica, thumbing at her friend. She was eager to reassure him, to make up for Shiara's inexplicable wariness.

"See, the reason I ask is there's a satellite qualifier in two weeks at Ragrattle Caves, not a hundred Ks from here—"

"I ain't heard of that one," Blane interjected. He'd been sidelined from the conversation too long and Cassica guessed he was feeling cut out. He was the head of the household, his word the most important, and though no one had mentioned it again, he was still sore from what those bikers had done the day before.

Harlan sensed it and addressed him directly, playing to his ego, but his words were angled at Cassica and Shiara. "The qualifiers you see on prime-time television, those are for Core League racers with big sponsors. The corps buy you a place on the grid, you show off their advert, see? Now, ordinarily I'd fix new racers up with a big sponsor and buy us one of those places, but a deal like that takes time we don't have. It's only luck brought me here to see these girls win, and if we want to make something of this, we've got to motor!" He leaned over the table, bringing them all in. "Now I'm sure I don't need to tell you, while those glitzy qualifiers are playing out, they run a whole bunch of satellite qualifiers in the Outer Leagues. They only show those in the dead of night, so most of them people don't even know about. Ragrattle Caves is the last one of the season round here. If we're quick on the paperwork, I can endorse you as your manager, and I'll put up the entrance fee. If you get a top-three place, you get a free pass to the last *proper* qualifier in Anchor City. And you'll have sponsors lining up then!"

"You want us to go straight for the Widowmaker?" Shiara cried. "Shouldn't we be, I dunno, payin' our dues in the Outer Leagues first? Racin' against that level of opposition?"

Cassica stared at her friend in exasperation. She couldn't understand why Shiara might have an objection.

"Why bother?" said Harlan. "You've got the ability, and you're the perfect age to go to the top! Listen, you ever wondered why hardly anyone out there on the track is much more than twenty? Because the others have either won a fortune and retired, or they got too slow. You know, they reckon teenagers have twenty per cent faster reactions and are inclined to be thirty-five per cent more daring than a driver in their twenties. True fact! From scientists! On the circuit, we got a different way of putting it: 'Twenty-six, out of tricks!' So you better get started, girls!"

"What about Dutton Rye?" Shiara argued. "He went on for years."

"That old warhorse? Well, there's always exceptions. And he never won the Widowmaker, did he?"

There was a clatter of cutlery, loud enough to silence them all. Melly was staring down at her bowl, her hand trembling. She folded it in her lap with the other and said nothing.

Blane said it for her. "Kids die in the Widowmaker. Kids die in the qualifiers. This ain't some badland runaround like Jessen Plains. They got Wreckers in those things. These are our girls you're talkin' about."

Harlan paused to survey them all. "I won't lie to you. You're too smart for that," he said, sombre now. "Maximum Racing is dangerous. One in ten racers don't make it to the finish line most races. Come the Widowmaker, it's one in four. But those that don't make it, I'll tell you this: most every one should never have been there in the first place. Kids pushed on to the track before they're ready, long-shots put in to make up the numbers." He sawed the air with his hand, face screwed up in disgust. "This business is full of amateurs and sharks, unscrupulous managers, taking a gamble with some precious kid's life just so they can get a payday. Well, that's not how I do it, Mr and Mrs DuCal. That's not how I do it, Cassica, Shiara!" He ignored Creek; Creek had no influence, and wasn't worth his attention. He raised a finger. "But those racers that have talent, those that are given the best equipment and the best advice ... well, *their* odds are very good indeed."

42

His confidence smothered Blane's objections. He had no footing for an argument. It was Harlan's world, his word.

"And I'm sure I needn't remind you of the prizes!" he said, his face lighting up, addressing Cassica and Shiara now. "The glittering prizes that await the skilful and the brave. Money enough to keep you and yours in comfort for the rest of your lives. Money to improve and expand this wonderful business you have here, or to move elsewhere if that's your desire. Money to enjoy yourselves. And if you should win the Widowmaker, ah, if you should do *that*! The greatest prize of all awaits. Two tickets to Olympus!"

He sat back, spreading his hands slowly like a sunrise, eyes distant as if he could see it all, the future coming real before him. "You'll be Celestials," he said, his voice building in volume as he spoke. "Your faces will be in every zine. Viewers will thrill to footage of your races. A generation of young women will be inspired by your courage. Up there on Olympus, you'll dine on foods you can't even imagine, wear dresses of diamonds and silk. You'll be among legends. You'll *be* legends!"

Cassica was dizzied by a sudden, violent expansion of her horizons. It had all come on her too fast. Not twenty minutes ago, her dreams of escape had been idle fancies. She'd never been more than a half day's drive from Coppermouth, and what she'd seen there hadn't been much different. The wider world she only knew from television. The endless forests of the Greenbelt, the towering spires of Anchor City lured and intimidated her in equal measure. It wasn't just a matter of getting up and going. She had no savings; nobody had. Without family, without connections, without support, she couldn't imagine how she might begin to live in such places.

But this stranger at their table had changed everything.

"We gotta think about this," said Shiara.

"What in hell is there to think about?" Cassica cried.

"We gonna *think* first," Shiara said, staring at Cassica hard. The air went taut between them.

"I can see this is all a lot to take in," said Harlan, his calm quiet tone defusing them. "It's a big decision, a *family* decision, and I guess you don't need me rabbiting on while you're making it. So I'll excuse myself, if I may."

He got to his feet and bowed his head towards Melly. "Mrs DuCal, that was a sensational meal. Thank you for having me in your wonderful home. I'll be staying at the Crab and Hook in town for the time being. Goodbye, Mr DuCal, Cassica, Shiara. I hope you'll do me the honour of thinking real hard on what I've said. No, no, I'll see myself out."

With that, he was gone, as commanding in his exit as he'd been in his conversation. He left behind a thick silence, which continued even after they heard the door shut downstairs, and they finished up their meals without a word.

There was a fingernail moon that night, and a deep gloom lay over everything, but Shiara could see Cassica's eyes shining, and she knew her friend was awake in the other bed.

"We gotta do it," Cassica whispered.

Shiara didn't reply for a long while. Eventually Cassica spoke again, as Shiara knew she would. Cassica had to say things out loud to work them through.

"When I was in the diner, they were showing when Lady Scorpion took out Pott," Cassica said.

"Pott and Rammson," Shiara said. No one ever remembered Pott's tech. It bugged her. "Two of 'em died, not just one."

"I'd have outrun her."

"Huh?"

"Pott tried to dodge the stinger. But Lady Scorpion never misses. They reckon that spear is magnetic or something. I think he was just afraid to go too fast. Couldn't risk ditching in a lava flow."

"Maybe." Shiara gathered her blanket round her, a pale ghost rustling in the dark. Through the window she could see the undersides of the clouds, pearled and sinister.

"You heard what he said," Cassica murmured. "If we're good enough, it won't happen to us."

"Pott and Rammson were good enough. They

45

could've won it."

Silence from Cassica. Then: "You think Blane will let us do it?" she asked. "If we decide to," she added quickly after.

"Reckon so," said Shiara. "Momma'll have plenty to say on the matter, but he won't stop me."

Part of her wanted him to. She wanted this choice taken from her. She wanted him to say *Don't go, Shiara. I couldn't take losin' you. You can have the auto shop, Creek can go shoot wolves or whatever he does up in them mountains, and we'll be happy ever after.*

He wouldn't, though. Because he loved her, and he knew she couldn't be kept, and there wasn't a whole lot here for her if she stayed. All she had to look forward to in Coppermouth was a life of thankless work playing second fiddle to her layabout brother.

The auto shop was supposed to have been Grayley's, but Grayley drank the water and caught something that killed him. Creek never wanted this place, but his younger brother Tedder wanted it less, and he got married and moved to the Eastern Seaboard Confederacy. Patten drowned in a shallow ditch after a storm, so drunk he couldn't lift his head.

Even though Creek would have preferred to give it away, the responsibility was his to carry on the family business. It couldn't go to Shiara. The customers would dry up and the place would fold. So it would be Creek's name over the door when Daddy was gone. The auto shop she loved would never be hers. Because she was a girl.

But out there on the track, when Maisie was roaring and the competition had been left in the dust, being a girl didn't matter the way it did in Coppermouth. They wouldn't be the first girls in Maximum Racing – though there was a sight less of them than boys – nor would she be the first female tech. But there was something in it, something worth a risk. To be accountable only to themselves, to be judged on their skill and nothing else. She'd never thought it could be that way; but tonight, for the first time, it seemed possible, and it made her heart beat hard.

"We probably won't even make top three in the satellite anyway," said Cassica. "It's just one race, right? And even if we win, we don't have to do anything after. I mean, we don't need to go to Anchor City. We don't need to try for the Widowmaker at all. We can always change our minds."

"Yuh, sure," said Shiara, sarcastic. "We gonna win the satellite and then you gonna give up. Sounds just like you."

"I'm serious!" said Cassica. "If we're in, we're in this together. We'll stop any time you want. I promise."

But Shiara knew her better than that.

05

Engines snarled and clattered. The air was greasy and stinging with fumes. The sun beat down on hot metal and baked earth.

Cassica adjusted her goggles while Shiara restlessly scanned the gauges on the dash. She sat back, apparently content, then suddenly reached underneath to make last-minute adjustments to the fuel enrichment system. Cassica made sure her helmet was on tight and checked her buckles. Little rituals, to steady her nerves.

When the race began, all her fears would dissolve. In the race, in the moment, she found a stillness she found nowhere else. The waiting was the worst.

She looked up and down the starting line. A motley clutter of racers waited alongside them. Gleaming streamlined speedsters that sat low between wide-set tyres; brutish off-roaders with three axles that could smash through obstacles or clamber over them; gristly all-rounders, their oily guts poking out through their chassis, their drivers hidden behind barred windows.

Maisie felt fragile and skeletal by comparison. She was light and fast, but not strong. A roll cage encased their seats, and there was a windshield to deflect the air, but that was all the protection she gave them. Only the trikes and bikes, suicidally fast and unsteady, had less armour. Most of her was taken up by the engine and a fuel tank, suspended on sprung axles between four fat tyres. But what an engine it was.

The tech's craft was a mystery to Cassica, who only understood the basics. Shiara could take a pile of scavenged and mismatched parts and make them cooperate. She could eke out every last bit of brake horsepower from the most unpromising materials. Every race Cassica burned Maisie out; each time Shiara built her new and better. This time, Harlan had helped her out with money and Blane with new parts. It was a rare bounty for someone used to working with scrap and guile. She'd barely rested the last two weeks, but she'd assembled a car that could compete with vehicles which cost ten times as much.

There were twenty racers, arranged in a row. Dusty, billboard-sized screens showed the feed from the cameramen as they moved between the drivers, focusing on each in turn. The commentator's voice was tinny through pole-mounted speakers. Officials buzzed around them, sweating in their suits.

A small crowd were held back by ropes and stakes, fewer than Cassica had imagined. Most would be at the finish line, watching on other screens, but still the turnout was disappointing. The race would be televised, but not at a time when anyone was likely to see it. She'd expected to be part of a spectacle, but the Outer Leagues seemed little different from the unofficial races she'd competed in. It made her feel insignificant and foolish. It had taken bravery to come here; they were proud of themselves for their courage. But the crowds only cared about the big races.

Set apart from the racers, wavering in a haze of heat and poisonous exhaust gases, was the Wrecker. He called himself the Rhino, after an animal that only existed in pictures now. His vehicle was a monster of grime and black iron, with a great spiked grille and a hide that was riveted and scorched. It didn't look to be carrying any weapon other than its weight; it was a battering ram, made to bludgeon opponents. If Maisie got in its way, it would crush her like a bug.

The Rhino looked out of the cab of his vehicle, and his eyes met Cassica's along the starting line. A trickle of cold spilled down her spine. His face was ridged with self-inflicted scars, dyed with crude home-made inks. Protruding from his forehead, implanted right into his skull, was a bony horn. His eyes were bright and crazed, and there was something absent in them, a lack of care or consequence, the psychopathic glaze of a skatch drinker. He bared rotten teeth and mugged at her, and she saw his tongue was dyed black.

She thought of Chabley Pott and Lady Scorpion, how she'd longed for the chance to face off against a Wrecker. She didn't feel quite so eager now.

Ahead was a shallow slope of hardpan, ending abruptly in a great bulge of red stone rising from the flat parched land. At its foot was a dark jagged entrance to a series of caves. What lay inside, they didn't know.

She recalled Harlan's pep talk as they waited in the sandbagged area that passed for the pits. His skin had shone as he leaned in close, talking in that over-eager way he had, long hands chopping the air as if to divide the information into digestible pieces.

"This is a blind race, okay? No laps, just one time through. You won't have much advance information, just a rough map through the caves. Only the Wrecker knows what's inside. Blind races are about speed of thought: reacting, not planning. Got that?"

Shiara hadn't liked that at all. Half the job of the tech was advance planning, calculating routes and fuel consumption, squeezing out an advantage by being smarter than the other techs. Cassica didn't like it for a different reason. Even by the standards of Maximum Racing, a blind race was terrifically dangerous. But if that was what they had to do to get to the top, then that was what they'd do.

"The secret to a blind race is control, not speed," Harlan had said. "Drive like a maniac, you'll crash in there. Just concentrate on getting through. If you come out the other side, you'll be in with a good chance."

In the end, Shiara had prepared as best she could by scouting the outside of the caves, comparing it to her map and making rough fuel calculations to ensure they were carrying as little weight as possible. She had the outline of a plan, ready to be changed on the fly. It settled her some, but not much.

Shiara finished her final adjustments. Cassica reached over and laid a hand on her shoulder. Shiara raised her head, and there was a look between them, like two animals caught in the same trap.

"Last chance," said Shiara. *Last chance to pull out. Last chance to change our minds.*

Cassica did neither. A tiny crease appeared in her forehead. She couldn't understand why Shiara would even offer her that last chance, or what she might do with it.

"Racers, ready!" the announcer howled through crackling speakers, and they faced forward, committed.

"Three!"

Racers gunned their engines. The crowd yelled, but Cassica could hardly hear them over the noise.

"Two!"

Waiting by the finish line, watching on a

screen, was Harlan. Cassica felt his eyes on her, felt *everybody*'s eyes on her. Adrenaline hit, and her nerves quit bubbling, like a pan taken off the boil.

"One."

The final second was a white blank, burning away fear and doubt. All that existed after was the here and now. Where Cassica needed to be.

A horn blared. Cassica hit the gas.

A few drivers fired their turbos the moment the race began, hoping to get ahead of the pack. Their wheels spun too fast to grip, burning rubber; they skidded left and right. Two of them cut their turbos and were left in the dust. A third slid out of control and into the path of a biker, who went straight over the hood and ended up in a heap on the other side.

Cassica ignored the chaos, accelerating smoothly. Shiara had put in the bare minimum of fuel, and Maisie was light on armour, so she began to pull ahead of the pack, outstripped only by the nimble bikes.

"Hold back!" Shiara shouted over the noise. "We don't want to be out in front!"

It was the plan they'd discussed. Stay behind the leaders, let *them* encounter the obstacles inside. Beat them on the final straight. But now it came to it, Cassica found it hard to give up a lead.

"Hold back!" Shiara told her, more firmly.

She eased off the accelerator, letting the slower cars

past her. The mouth of the cave rushed to meet them. She slotted into a spot in fifth or sixth and focused. Now came the unknown.

The world went from dazzling light to echoing dark. The ground dipped before her, a wide gravelly downslope lit only by the headlamps of the cars ahead. There was a terrifying moment of blindness as her eyes adjusted. She felt Maisie trying to skid and let off the speed some more. Others, less willing to use the brakes, began to fishtail as they lost control. The hollow roar of engines reverberated around the cave as the rest followed her in. Shiara checked the mirrors, anxious, looking for the Wrecker. Suddenly:

"Pull left!" she cried.

Cassica was already doing it. She saw how the cars ahead were lurching to the side and knew there must be a reason. A second later, she found out. The bottom of the slope was a wall of rock. The only way out was on the far left.

The leaders, who were travelling fast and saw it late, scrambled to adjust in time. One turned too hard: rear wheels slipped on gravel and swung out to the side. The car rolled twice before smashing hard into the wall. A biker lost control in his panic, tipped over and went sliding into the first wreck. He slapped against the metal like a rag doll.

Dead. The knowledge hit Cassica and slid off her. No time to think about it. Forewarned, she led Maisie over to the left and slipped through the gap, already grateful for Shiara's caution.

Beyond, they found sunlight again. The roof of the cavern opened up and they emerged at the bottom of an enormous sinkhole, drilled into the earth by some catastrophic weapon from the Omniwar. Left behind were fantastic formations of melted rock, shaggy with colourful mosses, shot through with strange metals created in the blast. Bats took flight at the sound of their engines, flocking out from the shadows and pouring into the hot blue bowl of the sky. Remote cameras swivelled towards them as they arrived.

Directly in front of the entrance, a fin of rock divided the racers. Cassica threw Maisie to the right, and was plunged into a maze of stone monoliths and hanging vines. Racers were all around her, in front and behind, glimpsed between gaps in the rock on either side.

There was no single route through the chaos. Cars criss-crossed each other's paths, battling for position. A racer cut into her, swerving out of nowhere. She hit the brakes and Maisie narrowly avoided getting her nose sheared off. Cassica swore loudly, her calm lost for a moment.

"Drag right," said Shiara, her face flitting from light to shade, light to shade as they passed through the shadowed alleys between the rock formations. She was looking at the map, which showed three ways out of the sinkhole. Shiara had decided the rightmost route looked more favourable; she reckoned it would be less jammed than the others.

Cassica checked her mirrors, waited for a gap in the stones, and then cut right.

Directly into the path of the Rhino.

A horn blared and her mirrors filled with black iron, a smoking monster bearing down on her from behind. Her heart lurched. She saw a gap to the left and swerved hard, desperate to be out of the Wrecker's path. Shiara was thrown against her harness as Maisie darted through, missing the flanks of the rock by inches, and the Rhino thundered past behind her, a terrifying tonnage of rage and ruin. Cassica caught a glimpse of a scarred face in her mirror, black mouth wide with laughter as he passed.

"Not that way," said Cassica. "Not that way," Shiara agreed.

They'd lost speed, and were falling behind in the order. The drivers in front were heading for a dark slash in the side of the sinkhole – the middle exit of the three. With no other choice, Cassica went for it, whipping past looming piles of melted stone and bubbled metal standing like witnesses aghast at the horror of past days.

The drivers were squeezed together as they raced through the exit. Beyond was a sepulchral cave, lit by the ghostly white glow of headlamps. They went out on to a narrow rocky bridge, spanning a black drop without limit. Night-vision cameras tracked them.

Overhead, at the far range of the light, the tips of many thin stalactites poked out of the dark.

They were on a thin path, barely wide enough for three cars abreast, with no barriers and death to either side. Only then did Cassica understand what they'd let themselves in for, what she'd been so eager to embrace when Harlan offered it. They'd put themselves entirely at the mercy of others, and those people – those who'd devised this course, those who arranged the race, those who watched it – didn't care if they died. Some, in fact, hungered for it.

They're trying to kill us, Cassica thought in shocked amazement. This was no race; this was a battle for their lives.

She fought to maintain her calm as that realization hit. Others failed. One driver jockeyed sideways to get away from the edge, and touched wheels with another. The two cars bounced apart, and the lighter of the two careered off into the void.

Cassica felt her heart in her throat as she saw it dive. Just for an instant, she was in that car, plunging to her doom. Just for an instant, she was Chabley Pott, consumed by flame after being hit by Lady Scorpion's stinger.

What am I doing here?

"Cassica!" Shiara cried. There was real fear in her voice. She was looking at the ceiling. Cassica followed her gaze up to the stalactites that hung over the abyss. She didn't know if it was the motion of the car, but they seemed to be visibly shivering. For the first time she became aware of a ringing sound, growing in volume, cutting through the bellow of the engines.

"They're singstones!" said Shiara. "Get us out of here!"

Shifting down a gear, Cassica stepped on the accelerator and Maisie roared. She swung out to the edge of the bridge, Maisie's wheels spinning inches from the drop, and powered past the car in front. As she passed, she glimpsed the driver's frightened face – he was blond, about seventeen, a wisp of a moustache on his lip. The darkness sucked at her, but she held her nerve.

The cars had bunched and slowed on the bridge, caution jamming up the pack. She nosed her way past another car, forcing it aside. Nobody wanted a collision here. All the time, Shiara kept looking towards the ceiling, and the ringing got louder.

Singstones. You'd see them in the badlands: weird rock formations found near craters left by orbital weapons. Cassica and Shiara had discovered one once, passed half an hour singing and shouting at it, laughing as it spoke back to them in a shivery, spectral whine. The louder you shouted, the louder the song came back, and if you kept at it constantly the song would keep rising in volume till the stone itself shook. In fact, they'd heard that if you made enough noise for long enough . . .

. . . they sang so loud they shook themselves apart.

Cassica heard a crunch from above, saw something plummet past in the dark. And then the stalactites started coming down, dropping like bombs towards the racers below. Panic bubbled up in her as the first stalactites fell into the abyss on either side. It boiled over when they started hitting the bridge.

Behind Maisie there was a wrench of metal as a stalactite came down square on the hood of a car. It smashed on impact, flinging shards and chunks of rock in all directions. Two racers swerved and went over the edge. Cassica heard their screams on the way down.

"Drive!" Shiara shouted, and Cassica threw all caution to the wind.

The bridge was chaos. Racers skidded this way and that as stalactites detonated around them. Cassica shot through gaps as they opened, driving aggressively, consumed by the need to get off that bridge. There was a screech of metal as cars collided. From the corner of her eye, she saw a trike go tumbling into the void, its rider flailing as he came free of its saddle.

Stone chips pattered against her helmet, speckled her goggles. She swung through the traffic, squeezing between cars, riding the perilous edge. Somehow, wherever she went, the way opened up before her. Somehow the falling missiles never found their mark. In her most acute moment of terror, she was most in control, and she sewed through the pack like a needle.

She burst loose of the group and covered the distance to the end of the bridge at speed. A tunnel swallowed them. After the empty expanse of the cavern, the tight space was a relief, the walls and ceiling bright with the glow of headlamps and the air pulsing with the growl of engines. She was close behind another racer, breathing his fumes. There was no space to overtake.

They were in the tunnel mere seconds before they saw the end. A dim circle, grey and murky. Shiara recognized what it was before Cassica did.

"Brakes! Slow it right down!"

Mist. Mist, down here underground. They plunged into a world of bleary shadows, warm and wet, and were dazzled by the reflected light of their own headlamps.

A dark shape loomed on their right. Cassica saw it too late to do anything but brace. The Rhino slammed into them, crashing the flank of his vehicle against Maisie. They were flung against their harnesses and knocked skidding away. Cassica's teeth clacked together, her neck whipped hard enough to dizzy her with the pain, but through it all instinct kept her fighting with the wheel. They spun through the muggy murky half-world, fishtailed wildly on slick rock, and came to a halt with their back wheels teetering in the air.

Neither moved, stunned by the impact. Unseen, other racers whipped past them, mosquito-fast.

Shiara looked over her shoulder. They were hanging over a bubbling pool, natural springs hot enough to boil them alive.

Dragged by the weight of her engine, Maisie began to tip backwards.

06

Shiara screamed as Maisie tilted towards the bubbling pool below them. But what she screamed was *"Turbos!"*

She ejected her harness and flung herself forward, adding her weight to Maisie's nose as Cassica thumbed the button. Maisie lurched forward, shoved from behind by the force of her boosters. She gave a lurching hop, and her back wheels found the stone lip of the pool. They bit, throwing her forward; her front wheels crashed down, and she stalled.

Cassica swore loudly as she battled to restart the engine. Shiara began frantically strapping herself in again, her mind awhirl. How to make back the time? How much turbo fuel had they burned? Had Maisie been damaged by the crash? She checked readings, adjusted this and that, but it was hard to hold on to any thought with all the death she'd just seen. She'd come a hair's breadth from getting boiled like a crayfish. Half of her didn't want Maisie to start again. Better if this was over right now.

But she'd built Maisie too well. The engine caught, and she gunned into life.

"Follow that guy!" Shiara said, pointing. They could see headlamps in the mist, the shadow of a racer's rear. It was the best idea she could pull out of the muddle. Let the others prove the path. Her priority now was getting them out alive.

Maisie tore off, chasing the lights. Shiara watched the dash, alert for signs of damage, but the impact from the Rhino hadn't been as bad as it felt. Just a sideswipe. It could have been much, much worse.

She raised her head, saw the edges of other pools to either side, bubbling away. They lay in wait as deadly traps for the unwary and reckless. She glanced at Cassica. Steam dewed her friend's forehead. She was angry; Shiara could see it.

"We're too far behind!" Cassica snapped, as if Shiara had complained about her speed. Shiara said nothing. She knew Cassica's moods, knew she was apt to be terse and rude when stressed. It rolled off her. She wasn't the kind to take offence.

They raced up a shallow slope, making time on the heavier car ahead. As they rose, they left the mist behind. Shiara looked back; the cavern, broad and flat, lay shrouded in steamy murk. She saw by the lights that there were still racers behind them, despite their delay. Cassica's heroics on the bridge had put them ahead of the main pack. But where the leaders were, or how many were in front of them, was a mystery.

They swept round a corner, through another tunnel, and suddenly the darkness turned to startling, dazzling light, bright enough to blind.

The car ahead of them skidded as the driver stepped on his brakes too hard. Cassica shot past him into a cavern filled with immense crystals, a field of transparent broken teeth whose angles reflected their headlamps endlessly. All around were the other racers, their own headlamps flashing, switching this way and that, refracted through a hundred prisms. The whole cavern was ablaze with shifting light, so that it was hard to see where they were going at all.

"Slow down!" Shiara said, but Cassica wouldn't slow now. Whatever they threw at her would only make her more determined to beat them. She slipped and skidded between the towering crystals, dodging lances of light thrown back by her headlamps as they moved, battling past the blindness.

Out of the disorder in her head, Shiara plucked an idea. She reached over and flicked off Maisie's headlamps, more as an experiment than anything else. It worked. Suddenly there was no longer light shining back at them, but the cavern was bright enough with the headlamps of the other racers to see where they were going.

64

"Genius," Cassica muttered approvingly, and put her foot down. Despite herself, Shiara felt warm at that.

Maisie tore through the cavern, overtaking other racers who'd been forced to slow because of the dazzle. They made good ground, enough that Shiara began to hope again.

There were two exits from the cavern: one at the top of a slope, the other at the bottom of a dip. Shiara had enough of a handle on the designers of this place now; she knew better than to choose the easy option.

"Upslope," she said, and Cassica obeyed.

One more tunnel and we're out, Shiara thought. Their crude map had told her that much. They'd broken the back of this course. She scanned around for the Rhino, but he was lost somewhere in the swarming light of the cavern behind them.

Into the tunnel, alone. There was no one ahead of them, it seemed, or they were so far ahead as to be out of sight. The leaders had headed for the other exit. No need to climb a slope with their heavy vehicles if it wasn't necessary.

But Maisie was a good climber, and what went up had to come down. They intended to come down fast.

There, ahead: sunlight! Shiara couldn't help a smile breaking on her face. Just to be out of this place felt like a win.

Maisie burst from the tunnel, and before them was the sky, banded with a sour rainbow of colour as it met the wide-open horizon. A long dry incline led down towards the distant finish line and the crowds in their bleachers, cheering as they turned from their screens to watch the racers emerge from the dark. Another tunnel, lower down, let out on to the flat hardpan, and other cars had already come through it, powering towards the finish. But Maisie had gravity on her side, and a bellyful of turbo fuel that they'd saved for this moment.

"Hit it," said Shiara.

Cassica whooped, let off the leash at last. Maisie surged forward as the turbos kicked in, and Shiara was squashed back in her seat as they went faster, and faster, and faster, until it seemed that Maisie wanted to rise up off the ground and float. Shiara adjusted the angle of the rear spoiler, increasing the downforce there, but even so, they were going so fast they were barely in control any more. It felt wild, throwing off all care like that. They were stripped of everything but velocity.

Maisie came off the slope and into the pack in sixth place, but she crept up on fifth and pushed past without opposition, and then they had their sights on fourth. First and second place were out of reach, they both knew that, but they only needed third to qualify.

They could catch third. Maybe.

Shiara got busy at the dash, making adjustments, tweaking Maisie's systems to squeeze every last bit of speed out of her. All the racers were blazing full turbo now, but Maisie had the edge, and she closed the gap on fourth. Wind buffeted them like the breath of an oven. In the distance, the tips of the crowd emerged from the heat haze.

They inched alongside fourth. Shiara saw the driver grimace, her teeth gritted as she tried to force more speed from her car. But she couldn't stop Maisie moving slowly in front.

Third place ahead. A low, lean speedster, dust clouding the sponsor's logos on its rounded flanks. The finish line was approaching fast, *too* fast: already the crowd were going wild as the winner drew close.

They weren't going to catch up in time. Shiara felt the realization settle on her like a weight. All they'd been through, and they wouldn't even qualify. Even if she wasn't sure she wanted to go to Anchor City, she wanted the choice.

Then the gap between them began to close, faster and faster, Maisie eating up the distance. Shiara looked at Cassica in wonder, unable to understand where she'd found the extra power. But Cassica was doing nothing at all; she was focused only on the win.

They weren't going faster. The car ahead was slowing down.

"The safety limiter!" Shiara said. The tech had miscalculated the distance, and the driver had pushed their turbos too hard until they overheated. Now the automatic cut-off had shut them down, to prevent the car blowing up.

"Go!" Shiara cried. "Go!" As if her encouragement might make Maisie move faster. Resurgent hope swept her along on a wave. Their car clawed forward, dragging their opponents closer, engine screaming as each part was taxed to the maximum. The cracked hardpan thundered beneath their wheels as they raced to the finish line. The cameras stuck to them eagerly, the announcer's metallic voice a frenzied babble on the wind, the roar from the bleachers growing.

Go!

They were wheel to wheel.

Go!

And edging forward.

Faster!

And the finish line was beneath them, and gone, and they heard for an instant the riot of the crowd and saw a flash of screens. Then they were slowing, slowing, the turbos cooling, everything spent and only fumes left in the tank. They rolled into a pit area marked off with a chicken-wire fence, where the winner was already getting out of his car. Only when they reached a halt did they let out the air in their lungs.

"Did you make third?"

Harlan's eager face thrust into Cassica's, his expression amazed, elated, desperate. He leaned into the cockpit, slapped them both awkwardly on their helmets in congratulation. "Great race, girls. Great race! Did you make third? It was too close to tell!"

Cassica was as bewildered as Shiara was. "Don't know," she mumbled. "It was too fast."

"Come on, we gotta see!" Harlan said, and he practically pulled Cassica out of her harness in his haste. Shiara unclipped and followed. Cameramen hovered around, capturing their uncertain faces for the crowd.

Harlan led them to a corner of the pits where a small screen, shaded by a tarpaulin, showed the race feed to the managers and medical crew. The announcer's voice came through the screen and the nearby loudspeakers at the same time, a disconcerting echo in the sky.

"And now I'm hearing that we have the results of the photo finish ready to show you!"

Shiara saw Harlan clutch Cassica's upper arm. Cassica didn't seem to even know he was there: she was fixed on the screen. It bothered Shiara somehow, that familiarity he had, so she looked away to her left and saw the driver and tech whom they'd been racing for third place. The tech, a freckled, pug-faced boy, gave her a rueful smile, a look that said: *well played*. Shiara nodded back. Drivers drove as enemies, but most techs felt like they were in it together, united by their passion for machinery and their willingness to live in the shadow of another.

A grainy photo came up on screen. They all looked. Shiara felt the blood leave her head.

Maisie was in front by inches.

"Third place ... Cassica Hayle and Shiara DuCal!"

The crowd cheered. Harlan hugged them and babbled congratulations, and those around them applauded. The pug-faced tech clapped Shiara on the shoulder; the driver stalked away, glowering like a thunderhead.

"You did it!" Harlan cried, his forehead glistening. "You're heading for the Core League qualifiers! Oh, you beautiful girls! What a race! What a race!"

Shiara and Cassica exchanged a glance, each reading the other. They'd been tossed into a meat grinder and come out whole. Many others hadn't. Only fools would volunteer for that kind of treatment again.

But Shiara saw the savage joy in Cassica's eyes, and knew her friend would forget the horror by morning. She wondered if they'd end up as fools after all.

07

Shiara lay on the hard warm stone, head pillowed in her hands, feeling the heat of the day on her bare arms and legs. She watched the sun through closed eyes, red through her lids, her heart bumping against her ribs. From nearby and all around came the splash of water, raucous laughing cries and shouted insults. Young voices: the youth of Coppermouth, strutting and flirting and jostling for favour.

I could stay here, she thought. *Like this*.

But she couldn't stay for ever, and she knew it.

She raised herself up on her elbows, eyes narrow as they adjusted to the glare. The riverside was busy this afternoon. Kids basked on ledges on the steep banks of red rock, or dived off into the brown slow waters beneath. On the far side of the Copper River, tanglefruit groves sprawled across the lee side of a range of broken hills. Beyond them was the ridge, the last barrier before the Rust Bowl.

It was a hot, drowsy day, the kind of day when it seemed nothing important should be done. Yet Shiara couldn't find it in herself to be restful. There was a decision to be made, and it weighed on her.

Harlan had a lot to say when she told him they might not go to the next round of qualifiers in Anchor City. The look of wounded disbelief on his face was something to behold. It was the first time she'd known him lost for words. Of course, pretty soon he got his tongue back, promising this and that, apologizing for what they'd been through.

"I didn't know it'd be that way! My heart was in my throat the whole time when I saw the traps those snakes had hid inside those caverns. Those Outer League cowboys, thinkin' they can do what they like just because there aren't any really big sponsors to answer to! That'd never happen in the Core League. When we get to Anchor City, I know people. I'll make damned sure the organizers never get near a Maximum Racing circuit again!"

But all his pleading and outrage didn't move her an inch. Shiara wanted time to think about it, and she wouldn't be swayed. Harlan invited himself over for dinner with the family the next day, but it soon became clear he was out to persuade Blane and Melly of the righteousness of his cause, so Shiara sent him packing. Now he was stewing in the bar of the Crab and Hook, waiting for their word and drinking more than was good for him, if the gossip was right.

Among those playing in the river, she found Cassica, trying to escape Card as he chased her through the water. Benno, Jann and Boba were flinging a ball about and splashing everybody. It looked like fun out there, but Shiara preferred to stay on the shore. She was pear-shaped and short, and even when she wore a long T-shirt to hide herself, the water made it cling to her curves unflatteringly.

She watched as Cassica let herself be caught, and they kissed, her hair sleek and seal-like as she held Card's face. Cassica, of course, looked great in a bikini; but that was Cassica.

Card had been on his best behaviour since the race. No more sulks, no passive-aggressive sideswipes. Cassica was confused but happy: she wasn't used to relationships that didn't involve arguments, and wondered why he was being so nice.

But Shiara knew. He sensed that soon he might lose Cassica. It was the same thing she was thinking.

Maximum Racing. The Core League. Anchor City. It was a dizzying, terrifying thing, to be given the key to all that. A temptation like she'd never had. And all it might cost was their lives.

Cassica wanted it, of course. She lived her life headlong, and Shiara got pulled along in her wake.

Since Cassica was taken in by the DuCal family at six years old, she'd been leading Shiara into some kind of trouble or another. But all the scraps and falls, the close calls and heartbreaks, hadn't tamed Cassica one bit. She forgot them and moved on, learning nothing. Bad outcomes happened to other people as far as Cassica was concerned. For her, the opportunity that Harlan offered was something to seize with both hands.

But Shiara remembered the race at Ragrattle Caves. The chaos, the speed, the screams as racers plunged to their deaths and singstone stalactites crashed down around them. The bubbling pool that almost boiled them alive. The Rhino.

The world on television scared her. It was a stark glittering land of wild glamour and danger. Celestials in sparkling dresses and fabulous cars; lowlifes jacked on drugs, waiting to take you down. A parade of stars hanging over a junkheap. Small-town folk warned their children about places like that. You could trust your own kind, they said, but you couldn't trust anyone from the cities. Deceit was in their blood.

And yet that was where the races were. *Real* races, not dirt-track boondock circuits or barely regulated suicide runs. Races with an audience of millions. A place where you could show the whole world you were good enough.

She thought of the faded billboard overlooking the

Point. RUTTERBY LAKEYNE DRINKS FAZZ! She wondered if one day it would be her and Cassica up there. Wouldn't that be a thing?

"It won't be like that last race," Cassica had told her. "Up there in the big leagues, they don't aim to kill half their racers. Viewers get squeamish: the sponsors don't like it."

"Uh-huh," said Shiara, sarcastic. "Remember the Slaughter Year?"

"I don't, and nor do you. But that's history, and they learned from it. You heard what Harlan said. If you're prepared, if you're good enough, you'll make it through. And we *are* good enough!"

But here in the sun by the river, it seemed crazy to dream of leaving this place for the unknown perils of Anchor City. This was an honest town with honest folk. A simple life, but a decent one, with a family that loved her. Her future laid out, fixing cars for Daddy, and later for Creek. It wasn't glamorous, but then, it wasn't likely to be fatal either.

There was a splash and patter as Cassica pulled herself from the water and up on to the ledge where Shiara lay. She came padding over, dripping, wiping water from her face.

"You been lolling about up here long enough," said Cassica. "The boys want a game of duckball and we need another player."

"I'm alright here. Don't even like duckball."

"You're making out like I'm giving you a choice,"

said Cassica, a mischievous grin spreading across her face.

"You better not!" Shiara warned, seeing her intention. Then she shrieked as Cassica squeezed out her hair all over her, splattering her with water.

She sprang to her feet, laughing. "You gonna frickin' pay for that!" she cried, but Cassica seized her by the arm while she was off balance and started dragging her towards the river.

Though she was stronger than Cassica and she really didn't want to go in the river, she let herself be pulled, squealing in outrage all the way while the boys in the water laughed along. You couldn't say no to Cassica when she was in this kind of mood. By the time they reached the lip of the ledge, Shiara had given up resisting.

Cassica took her hand, and their eyes met. When the two of them jumped, they jumped together.

As night approached, fires were lit on the scrub-covered hillside, and they lounged around in towels, drying themselves. Someone played a guitar nearby, and the distant, sad howls of jackwolves drifted down from the ridge.

Shiara, cross-legged, gazed into the flames. Cassica sat close, leaning her head on Shiara's shoulder, her eyes closed. A rare moment of stillness. There was something childlike and trusting in it that touched Shiara.

Cassica had never been officially adopted, since there wasn't much use wasting time on legal matters in Coppermouth, but she was close as kin nonetheless. They had the thoughtlessness of sisters: affection came easily to them, but they were apt to take each other for granted, because they both felt, deep down, that the other would always be there.

Except suddenly that wasn't true any more. For the first time, Shiara faced the possibility that her best friend was going to leave.

No, she thought, as she stared into the snapping fire. *Ain't just a possibility. It's certain.*

Over the last few days, they'd talked of nothing else but going to Anchor City. Sometimes Cassica got impatient, wanting a decision from her, and then they argued. She said Shiara was holding them back, that this was the chance of a lifetime. Shiara couldn't disagree. When Cassica calmed, she apologized and told Shiara she didn't mean what she'd said. But she wasn't being honest with herself. She meant every word, and she was right, and Shiara felt terrible for that. Yet still she feared to leave the world she knew for the dangers of the unknown.

Then, last night, Shiara had come to a realization, one so sharp it pricked her from sleep. She sat up quickly in her bed and looked across the moonlit bedroom to where Cassica slept, as if Cassica had spoken it aloud.

Cassica was leaving, with or without her. Maybe

not today or tomorrow, but eventually. If Shiara refused to go to Anchor City, Harlan would offer to take Cassica alone, find her a new tech to pair with. Cassica might stay out of loyalty, but the damage would be done. Coppermouth only held her because she'd never seen a way out of it. This town was a cage to her, and Harlan had thrown open the door.

Sooner or later, in a few days or a few years, Cassica would go. And if Shiara didn't go with her, she'd be left behind.

The crunch of boots caused Cassica to stir against her shoulder. Card was approaching, skirting the firelight. He was carrying his goat-herd kit, a whistle round his neck and a shotgun in his hand. He squatted down in front of them, putting the gun across his knees.

"I oughta be off," he said to Cassica. "Jackwolves are apt to snatch a kid this time of year, and old Karby'll rip me a new one if I lose any."

Cassica gave him a drowsy smile and a nod. "See ya," she said.

Confusion flickered across his face. He wanted a goodbye kiss, perhaps; he wanted her to express regret that he was leaving. But they were things he couldn't say without embarrassing himself now, so he stood up stiffly. "Uh-huh," he said, by way of a farewell; then he headed off up the hill into the dark.

Shiara felt a little sorry for him. He didn't know Cassica like she did. All his efforts to keep her were wasted. She was already detaching herself, readying to leave him behind. He wasn't part of her future. Too late, he'd realized he wanted to be with her, but she was already leaving in her mind.

Shiara was seized by that dreadful feeling again, the same one that had woken her in the night. One day, the same thing would happen to her, and she'd be left alone in this town. That idea frightened her more than anything.

In that moment, the decision was made. She'd rather be with Cassica anywhere than without her in Coppermouth.

Cassica was looking up at the ridge, her face lit by the fire, hair unbrushed and tangled, her eyes far away. Shiara followed her gaze. There, in the last light, the dust was visible as a sifting haze, blowing off the Rust Bowl over the town. The killing dust that had taken Cassica's mom.

"Let's do it," she said.

Cassica's head snapped around to face her. "You better not be kidding me," she warned, excitement and hope in her voice.

Shiara let out a long breath. It felt like a weight had lifted. The decision was made. She smiled. "I ain't kidding. Let's do it. Let's go to Anchor City."

Cassica let out a strangled cry of joy and disbelief, and pounced on Shiara, bearing her to the ground in a hug. "Yes! Yes! Yes! You're the best!"

Shiara laughed and struggled. "Alright, alright,

it ain't *that* exciting!" she protested, even though it really was.

"We're gonna be famous!" said Cassica. "You and me! You and me!"

You and me, thought Shiara. And it felt right.

08

The days following their arrival in Anchor City were fast and dizzy as first love. The streets amazed them: the people without number, the din of hawkers and traffic, the fizzing neon signs scrawled across the night. The energy was overwhelming. They went to bed excited and talked into the small hours, and all their talk was of the city, and what a place it was. They could scarcely believe they'd once considered staying at home.

Harlan was often absent – "Cutting deals, girls! Lots to do!" – so they were left to their own devices for the most part. They used their time to explore, walking the boulevards beneath the billboards where Celestials advertised scents they could only imagine, foods they'd never heard of, cars of impossible beauty. Shiara kept a lookout for Rutterby LaKeyne, but while there were advertisements for all kinds of fazz, different Celestials held the bottles now.

They toured the shopping districts, marvelled at fantastic confectionaries, and Cassica tried on dresses when she dared. They felt like intruders then, guilty in the knowledge that they could never buy such finery. With Cassica's encouragement, Shiara tried a few herself, but she felt awkward and her reflection was unfamiliar. She preferred to stand by while Cassica twirled before the mirror, enjoying her friend's pleasure. Cassica wore the clothes like she was born to them.

Afterwards, Cassica insisted they go to an auto parts showroom so Shiara could run her hands over the latest intercoolers and gearboxes. It was a sore test of Cassica's patience, but though she drummed her thumbs against her legs and flitted about like a bird in a cage, she protested that she was perfectly content until Shiara had mercy on her and they left.

On their fourth day in the city, they awoke to find a note in an envelope pushed under the door of their room.

"Meet me at twelve-o, Reunification Plaza, by the statue of Wolkerston," Shiara read aloud. "Harlan."

"He surely is a mysterious sort," Cassica observed, twining her fingers together over her head as she stretched.

"He's left us more money too," said Shiara, pulling out a handful of notes.

"That's breakfast taken care of, then."

Their hotel and the area surrounding it were not

as glamorous as the shopping districts. There was a bare, unfinished look to the buildings, and the people were coiled and unpredictable. They hung on corners dicing, or moved in furtive groups, and there was a watchfulness about them that Cassica found predatory. More than once they'd been catcalled and had quickened their step to escape. Another time they'd been followed for half a dozen blocks before they came to a busy street and their pursuer gave up.

"It's just for a few days," Harlan told them. "Only till I get something fixed up." But they were having such a good time, it didn't occur to them to be worried.

They found breakfast at a street stall and sat outside eating rabbit skewers and spiced eggs with the space elevator rising above the buildings nearby. There was hardly any place in Anchor City you couldn't see it, dividing the sky, casting a narrow shadow to the horizon and beyond: a massive cable fifty metres across, stretching upwards, thinning and thinning until it was lost to sight.

Somewhere on the edge of space, the Celestials lived in a vast and wondrous habitat, far from the cares of those beneath. The technologies that built and maintained that place were beyond the understanding of the greatest minds of the day. It was a relic of the old world that had somehow survived the Omniwar, a place of almost unimaginable luxury, where every whim was catered for. You could have your food prepared by the greatest chefs alive, wear clothes tailored specially for you by leading designers. Concierges waited on your command; everything was at your disposal. Nothing was ever less than fabulous. There, the most famous and popular people in the world mixed and mingled, while their lives, loves and losses were chronicled daily for the earthbound on *Celestial Hour*.

They called it Olympus.

After breakfast, Cassica and Shiara took the bus into the city, where they roamed the streets until at last they came to Reunification Plaza, a pillared circular expanse of stone, garden and glass. Tourists roamed between monuments commemorating heroes of the Reunification, when the world dragged itself out of the mire of the Chaos Age and the four great nations that shared the continent came to be. On the floor was a map cut from bronze, showing the divisions. Pacifica dominated the west coast, Kurtisland the north and centre, while the Eastern Seaboard Confederacy had everything on the other side of the mountains. Texico took the south, all the way down to the half-drowned and storm-lashed wastes of Panamania.

"Don't you miss Card?" Shiara asked, as if reminded by the map that there was a world outside Anchor City.

Cassica looked back at her friend, who was regarding her with one eye asquint against the bright midday.

"I really don't," she said, and she put her arm round Shiara's shoulder and gave her a squeeze. "I got you."

Twelve-o came about, and they headed to the statue of Wolkerston, which stood on a pedestal on the edge of the plaza where the road ran close. Shiara reckoned he was some kind of general by the gun he carried and the way he was standing, but Cassica didn't care much for history. They watched the road instead, remarking on the cars that passed. Never had they seen such a variety of vehicles until they came to Anchor City; back home, everything was rugged and functional, built for strength over beauty. They even spotted a Celestial car, one so sleek and sculpted it might have been designed by some alien engineer, moving silently among the traffic.

The snarl of an engine distracted them, and a Braxford Interceptor pulled up to the sidewalk. Harlan leaned out of the window and grinned.

"Hey there, girls! Like the ride?"

Shiara was already hurrying up and down excitedly, examining it from all angles. The bodywork was bright red and flowed like a wave over the wheels. Large-bore turbo exhausts shone in the sun. It sat low on its chassis, purring with power. Cassica could tell just by the sound that it had a monster of an engine, and it made her heart flutter.

"Tell me that's for us," she said reverently.

"Want to take her for a spin?" Harlan asked.

Cassica and Shiara locked eyes in a frozen instant of joyous disbelief. Then they squealed like children and jumped into each other's arms.

The speedometer edged into the red as the Interceptor tore down the straight, turbos blazing. Cassica held on to the wheel, calm as a stone on the outside, quivering with excitement within. Shiara, in the seat next to her, had a great big smile plastered over her face. She scanned the gauges on the dash, eyes greedy for information as she scribbled down notes on a pad.

"The stresses this thing can take are insane!" she yelled.

"How long do you think I can go before the turbo explodes?" Cassica asked happily.

"We're not even near the cut-off point," Shiara replied.

"Turn off the safety limiter! See how far we can push it!"

Shiara gave Cassica a look. Cassica grinned. "Kidding!" she said. Back in the days before safety limiters were introduced, racers used to regularly blow themselves up by overheating their turbos.

She cut their speed and swung into a series of turns. Floodlights blazed as they passed; behind them, the space elevator was a string of white dots against the dark, ascending to infinity. Night had crept up while they'd been putting the Interceptor through its paces, yet it seemed as if they'd only just got here.

The track lay inside an empty stadium in the heart of the city, a snaking loop of tarmac used for time trials, junior qualifiers and other motorsports less lethal – and less popular – than Maximum Racing. Today was a designated practice day, and there had been two dozen cars out on the track, testing their engines and race set-up before retreating to the pits to make adjustments. Most had left by now, but Cassica and Shiara's thirst was undiminished. They could have gone till dawn, if the track didn't need to close.

They pulled into the pits and backed the Interceptor in next to Maisie. Harlan had hired them garage space at the track for the week leading up to the qualifier, so they moved the old car in with the new to allow Shiara to run comparisons. Maisie looked shabby and battered next to the Interceptor, but Shiara intended to tinker with her anyway, when she got the time.

"What's the point?" Cassica asked when Shiara said as much. "We've got the Interceptor now."

Shiara shrugged. There was no point. The Interceptor was superior in just about every department. But this was Maisie, the car Shiara had built and rebuilt a dozen times. She was a comforting habit.

They climbed out of the Interceptor's cockpit, removed their helmets and began poring over Shiara's notes, looking for ways to improve. Harlan was elsewhere; once he'd got done basking in their gratitude, he'd gone to the bar, leaving them to speculate how he'd laid his hands on such a fine vehicle. As ever, he'd been evasive when they asked.

"You're the talent," he told them. "All you need to worry about is racing. Leave everything else to me."

Shiara could barely wait to let the engine cool before she opened the hood and started fiddling. Cassica read out numbers from the notepad. She'd only got a few lines down when she noticed someone watching them from the garage entrance, a boy of seventeen or so, dressed in racer leathers and leaning against the jamb.

"'Scuse me," he said, once he saw she'd noticed him. He had a flat Greenspan drawl, from north Kurtisland. "Just came by to see who it was throwin' that Interceptor round the track all day."

He approached them and extended his hand. Shiara noticed he offered it to Cassica first. Everybody did.

"Name's Sammis," he said.

"Cassica," she replied, and shook.

He offered his hand to Shiara. He had a broad easy face, plump in the cheeks, with a scattering of freckles across his nose. Shiara looked at her hands helplessly: they were streaked black.

"Oh, I don't mind a bit of grease if you don't," he said, so Shiara shook with him too.

"You a racer?" Cassica asked.

"Driver, yeah. My tech's elbow-deep in our car

right now." He looked at Shiara. "You guys love to tinker, don't you?"

His wry smile embarrassed her; she wasn't sure if he was making fun. She felt herself flush and looked away. Blushing was agony to her. On others it looked pretty, but for Shiara, with her too-pale skin, it was a curse, an angry red glow that had always attracted laughter and mockery from her brothers.

Sammis didn't laugh, though, because Cassica was talking to him now. He probably didn't even see.

"You gonna be in the qualifier?" she asked.

"That's right," he said. "Last one before the Widowmaker. Only just made it through the regionals in time. I guess you two will be racing as well?"

"Yep," said Cassica. "All the way to Olympus."

His laugh was tumbling and kindly. "I like your confidence. Forgive me, I usually keep a close eye on the regionals best I can, but I haven't seen you guys before..."

"We came up through the Ragrattle Caves race."

His eyes widened. "I heard about that! Damn fools, running a race that way. What was it, sixteen out of forty participants dead? Thought we'd left those kind of numbers behind in the Slaughter Year."

"Yeah, well," said Cassica, as if to say: *What's to be done?* "We made it through, anyway."

"Without a scratch too," said Sammis, admiring the Interceptor.

"We made it through with *her*," Shiara told him, pointing at Maisie.

He looked at them both to see if they were pulling his leg, then whistled to show how impressed he was. He walked around Maisie, examining her. Shiara felt faintly annoyed at the way he sized her up, like his opinion meant all that. Then she got annoyed at herself for giving a damn what he thought.

"I'm no tech, but this looks like you built it from the ground up. That so?" he asked Shiara.

"Uh-huh," she said, sullen with suspicion.

"Girl's a sorceress when it comes to such things," Cassica added, and Shiara blushed again.

"Well," said Sammis. "I see she ain't carryin' any sponsors, either. My deepest respect for makin' it here under your own steam. Too many folks in Maximum Racing just buy their way in these days. Used to be it was about how good you were. Now it's just about who looks best on the television, who's got the most expensive car. Race sexy, leave a pretty corpse."

That surprised Shiara. She hadn't expected a cynic when this farmboy from the Greenbelt walked into their garage. He seemed about to say something else when they heard running footsteps, and Harlan appeared, shiny and flustered. He relaxed visibly when he saw them.

"All here? Good. We gotta go." He noticed Sammis and disregarded him as quickly. "*Now*, girls!" he said, clapping his hands.

"What's up?" Cassica asked.

"We got an appointment, that's what. And we're late."

"Who with?"

"Will you just get moving?" said Harlan, with barely contained exasperation. "I'll explain on the way."

"Think I'll get out of your hair," said Sammis. "Hey, I never caught your name..."

Shiara belatedly realized he was speaking to her, but before she could answer, Harlan answered for her. "That's Shiara, and we're going!" he said rudely. He began shutting the garage door. "Come on, it's all gonna be locked up. Out that way. Out!"

They'd never seen him in such frantic haste. Sammis raised an eyebrow at Shiara – *what's his problem?* – and ducked out before the door came down. Shiara and Cassica were hurried out of a side entrance.

Harlan had his own car parked outside the stadium, a third-hand thing that looked better than it ran. He said he didn't like driving around in new cars: a good manager had no business outshining the talent. Once they were on their way, he made a call to confirm their appointment.

"What?" he yelled into the phone. "What do you mean, cancelled? I just dragged my best racers out of their practice and you tell me it's been cancelled?"

He apologized profusely after he hung up. "People

in this town," he said, shaking his head. "I'll drive us back to the hotel."

But neither Cassica nor Shiara were fooled. Harlan was no actor. They could tell by the hammy way he spoke; there was nobody on the other end of that phone call. There'd never been any appointment.

So what had caused him to hurry them out like that?

09

"Don't I bring you to all the best places, girls?" Harlan asked, an arm draped over each of them.

They stood on the edge of a hall heaving with glitz and throbbing to the dirty grind of a Kellis Osten beat. Pretty women served drinks in clothes that sparkled and showed more than was decent. A brand-new Siyatsu racer, polished to a mirror sheen, rotated on a platform in the centre of the room.

Everywhere they looked, they saw people they knew: famous drivers, minor actors, politicians, music stars that hadn't yet made it into legend. Celestials in waiting. Between them moved the newsies with cameramen at their shoulders – "Just a few words about your new film, Ms Fayette!" – and the paparazzi, slinking like eager weasels through the flock – "Give us a pose, love! Now like that! A kiss for your fans!"

Harlan basked in it all, enjoying their awe, smug with power. "Didn't I promise you the big time?"

The girls were so stunned by the sight and sound that they hardly even noticed his arms lying heavy across their shoulders, the hot sour smell of him so close.

"Come on," he said. "Let's get down there, get you some drinks, loosen you up a little. You look like a pair of rabbits about to get hit by a truck." He released them, patted them both on the back to spur them onwards. "Better get used to this. Lot more where this came from."

Cassica had been frantic with nerves from the moment Harlan announced he'd got them into a press event to promote the next race. He made out it was no big achievement on his part, though he did it in such a way as to imply that it really was. "Some managers just got the connections," he said.

The preparations had begun immediately. They were going to be on television, their pictures in the zines; they needed to look the part. He'd booked them in to a stylist who'd take care of everything, from hair to make-up to clothes. She was an elegant lady named Alia who moved with impossible grace and looked like she'd never had an emotion in her life.

Shiara treated it all as if it was something to be endured rather than enjoyed. She said nothing and let Alia do as she liked. Sometimes Cassica envied her ability to submit to the future, to shrug and get on with it. She herself was in torment, caught in an agony of choice. What should she do with her hair? What jewellery should she wear? What dress?

In the end, it didn't matter. Alia made a polite show of considering her suggestions, then said, "Why don't we try it *this* way?" And that was the way they'd do it. Cassica was left delighted by her transformation, but embarrassed by the process. She felt used, dressed up like a mannequin, her own opinions treated as worthless. And yet, when she saw herself, she realized how trashy and gaudy her own ideas were. A boondock girl, aping sophistication. Alia was right to ignore her.

Her stomach knotted as they walked into the crowd. She was an imposter here, and they all surely saw through her illusion.

They made their way towards the centre of the room. Harlan snagged them drinks from a passing waitress whom Cassica thought beautiful enough to be famous just by virtue of her face and figure. He gave them a glass each, then took two for himself, downed one and put it back on the waitress's tray. At Harlan's urging, they sipped their drinks. Afterwards they couldn't even remember what they tasted like.

"Look there," said Harlan. "Bet you know who that is."

Of course they knew; they'd just never expected

to be in the same room. It was a jolt to see him with their own eyes. Curiously, it felt less real than television.

He was a withered old turtle of a man, dwarfed by hulking bodyguards, his bald head patched with liver spots. His eyes were hidden by absurdly large shades with acid-green plastic frames, an affectation so tacky that only a man of great wealth and power could carry it off. And they didn't come much more wealthy and powerful than Dunbery Hasp, the media mogul who owned Maximum Racing. Every race, every broadcast, every deal was licensed through him. He'd bought it lock, stock and barrel twenty years ago and turned it into a phenomenon. Here was the mastermind behind the sport that consumed the world, the genius that made it all happen. Frail and ancient though he was, he still seemed more important than everybody else in the hall.

"Right, let's find you girls a camera," said Harlan, casting about for a likely target. "Just be honest if anyone asks you a question. Your story's gonna sell itself."

"Our story?" Cassica asked, who wasn't aware of any story.

"Hup! This way!" Harlan took Cassica's arm and led her off briskly in another direction. "No sense wasting time talking to *them*."

"Who?" She looked around but could only see a finely dressed couple in their sixties shaking hands with a group of smart young men who seemed very happy to see them.

"The Cussens," said Harlan, a note of disgust in his voice. "Dridley and Prua. Desperate folk. Won't do us any good to be seen with them. "'Sides, they'll bore you half to death."

Cassica looked back as they were led away. Dridley Cussens was a plump, balding man with an ingratiating smile who mopped at his brow with a hankie; his wife was a narrow lady in pearls, bird-boned and sharp. They bade farewell to the young men and turned away. The young men lost their pleasant faces and exchanged smirking glances of mockery.

Shiara caught Cassica's eye, and Cassica knew what she was thinking. *City folk. They'll say one thing to your face and another behind your back.* It was a common refrain back home, though in Cassica's experience they did it plenty in Coppermouth too.

She searched the crowd, amazed by the company she was mixing with. Harlan was right: she had to relax, blend in. Stop looking so awestruck. They were here because they deserved to be.

She finished her drink and took another, enjoying the decadence of taking without paying, of being served by someone so glamorous. But she couldn't quite manage to do it without saying thank you, the way they did in the movies. She'd have to work on that.

Her drink was halfway to her lips when she froze.

Through the lights and the people she saw a familiar face. Familiar because it had haunted her fantasies these past weeks. The racer she'd seen on television in Gauge's Diner.

Kyren Bane.

"'Scuse me," she said to Harlan and Shiara, and then she was away. She acted without thought, her decision instant, the way it had to be on the track sometimes. By the time doubt caught up, it was too late to turn back.

"Hi," she said, intercepting him as he made his way across the room alone. "I'm Cassica. You're Kyren Bane, right?"

Up close, he was even more beautiful than on the screen. Dark hair spilled over dark eyes. He wore the studied disdain of a rebel. He pulled on his cigarette, took it out, and let smoke seep between his lips while he looked Cassica up and down.

"Yeah," he said, finally.

"I saw your race. That qualifier you won."

"Oh, yeah?"

"I'm a driver too. Racing in the next qualifier. Going for the Widowmaker, y'know?"

"Is that so? Cool." His tone made it sound like it was anything but. His attention skated away from her, flicked back, skated away again.

Cassica felt the heat rise in her cheeks. She wasn't used to indifference from boys. It only made her try harder. "Yeah, we made it through on a blind race.

Ragrattle Caves." But now she sounded boastful, now she was conscious of every word, and each one sounded worse than the last.

"Oh, yeah?" he said, looking over her shoulder as if for someone more interesting. "Don't know that one."

An awkward silence ensued. Cassica felt herself floundering. She was frustrated and embarrassed and didn't know how to get out of it with her dignity intact. To leave would be to admit defeat, but she wanted to win.

"And who's this, Kyren?" said a gruff voice, as two more joined them: a teenager and an older man in his fifties.

The teen was Kyren's tech; it couldn't have been otherwise. Both had the same crafted style, the same arrogant poise, perfectly matched without matching. The older man had a big face with a broken nose and haggard, sad eyes. He seemed kind and hard all at once.

"Anderos Cleff," he said, when Kyren didn't introduce him. He held out a calloused hand and Cassica shook it. "And this is Draden Taxt."

Draden nodded at her. It was clear what he thought, what Kyren thought. Boys that looked like that, famous boys, there'd always be girls who flung themselves at them.

I'm not some damned groupie, Cassica thought, and the anger made her feel less embarrassed.

"And you're Cassica Hayle, I think?" said Anderos.

Belatedly Cassica realized she hadn't introduced herself. "Yeah," she said, and then frowned. "How do you know?"

"That was a hell of a drive you did at Ragrattle Caves."

"You saw that?"

"Well, it was on late, but it's my business to keep an eye out for talented new racers," he said with an indulgent smile. "I'm a manager, in case you hadn't guessed. Manage these two fine boys here, among others." He slapped his hands down on his racers' shoulders. Kyren looked away like a sulky teen annoyed by a parent, and blew out smoke; but he glanced back at Cassica afterwards, and there was new interest in his eyes. *Talented new racers.* Cassica took a small victory from that.

"There you are!" said Harlan, hurrying up alongside her. He took her arm. "Come with me. Alpha Sports want to talk to you."

"Harlan," said Anderos, by way of a greeting.

"Anderos! Didn't see you there," said Harlan, fooling no one. "Not tapping up my new protégée, are you?" It was pitched as a joke, but it evidently wasn't.

"Not my style, Harlan," said Anderos, with a careless lazy smile. "I only take on clients that ask me."

"Well, I'm gonna have to steal her away from you

now," said Harlan, still holding possessively on to her arm. "See you by the track!"

"Look forward to it," Anderos replied. He smiled at Cassica. "Goodbye, miss."

"Pleasure to meet you, Mr Cleff," said Cassica, pointedly ignoring Kyren and Draden. "Glad there are *some* gentlemen at this party."

Anderos's surprised laughter followed her as Harlan led her away, his eyes searching the crowd, agitated. "What was that about?" he demanded. Then: "Never mind. We need to catch the Alpha Sports people before they find someone else. Where's Shiara got to, anyway?"

Shiara wandered through the babble like a lost child, looking for something familiar, something to make sense of it all. Around her, people smiled and air-kissed and chatted and posed for photos. They all seemed to know one another, and they dressed in finery that would outshine a wedding back in Coppermouth. A bass beat pulsed through machine-cooled air. Shiara felt as if she was a member of a cinema audience that had stumbled through the screen into the movie, a creature from the world outside, so utterly foreign that they couldn't even see her.

It had been no surprise when Cassica ran off – she always did at parties – but when Harlan left her to talk to some newsies, she'd found herself anchorless, and gone roaming.

"Hey there. You look as lost as me."

The voice belonged to a tall blonde woman in her early twenties, with huge blue eyes and an eager smile. Shiara thought she looked rather like a doll.

"Not really my thing," she said, gesturing at the party around them.

"Mine either. Hell, I don't think I know a soul here 'cept for my manager and my tech."

She spoke rapidly in a Texico accent, which Shiara found unaccountably charming. She'd never met anyone from Texico before. "You're a driver?"

"I am." She extended a hand, cocked her head to one side. "Linty Maxxon."

"Shiara DuCal. Tech."

She clapped like an excited child. "I just *knew* you were a racer! Don't ask me why, I could just tell. I love your hair, by the way. What a colour!"

"Thanks," said Shiara, feeling faintly embarrassed. "That's just how it grows."

There was an awkward pause as they looked at each other.

"I bet I know what you're thinking!" Linty said. "You're thinking: isn't she kinda old to be starting out in racing?"

Shiara blinked. "That *was* what I was thinkin'."

"Everyone does. But I think all that razzle-dazzle the scientists say about 'reactions' this and 'aggressive driving' that is all just bullshine! I think they all just believe it 'cause so many people have said it for so long. And I'm here to show 'em that someone like me is just as good as some cocky sixteen-year-old who never uses the brakes 'cause they think they're invincible. Am I right?"

"Uh ... yeah," said Shiara. Talking to Linty was like being verbally machine-gunned. She hadn't really wondered before why all the racers in Maximum Racing were so young. She'd just accepted the reasons that everyone had given her: that teenagers had faster reactions and drove more aggressively.

"Hey, did you know they've got this big old museum of cars up on the north side of Anchor City? Like, pre-war cars going back a thousand years?"

Shiara was momentarily wrongfooted by the change of subject. "I'd like to see that," she said.

"Oh, me too! Wanna go?"

Shiara hesitated. "Um..."

"Told you, I don't know a soul here!" Linty said. "Oh, come ooooon, it'll be fun!"

Shiara eyed her dubiously. But then she thought of all those old cars, and how bored Cassica would be if she went, how she wouldn't last ten minutes there. "Sure," she said. "Why not?"

"Great!" said Linty. Just then her manager appeared, a whiskery old man who informed her she was needed for an interview. Linty made a face at Shiara. "Sorry," she said. "Gotta run."

Before she left, she borrowed a notepad from her

manager and scribbled down an address. "That's where I'm staying," she said. "Call by!"

She was led away into the crowd, leaving Shiara a little bewildered, but rather pleased. On balance, she thought she liked Linty Maxxon. Maybe she would call by. So she folded up the address, looked for a pocket, realized she didn't have one, and stuck it in her shoe instead.

She wandered away. Her feet took her to the edge of the room, where a thin crowd had gathered at the top of a short set of steps, observing something below. The sound of raised voices drew her.

At the bottom of the steps was a pair of glass double doors, standing open – a side entrance to the hall. Two security men guarded it, their backs to the crowd. They stood impassive while an old man in a shabby suit shouted at them.

"Move yourself, you damned pair of apes! Don't you know who I am?"

"Your name's not on the list, sir," they told him, their words more polite than their tone. "So you don't get past."

"I don't need any list! You know my face, don't say you don't!"

"If you're not on the list," they said, "you're not coming in."

"Ah, get out of my way!" snapped the old man. He made to push past them, but one of the guards planted a hand in his chest and shoved him backwards. It wasn't a hard push, but the old man tottered and fell to the ground hard. There was a ripple of shocked laughter from the crowd at the top of the stairs.

The security guards seized the old man by the arms and began dragging him away. Shiara looked around at the faces in the crowd, expecting a reaction, and was amazed by what she saw. Some were amused, some scandalized, some appalled, but all of them were just watching.

"Ain't anybody gonna *do* anything?" she cried. But they just looked at her, surprised or disgusted by her lack of manners. Some of them seemed offended, and some smirked into their glasses.

At that, her outrage boiled over. She pushed past them and down the stairs, through the doors, and caught up with the security guards in the corridor beyond.

"You let him go!" she snapped at them. "You let go of him!"

The security guards looked over their shoulders, surprised to be addressed by a girl half their age. They took in her dress and shoes, and though they didn't know her they couldn't be certain she wasn't important, so they dropped the old man and stepped away.

"Ain't you ashamed of yourselves?" she demanded, as she helped the old man to his feet. "Pickin' on an old man like that. You treat your grandfathers this way?" She was flushed and red and too angry to care.

"You like him so much, take him out of here," said one of the guards. "Save us a job."

"I'll do that!" she snapped. She turned her attention to the old man. "Come on, sir. You don't wanna be mixin' with the kind of people they got in there anyways." She said it loud enough for the crowd at the top of the stairs to hear. Then she lent her arm for the old man to lean on and he, dazed and subdued by his fall, allowed himself to be helped outside.

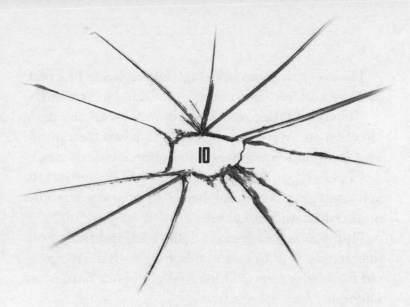

10

She took him to a diner across the street, bought black coffee for them both. They sat opposite each other in the stark fluorescent light, a Formica table and a laminated menu between them. Over his shoulder Shiara could see a television on a wall bracket, showing live guest interviews from the party they'd just left.

The old man hadn't said a word since she led him out. There was a shamed, defeated look in his eyes. His clothes had probably once been fine, but they'd been worn too hard and too carelessly, and there was a musty smell about him like an animal lair. He had the folded and frayed look of a man who'd lost his way and kept on down the path long past the time he could have turned back.

"You're Rutterby LaKeyne, ain't you?" said Shiara. She couldn't think of a more elegant way to broach the matter.

His eyes rose from his mug and met hers. The first flicker of interest she'd seen from him. He grunted.

"There's a billboard of you in my town," she said. "Reckon you were a sight younger when they put it up. Guess those meatheads don't watch old movies."

"They recognized me, alright," said Rutterby. His voice was deep, rich, touched with hoarseness; some of its power still remained.

"But you're a Celestial. . ." she said, and trailed off uncertainly. It didn't seem to square with the raggedy old man before her. "Don't you got better parties on Olympus?"

He took a sip from his mug, grimaced and set it down. "If I was on Olympus, you think I'd be drinking coffee this bad?" Then he seemed to realize what he'd said, and his eyes creased in a weary smile. "Apologies," he said. "Where are my manners? I'm grateful to you, miss, for the assistance and the coffee. What's your name?"

"Shiara DuCal."

"Pleased to meet you, Miss DuCal." He held out a seamed hand and she shook it.

"Never shook hands with a Celestial before," she said, with a tinge of self-conscious pride.

"And you still haven't," said Rutterby. "I'm no Celestial, not any more. There's not a word for what I am. They never talk about what happens *after* Olympus."

"They kicked you out?" Shiara couldn't believe

it. Rutterby LaKeyne, who drank fazz over Coppermouth, whose movies her mom adored?

"There's only room for a thousand up there. Every year, new Celestials go up. That means some people have to come down."

"I didn't know *you* came down, though. Did it happen recently or somethin'?" The look in his eyes told her it hadn't. She felt like she should apologize for not noticing. "I seen the shows and zines and adverts and all, but I ain't no Celestial-watcher. Seems pretty much everyone else is, though. Specially the kids."

"Yeah, everyone here in Anchor City wants to be up there," he said. "They see the parties, the clothes, the award ceremonies. They dream of that. Not many think about what it takes to get there, or what happens when you do." There was open bitterness in his voice, and he caught himself and stopped.

Shiara waited while he decided whether to go on or not. For the first time she realized he was drunk, and not just slowed with age. He held it so well, you almost couldn't tell, but the spite in his tone kept creeping through, and then you knew. The kind of fury that only the drunk and wronged could spit out. He was still recognizably the man on the billboard, but his features had suffered the landslide of years. Shiara wondered at the sequence of events that might have brought him to this pitiable state.

Finally he cleared his throat. "Getting famous

isn't the thing," he said. "It's *staying* famous that kills you." He rocked back in his chair and looked up at the roof as if he could see beyond the stained ceiling tiles to the sky beyond. "Up there, it's like nowhere on Earth. Everything you want, you can have." He trailed off and his eyes took on a distant sordid look that Shiara didn't much like. When he continued, his voice was hateful. "Nobody ever says no to you. Can you imagine what that does to a person? When every ridiculous, dishonourable thought goes unopposed?" He shook his head and closed his eyes. "Rots you. Right out from the inside."

Shiara was taken aback by that. She hadn't expected to be having a conversation like this with a Celestial, or even an ex-Celestial. People back home didn't expose their hearts quite so readily to strangers; it made her feel awkward.

"You've seen *Celestial Hour*, right?" he said.

Shiara gave him a look. You'd have to be blind, deaf and live on Mars not to be aware of *Celestial Hour*. It was the highest-rated television programme on the globe, the only reality show with access to Olympus itself. Through their daily dose of *Celestial Hour*, the rest of the world could participate in the loves and lives of the famous. Scandals, feuds, joy and tragedy played out on screens all over the Earth. Even people who'd never owned a television knew what happened on *Celestial Hour* – Celestial news was more interesting than the real news to most.

Everyone remembered the day when Rica Shawno's web of lies finally came undone; when Jesper Go and Ibsen Tarn at last admitted they loved each other; the agony of Shindra Cone, who bore a child on Olympus that there wasn't space for, and who had to give it away to be raised on Earth because she couldn't bear to leave. Shiara felt sad that Rutterby LaKeyne's fall from grace went by virtually unnoticed amid all of that.

"You think it's utopia," Rutterby said into his mug. He grimaced again, set the coffee aside for good this time. "But that's not what it is. It's a stage. And everyone gotta perform for the crowds."

Shiara took a swallow of her own coffee. It wasn't that bad. Better than she was used to, anyway. "I'm guessin' you didn't perform?"

He chuckled, but there was no humour in it. "I was up there a long time. Long time. Loved a lot of ladies, broke some hearts. Acquired a fondness for drink that'll kill me sooner or later. But one day you realize it's just the same thing over and over again. The parties, the women, all of that. Same betrayals, same feuds, same tragedies, just different faces. So I gave it up. Gave up the friends I had, the people that were bad for me. Kept to myself, tried to take it easy." He snorted. "The viewers didn't like that. When Celestials get to be old news, they gotta make way for the new. And I was old news."

He was silent for a time, and then he smiled sadly

111

to himself. "You ought to see how the kids do it these days. How desperate they are to get your attention. Leilee Baba wearing a coat of human skin. Jalin Hanson eating a pregnant cat live onstage at one of his gigs. Rince, who had his ears and mouth sewn up as a protest against the music industry, and now he only communicates through sign language and a masked albino interpreter." He'd started laughing by the time he got to the end of the sentence, but he ended up coughing instead. "Can't compete with that, and I don't want to. Still got *some* dignity." He sighed. "They'll do anything to hold on to Olympus, you know. They'll kill for it if they have to. They're so scared."

"Scared? Why?"

"Because they know that once you've been there, there isn't anything after." His voice cracked, and his eyes filled, and he looked away.

Shiara looked away as well. The grief of the old always seemed saddest to her, because they grieved for lost things that couldn't be found again, the way Mom did. She sought the television on the wall behind Rutterby, and there she found Cassica.

It was a shock to see her up there, in front of the camera, smiling at the interviewer, chatting with that happy enthusiasm she had. She seemed transformed by the screen, made important by it. In that dress, in that moment, she looked more elegant and adult than Shiara had ever known her.

If she wasn't my friend, I'd think she was one of them.

She felt a pang of petty jealousy: why wasn't *she* up there? Why was it Cassica they all wanted to talk to? But then she remembered how she'd walked out of the party, and she felt foolish for blaming her friend. If she wasn't up there with Cassica, it was her own fault.

"What are you, anyway?" Rutterby asked her suddenly, jolting out of his reverie. "No, let me guess. You've got an accent and an overblown sense of decency, so you're not from Anchor City, that's for sure." She smiled at that. "It's a press event for a qualifier, so... You're a racer? A driver? Don't think you're sponsored, so that means you got there on merit. Girl from the boondocks done good. That's an angle they can get behind. Am I right?"

"Why do you think I'm not sponsored?" she asked.

"You just don't have the look," he said.

She bristled at that. He'd said it thoughtlessly, but there was a weight of meaning in that comment. *You just don't have the look*. You're not beautiful enough, slender enough, stylish enough. Not for the sponsors. When it came to girls, they only want the pretty ones.

"Well, I ain't sponsored, you got *that* right," she said, unable to keep the anger from her tone. "And I ain't the driver neither." She was looking over his shoulder at Cassica as he said it, and he saw her expression and turned around, following her gaze to the television.

"*She's* your driver?" he asked. He raised an eyebrow at her. "Reckon you've got a chance after all."

"Hoy!" Shiara snapped. "We've got a chance 'cause we're *good* at this!"

"No," said Rutterby. "First you have to be good. Then you need a sponsor. Best racer in the world can't beat one who's got money. You know how much it costs to run those fancy cars? You know you're gonna need at least three of them if you want half a chance of winning the Widowmaker, right?"

Shiara sat back, fuming. She hated that idea. Hated that it wasn't just about talent and hard work, that they had to make it about something else too. Hated that he might be right.

Rutterby held up his hands, gave her a disarming smile. "I can see I've offended you. I tend to do that, given long enough in someone's company. Apologies." He pushed back his chair, got unsteadily to his feet. "I should go. Goodbye. Thank you for the coffee."

Shiara said nothing as he left. As he passed her, he paused and turned back, and when he spoke there was a note of pleading in his voice that she hadn't heard before.

"You're a nice honest girl. Don't let them change you. It's not worth it."

Then he shuffled out into the neon-lit street, and Shiara finished her coffee.

Shiara screamed and shielded her face as a wall of flame bore down on her like the opening of Hell's gate. The fine blonde hairs on her forearm twisted as the heat seared her through the Interceptor's mesh windows. She was filled with the terror that came with knowing she'd die by fire.

But the Interceptor slewed right, and the flames drew back, and to her surprise, she lived on.

It took her a few seconds to collect herself from the shock. Not Cassica, though. She was still driving, steel-eyed, as if it hadn't even been a thing.

Anchor City surrounded them, a nest of lights woven through the dark. The racetrack was a floodlit ribbon overseen by billboards with images that moved disconcertingly as they passed. Beyond the barriers, a throng of thousands lined the track, here to see the final Core League qualifier before the Widowmaker.

To their left, now separated from them by a low divider in the road, was Hotwire. The speciality of that particular Wrecker was cooking his victims with jets of flame that fired out sideways from his undercarriage. Coming up behind them was Slick, who used oil as his weapon. Ahead, a gate straddled the track, where huge mechanical jaws clashed together in a steady rhythm, chewing up the distance between them.

Welcome to the big time, Shiara thought to herself, and let out a sudden laugh that was more hysteria than humour.

"Shiara!" Cassica snapped.

Her tone stung Shiara out of her shock. She forced herself to concentrate. She checked the mirrors and the read-outs on the dash, then looked up at the gate and began counting seconds. Timing their approach.

Another racer was ahead of them, and beyond that, another. The rest were too far away to be seen. Cassica and Shiara were in fifth place and needed to make time, but the Wreckers had ganged up on them, and they had to be dealt with first. They couldn't win the race if they were fighting a running battle the whole way. And they needed at least third place to make the Widowmaker.

Shiara glanced to her left. Across the divider, Hotwire kept pace in his red-and-yellow car, waiting for the next gap so he could get closer. He was skinny, pale, red-haired and red-eyed as if from weeping or lack of sleep. Smoke seeped from the rack of flamethrower nozzles between his wheels.

Shiara had never had anyone try so hard to kill her before. Even their clash with the Rhino had been over in an instant, more like an accident than premeditated murder. But the Rhino had been a small-time Wrecker, and Ragrattle Caves a minor race in the Outer Leagues. They were in the Core League now; the Wreckers were twice as deadly. And Hotwire was determined to burn them. His malice made her weak with fear.

Cassica swerved to block off Slick, who was trying to pass on their right. His car was much faster than theirs; if he got ahead of them, he could lay oil in their path. Cassica was determined not to let him.

"Gap comin' up on the left," said Shiara. "Hotwire's comin' over."

"I got it," said Cassica, barely audible over the roar of the engine. The confidence in her voice reassured Shiara, helped armour her against the thought of the fire. Once the divider was no longer between them, Hotwire could use his flamethrowers again.

Cassica drifted right, away from the divider and towards the edge of the track. Crowds and lights blurred together in a jumble. Slick's black racer slid back and forth behind them, searching for the moment to make his move. Hotwire glanced over, and Shiara met his eye. He was hungry to kill.

"Gap coming up . . . *now!*"

Cassica stepped on the brakes and swerved left through the gap just as Hotwire swung the other way. They crossed over in the gap, Hotwire's tail missing their nose by inches. Slick swerved as Hotwire cut across him, and the two Wreckers almost collided. Then the divider rose up in the middle of the track again, with Hotwire and Slick on one side and the Interceptor safe on the other.

Shiara slapped the dash. "Punch it!" she yelled, and Cassica activated the turbos. The Interceptor surged forward with thrilling force and acceleration that put Maisie to shame. The Wreckers' near-collision had cost them speed, and the Interceptor raced away from them, in the clear now, leaving Shiara free to concentrate on the crushing jaws of the gate ahead.

She'd kept counting all through the chaos. Four seconds between each bite. She made a quick calculation of speed and distance; the rest was guesswork.

"Turbos off when I say..."

The racers ahead of them nipped through the gate, one after the other.

"Now!"

Cassica killed the turbos, and immediately the drag began to slow the Interceptor down. It seemed crazy to decelerate when instinct told them to speed through, but Shiara could be as calm as Cassica when it came to mathematics. Numbers didn't trip you up.

She kept counting as the jaws crashed together with

a mechanical screech. Each bite was louder than the last: the howl of hydraulics, the terrible din of impact. Once they clashed, twice, the third time deafening as the jaws met right in front of the Interceptor's nose. Just for an instant, Shiara thought she'd got it wrong, that they were too fast, they'd hit the gate and their world would come to a dead black stop. But the jaws parted and they shot through, and it was on to the next thing without a moment's respite.

Now the track split, one way looping up into a high overpass, the other staying level and bending away right. The racers ahead of them took the rightmost route. Shiara told Cassica to take the other. It was vital to force the Wreckers to make a decision. They needed to shake them off.

Her plan half worked. Hotwire split right, searching for less troublesome prey, but Slick stuck with them, following them on to the overpass.

Shiara cursed under her breath. She looked in her mirror and saw him, a dark face in a dark car, eyes hidden behind shades, black hair pressed close to his skull and gleaming with grease. He was hunched inside an oilcoat, its collar turned up high.

"You got an idea to get rid of him, now's the time," said Cassica.

Slick's turbos boomed and he raced up behind them. His car was all about speed; they couldn't hope to beat him on open track. He wanted to get ahead of them so he could use the oil sprayer mounted on his rear. Cassica tried to hold him back, but he darted and probed till he surged up alongside them.

He looked at them out of his window. Eyes blanked by reflective shades. He grinned, showing white teeth crowded like tombstones. Then he gunned his his turbos again and surged off ahead.

"Don't," said Shiara, as she saw Cassica's thumb straying towards the turbo stud on the wheel.

"We can't let him get in front!"

"We need those turbos."

They'd used them too much already just by fighting to keep up. The pace and skill of their opponents had been a surprise; the racers here were much better than the racers in the Outer Leagues. She fiddled with the settings on the dash, trying to eke out extra speed.

A screen blurred past; she saw their names. Still fifth. Fifth place, and they were nearing the end of the race. It wasn't enough.

"So what do we do?" Cassica cried, as she maneouvred away from Slick, to make sure she wasn't caught directly behind him.

"Magnet trap ahead," said Shiara.

"What good does *that* do us?"

"He's got to let off his turbos before he uses the oil," said Shiara. "He'll set fire to himself otherwise." It something Shiara had deduced from studying old tapes and reading up on their opponents. A tech's job was to give their driver any advantage they could.

"So?" Cassica demanded, but then her face cleared and she saw what Shiara meant.

"Can you do it?" Shiara asked her.

"Just count me up to the magnet trap," Cassica replied, settling herself again.

"Thirty seconds, more or less," Shiara replied without thinking. She'd be more accurate as they neared.

Cassica slid over to the left of the track. Slick was ahead of them now, burning turbos in order to get enough distance to deploy his weapon. Shiara's heart punched at her ribs as they sped up the overpass, the city falling away to either side. If they hit oil at the speed they were going, they'd surely crash and likely not survive it.

The narrow line of the space elevator was a string of stars leading upwards for ever. The roar of the crowds, the lights flashing past, the engine thundering at her back, all of it sank into the background of Shiara's mind. The only thing she could do was keep the count. It was Cassica against the Wrecker now, and Cassica was waiting, waiting, trying to divine her opponent's mind. A battle of timing and nerve.

"Twenty seconds," said Shiara. The magnet trap was visible in the distance: a long row of enormous metal disks on either side of the track, with massive machines of pipes and wires behind them. Cassica was over on the far left of the track, and Slick was drifting across in front of them. Shiara's eyes fixed on the flames licking from Slick's exhausts. He was taxing his turbos hard, and would soon burn all his fuel; but then, Wreckers didn't need to win races. They didn't even count in the race order. They were just there to cause mayhem.

"Fifteen."

The flames from Slick's exhaust went out. Cassica threw the Interceptor to the right and thumbed the turbos just as black jets of oil spewed from the rear of the Wrecker's car.

She cut it fine. The Interceptor's wheel touched the edge of the oil spray, squealed and threatened to slip; but then rubber bit and they surged forward, swinging right across the track. Slick was taken by surprise; he swung to the right to cut them off, but in his alarm he turned too hard, and had to brake in panic to avoid a skid. They shot past him, striking sparks off his front right fender, and sped into the alley of huge electromagnets that pressed close on either side of the track.

"Yeah!" Cassica cried, but Shiara just glanced in her mirror.

"Not over yet," she said.

Slick had regained control and engaged his turbos. His car was fragile, but so very fast. He had the best engine in the race.

"Keep on the turbos!" Shiara said, because it was all or nothing now. They'd pay for it later, but if Slick got ahead of them before they reached the end of the magnet trap, they were done.

The Interceptor shuddered and howled as the temperature gauge rose into the red. The world was a blur of speed and wind. But still Slick crept closer.

"Trigger! Far right!" Shiara called. By good fortune, they were already on that side of the track. Cassica saw the pressure plate in the road, placed at the end of the alley of electromagnets, and she ran the Interceptor right over it.

The effect was immediate: a hum like the drone of a swarm of bees. The very air seemed to shake and warp in their mirrors. Behind them, Slick was caught in between the rows of powerful electromagnets that had suddenly activated. His car slewed left and right, wheels smoking and screeching, pulled this way and that by immense forces. He fought it as long as he could, but one of his axles broke and the car slumped down on its nose. It skidded along the tarmac, shedding metal until it ground to a halt against the side of the track.

By then the Interceptor was already out of sight, over the hump of the overpass, plunging down towards the finish.

Shiara yelled for joy and Cassica whooped as they tore along the track. They'd taken down a Wrecker! The crowd seemed louder, frenzied with cheering.

They passed a screen showing Slick running away from his vehicle, the flash of an explosion knocking him flat as the oil tanks went up. There in the corner was the race order, and there were their names in third place.

"We're in third!" Cassica cried in disbelief. "We're ahead of the others!"

"That, or Hotwire got 'em," said Shiara grimly. She glanced at her dash. "Lay off the turbos. We're too hot."

Cassica didn't respond with her usual speed. She wanted to win. Wanted to win so bad.

"We're too hot," Shiara said again, more gently. Because you couldn't argue with physics, and they were about to hit the safety cut-off point.

Cassica disengaged the turbos. They had little fuel left, but they likely wouldn't get time to use it all before the end of the race, because the turbos couldn't cool fast enough. That would leave them short on the final straight. They just had to hope that the other racers hadn't saved their turbos, or third place might quickly become fifth again.

One more obstacle before the end. A choke point, where the track narrowed until it was barely wider than a single car.

The overpass curved down, joining the track a short distance before the choke point. As they approached, they saw another racer speeding up from the other way: a white car with blue spoilers, a Cobratech logo on the hood. Shiara knew that car and its driver. Linty Maxxon, the fresh-faced, friendly girl Shiara had met at the press junket. She felt an absurd stab of guilt: she'd meant to call on her, but in the preparations for the race it had entirely slipped her mind.

Hotwire was some way behind Linty, too far back to be a threat. There were two other racers ahead, slipping through the choke point one after the other. In second place was Sammis, the boy who'd spoken to them in the garage earlier. His broad, kindly face appeared in her mind, and she found herself oddly glad to see him make it through.

The Interceptor slid on to the track in front of Linty. Linty saw them coming and activated her turbos. Cassica hit the turbos too. The temperature gauge had barely dipped out of the red; now it crawled upward again. They'd get a few seconds out of it, but not much more.

"Take off the safety," Cassica said. She'd joked about it in practice, but this time it didn't sound like a joke.

"Don't be stupid," Shiara replied.

"They always set it way too low. We can get another thirty seconds' burn!"

"Yeah, and every second makes it more likely you'll explode your engine. They set it low so damn fools like you don't blow 'emselves up and take their techs with 'em!"

Ahead, the walls of the track pinched together. Linty was close on their tail, riding up their slipstream.

"Do it!" Cassica demanded.

"I ain't doin' it!" Shiara shouted back. It was dawning on her that Cassica really did mean to take that risk, that she would if she could. She'd gamble with their lives just to keep them ahead.

Cassica shot her a blazing glare, but Shiara was unmoved. She sat back from the dash, held her hands up. "I ain't!" Then there was a buzz from the dash, the safety limiter kicked in, and the turbos cut out.

The Interceptor's speedometer began to come down steadily now the extra thrust was gone. Cassica switched her attention to the mirrors. Linty, still under full turbo, began catching them up, slowly at first and then faster as they slowed.

"She's gaining on us!" Cassica yelled angrily.

Shiara searched for a solution but came up empty. There was no way to get more speed. The choke point was too far away; it would be close, but Linty would overtake them and nip in ahead. With the advantage of turbos, she was too fast to block off.

Shiara gripped her hands together in frustration as Linty's engine grew louder, drowning out the Interceptor's. Should she have listened to Cassica? When they were old women in Coppermouth looking back on their lives, would they remember this as the moment they missed their chance to make it? The moment Shiara didn't dare?

She watched helplessly as the car drew up to them. Linty was in the cockpit, her face creased with a determined frown, her tech yelling encouragement at her. The choke point was coming up fast, but not fast enough. Linty moved on, almost past them now.

Then the world lurched as Cassica swung the Interceptor sideways, into Linty's car.

It only took a nudge in the right place to send a car fishtailing when it was under full turbo. Cassica gave her more than a nudge. The crash threw Shiara against her harness, whipped her head against her shoulder. Shreds of fender spun up in the air; Linty's spoiler tore free. The Interceptor rebounded, shaken like a rag in a dog's mouth as Cassica fought the skid. Through the meshed windshield, Shiara saw Linty's broken tail end slewing wildly across the track, turbos still lit.

Linty smashed into the side of the track where it narrowed. Metal panels punched in with a dull crunch; car parts exploded outwards and a wheel rolled away. Shiara only had time to see the moment of impact before Linty's vehicle was obscured by the wall, as Cassica steered their swerving car through the choke point and out the other side. Ahead of them was a short straight to the finish line. The crowds cheered wildly and Cassica screamed in raw-throated triumph.

But Shiara didn't care about the finish line. She was staring in the mirror at what they'd left behind. Beyond the choke point, she could still see the wheel rolling and bouncing down the track. The world had suddenly become very small and very cold.

"Where's Harlan?" Cassica cried, in the chaos that followed. "He should be part of this!"

When she got no reply, she turned around, to find Shiara had disappeared too. Cassica looked for her in the press of bodies that surrounded them, but saw no sign of her.

She didn't give it another thought. She was too caught up in all the congratulations to let it trouble her. The pits had been invaded by well-wishers and fans; security men struggled to keep them out. Strangers pressed around her, clapping her back, grinning.

The Widowmaker! They were going to the Widowmaker!

Camera flashes went off all around her. She couldn't keep the smile off her face. The adulation warmed her like fire: everyone's eyes were on her, and it felt *right*. She saw herself on screens around the pits, a live feed from the cameramen that were struggling to get to her.

Where *was* Harlan, anyway? Strange that he hadn't been there to meet them after they won. He was never far off when there was an opportunity for publicity.

Sammis pushed through the crowd to her side, and shook her hand warmly. "Well done! Looks like I'll see you in the Widowmaker!"

"Thanks. Good race yourself."

He frowned, craned his head and looked around. "So where's Shiara?" he said with a forced casualness that made his real intentions obvious.

"Was kinda wondering that myself," she said.

He seemed disappointed, but he made an *oh, well* kind of noise, congratulated her again and headed off into the crowd once more. Cassica smiled to herself.

She shook more hands, accepted more compliments, but she soon began to feel slightly uneasy. She had a niggling sense that Shiara should be here to take her share; it took the edge off her mood. So she slipped off through the crowd and went to look for her.

Shiara was on the edge of the pit area, next to the track, standing with her arms crossed over her belly as if holding herself. She had the skill of being invisible in crowds, and nobody was paying attention to her. She was watching the activity on the track, where fire crews and paramedics hurried about, dealing with wrecks, ferrying in casualties from further up the track.

Cassica called her name as she walked up behind her, but Shiara didn't hear. Her attention was fixed on a gurney that was being wheeled towards the open doors of an ambulance. Lying on the gurney, her head in a brace and her face bruised almost past recognition, was Linty Maxxon.

"Hoy," said Cassica softly, and laid a hand on her arm.

Shiara jumped at her touch, spun around and glared at her with such fury that Cassica was momentarily frightened.

"Don't touch me," Shiara said in a tone Cassica had never heard before. Then she stalked away, out on to the track, leaving Cassica gaping, shocked, offended. Uncomprehending.

What was *that* about? They'd won, hadn't they? Shouldn't she be happy?

"Miss Hayle!"

The voice came from behind her. A newsie was making his way over to her, with a camerawoman in tow. "Miss Hayle! What a race! A word for our viewers?"

Cassica looked back at Shiara, still walking away. She should go after her, that was what she should do. But the camera was on her now, and it would look bad for both of them. She could imagine how the news shows would devour the footage of an argument.

So she put Shiara from her mind and put on a smile. "An interview?" she said. "It'd be my pleasure."

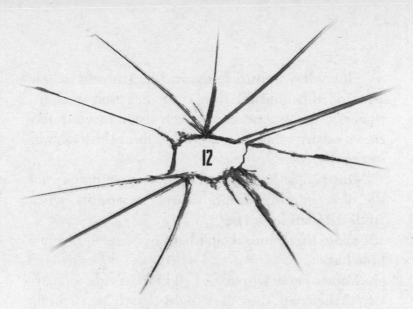

12

Harlan didn't show that night. Not after the crowds had gone, not after the pits closed and the corridors emptied and everything went eerily quiet in the racers' compound. Shiara was nowhere to be found either.

After two hours of interviews with newsies and radio jocks, Cassica was exhausted from smiling. Later, people started coming to her with questions she couldn't answer. Where was the Interceptor going to? Who was signing for the tow crew? Who should sponsors' representatives be talking to and how could they get in touch?

She floundered and sent them elsewhere. Harlan handled the business side of things; Cassica and Shiara only had to turn up and they'd find their car waiting, passes that would whisk them through security, ushers to guide them everywhere. She had no idea what went on among the army of people who toiled behind the scenes: construction workers, riggers, runners, bureaucrats, television crews, safety crews, security staff, and more and more. Her job was just to drive.

Most people had packed up and gone home, and she was hunting around empty corridors when Anderos Cleff found her.

"Hello there, miss. Can't help noticin' you seem a little lost."

"I don't know where the hell Harlan's got to, that's why!" she cried; then she caught herself and held up a hand in apology. "I'm sorry. Mr Cleff, right? I just had people after me all night for stuff he should know about, and he ain't here."

Anderos looked sympathetic. "Why don't I get one of my people to drive you home? You shouldn't oughta be dealing with this. I'll take care of your car and such."

Cassica hesitated at that: it seemed wrong. This was Harlan's territory, and there was something suspicious about letting a rival manager near their car. But by then she was too stressed to care, and she just wanted to be done with the night. Her victory had been spoiled by Shiara's attitude and Harlan's absence.

"That's kind, Mr Cleff," she said. "I'll take you up on that."

Anderos led her to a glass-fronted VIP box

overlooking the finish line, where a party had recently ended. Staff were cleaning up glasses and plates, and the last guests were leaving. Anderos caught one of his retinue and instructed him to take Cassica back to her hotel.

As she was escorted away, Cassica wondered if Kyren Bane had been here among the revellers tonight, whether he'd seen her cross the finish line. It gave her a nasty sense of triumph. *You won't ignore me next time*.

When she got back to her room, she found Shiara already there, asleep. Cassica wanted to wake her up, but she still hurt from that last look Shiara had given her, so she went to bed instead.

There was no sign of Harlan the next day either. Cassica and Shiara were awkward with each other all morning. Cassica tried to smooth things over – she couldn't stand that there was something between them – but Shiara shut her down. It was plain she didn't want to talk, and so the tension remained.

Anderos Cleff dropped by their hotel around midday to tell them that their car was back in the garage at the practice stadium, and to enquire if they'd heard from Harlan. He seemed concerned, and his heavy, scuffed features were grave. Shiara was polite at first, but when she found out he was a manager, she turned cold.

"We'll tell him you were askin' after him," she said, in a tone that said: *Time for you to leave*.

"Please do. And if there's anything I can provide, any help I can offer, just let me know."

"Harlan's our manager, Mr Cleff. He'll see to us." And Shiara closed the door on him.

"He'll see to us?" Cassica said, after Anderos had gone. "*He* ain't here! Do *you* know what we're supposed to do now? Do we need to fill in some entry form for the Widowmaker? Don't we need sponsors or something? How we even gonna get there?"

"I dunno," said Shiara. "I just do what I know how to. And I got a car to fix."

They took a taxi to the practice stadium. Shiara paid the driver while Cassica got out, shaded her eyes against the sun and looked up at the curved walls towering over them.

"You remember that time Harlan hustled us out of here, like he was in one awful hurry? You think that 'n' this are connected?"

"Might be," said Shiara, walking past her. "Might be he's just drunk somewhere."

They found the Interceptor waiting next to Maisie in the garage, just as Anderos has said.

"Least *someone* does their job," Cassica muttered.

Shiara ignored the comment. She walked over to the Interceptor and studied the damage to the front left side, where Cassica had sideswiped Linty

Maxxon's car. She stared for a long time, until Cassica couldn't take it any more.

"Alright, say it!"

Shiara turned and looked at her flatly. "I ain't got nothin' to say."

"Think I can't tell when you're judging me? Girl got hurt; so what? Think I'm proud of it? I ain't! But you had the chance to take off the safety, and you were too scared. So I did what I had to. She'd have done it to us."

"You reckon?" Shiara's face showed nothing. "Guess we'll never know." She picked up a case of spanners, walked over to Maisie and opened up her hood.

Cassica fumed. She was spoiling for a fight, and Shiara wouldn't give her one. Card always used to; at least he was good for that. But Shiara refused to engage, and that was insufferable.

"It ain't Maisie that needs fixing," Cassica said. "We need the Interceptor in good shape. You wanna race the Widowmaker or not?"

"Oh, sure, I wanna race it," said Shiara. "Just fancy workin' on something *I* built instead of somethin' bought for us. You know, somethin' *honest*."

That was too much for Cassica. "Yeah, you better keep her tuned!" she sneered, as she stalked out of the garage. "Gonna need an honest car to drive your hayseed ass back to Coppermouth!"

Shiara didn't reply, of course. Insults and ire just

rolled off her. Cassica could rage and scream all she liked and Shiara would just sit there like some dumb placid mutt and it wouldn't affect her one bit. Some days Cassica just wanted to punch her, see if she could get a rise.

She stormed through the grey stone corridors of the stadium and out on to the street. Here the roads were wide and dusty and hardly trafficked. Warehouses and yards overlooked empty sidewalks. A truck rattled past her as she emerged, but it was the only vehicle out in the midday heat, except for a black car parked a little way from the stadium entrance.

She heard its engine start, but she was too wrapped up in her fury to think anything of it. She heard it drive closer, but she was concocting things to say to Shiara next time they met. It was only when it pulled up ahead of her that she felt the first tugs of alarm. Two men got out, one in front of her, one on the far side. The man before her was tubby, with a heavy brow over small eyes and the grim witless look of a thug.

Now she knew they had something in mind for her, and she turned to run. But the other man was quickly round the back of the car, and he seized her arm as she fled. He was wiry and strong and had nails implanted in rows along his bald head and cheekbones.

Panic took her. She drew in air to shout for help, but Nail-head drove a fist into her belly and she lost her breath in the shock and pain. Then they were all over her, bundling her into the car. She gasped for air and struggled, but they were too forceful. She struck her head on the edge of the open rear door as she was pushed into the back, and that knocked the last of the fight out of her.

Doors slammed, an engine revved, and they moved off. Nail-head pressed up close beside her, a knife in his hand.

"Sit tight and shut up."

Cassica, already terrified beyond reason, obeyed. The sight of the blade made her panic worse. She was still winded from his punch. Her eyes bulged as she tried to suck in air, and she thought she was suffocating. But at last her lungs relaxed, and she breathed again, and soon hot hysteria turned to cold fear.

The thugs didn't speak again, and nor did she. Wild plans of escape slipped and slid through her mind. Fear kept her from moving, like a rabbit in the jaws of a fox. She could go nowhere, do nothing, entirely in a stranger's power. Never had she felt so out of control.

Their journey took them through industrial areas and ghettoes, a seamy desperate land of water-stained brick and chain-link fencing, tramps digging at bins like shabby crows. At last they stopped in an alleyway scattered with rotten mattresses and broken furniture. Cassica was led through a metal side door and the bare stone rooms beyond, until they came to a wide area that might once have been a factory floor. Tall windows made up of grimy square panes let in sunlight to drive back the warm gloom.

Tied to a chair, half his bloodied face lit blindingly and the other half in shadow, was Harlan. He'd been beaten, eye swollen and lip split. He looked up at Cassica as she was led in, then looked down, shamed.

Cassica searched for some explanation. There were other men in the room, some in darkness, some in light. Some had guns.

She heard the scrape of a chair behind her, and she was pushed down into it. Her own hurts were all but forgotten. She'd suffered worse in crashes.

One of the men walked over to Harlan, put a hand on his shoulder. "That her?"

Harlan nodded without raising his head. The man straightened up. He was lanky, hangdog and unshaven, with a horse-like mouth that showed his gums when he spoke.

"Tell her," he said.

Cassica looked from one man to the other, dreading the news to come. "No?" said the man, when Harlan didn't respond. "I'll get you started, then."

He walked over to Cassica. There was something clownish in the gangly way he walked, but Cassica didn't feel like laughing.

"Name's Scadler, miss," he said. "Your manager

got himself in some trouble. I'm guessin' you don't know the half of things, so let me fill you in."

He squatted down beside her and pointed at Harlan as if aiming at him.

"You manager was a big shot once," he told her. "He discovered Liandra Kesey. You heard of her, right? Everyone has. Well, he found her singin' in a club and made her famous. But Liandra's head got turned; she wanted more, and more after that, and Harlan couldn't give it to her. So she went to Anderos Cleff, biggest manager in town. Left Harlan up to his neck in debts and favours owed that he'd taken on to get her to the top." He scratched one unshaven cheek. "Ain't no room for sentimentality in show business."

Harlan sat motionless in his chair. He never once looked up, but stared at the ground between his feet. Cassica might have pitied him if she hadn't been so scared. What did any of this have to do with her?

Scadler unfolded himself straight again. "Well, those debts left a lot of bad blood, so Harlan there, he was pretty much cut out of the entertainment game. He went into Maximum Racin' instead. Trouble is, he ain't very good at it!" He began counting off on his fingers. "Jebson and Trey – dead; Osger and Robbin – dead; Rubble and Tamkin – one dead, one that ain't gonna walk again; Rapp and Espin – you heard any of these names before, miss?"

Cassica shook her head.

"Yeah, that's cause they never amounted to nothin'.

None of 'em got past the qualifiers. Point I'm makin' here is that your manager got a habit of backin' the wrong horse, and that's an expensive habit. He's been borrowin' all over town. Lives are cheap in Maximum Racin'. Cars ain't."

Cassica's gaze hardened as she looked at Harlan. She was beginning to understand now. How much he'd duped and dazzled them. She remembered his speech the night they first met, delivered at the DuCals' dinner table:

This business is full of amateurs and sharks, unscrupulous managers, taking a gamble with some precious kid's life just so they can get a payday. Well, that's not how I do it, Mr and Mrs DuCal. That's not how I do it, Cassica, Shiara!

But that list of dead and crippled kids said otherwise.

Anger helped her find her voice. "He owes you money?" she asked Scadler.

"Oh yeah. A lot of it."

"That's nothing to do with me."

"He's made it so it is. And since you're involved, I reckoned you ought to be in on our chat. Otherwise this feller might spin you any old tale he likes." He scowled at Harlan. "I like my business honest."

"What's he said to you?" Cassica asked.

"He and I, we cut a deal. In recompense for what he owes, he's gonna let me arrange your sponsor for the Widowmaker. An' he's gonna let me keep all the money from the deal, which might otherwise go to your pocket, or his, and on spares and repairs and what-all else."

"That money's not his to give!" Cassica cried.

"Life ain't fair," said Scadler. "But a man's gotta claim what he's owed. Who'll respect him otherwise?"

Cassica fought for an argument, something that would undo what Harlan had done. She wasn't thinking about riches. She was thinking about all the things that were necessary to stand a chance over the three days of the Widowmaker. Backup cars, replacement tyres, fuel, spare turbo systems, navigation gadgets, medicines, and only Shiara knew what else. Sponsors put up the money to help the racers equip their extraordinarily expensive vehicles, in return for advertising their brand. The better equipped the driver, the longer they were likely to be in the race and the more screen time the sponsor's logo would get.

Everyone in the Widowmaker got sponsored by somebody. If they didn't have access to that gear, they were already at a big disadvantage.

"You ain't heard it all yet," said Scadler. "That about covers his debts. But it don't account for the additional impertinence of fleein' the city to hide out in some backwater so as to avoid his responsibilities. With regard to that ... well, I'm a man enjoys a gamble, so here's how it's gonna go. I say you can win the Widowmaker even without that sponsor money. If you do –" he held up his hands "– then all is forgiven. If you don't. . ."

He motioned to a man in the shadows, who stepped forward, brandishing a huge pair of wire cutters. He snipped them in the air. Harlan flinched.

"If you don't, I'm gonna cut off the fingers on his left hand."

Harlan raised his head then, his eyes pleading. Cassica stared at him, strips of blazing sunlight lying between them, divided by shadow. The worldly man with his city wisdom and his fancy words was gone for ever. For the first time, she thought him pathetic.

"Say I don't agree with the deal he made. What then?" said Cassica.

"You don't get that choice. Sponsors only gonna pay me if you get out there and race." He shrugged. "Course, once you've started and I've got my money, I don't care if you win or lose." He wiggled the fingers of his left hand at Harlan. "But I'll wager *he* does."

Cassica felt the weight of that come down on her. Not a person, not in control: a commodity now, a chip to be traded and bet with. A girl without a choice.

She glared hatefully at Harlan. He couldn't hold her gaze.

"You're a damn fool," she told him. "Why'd we ever get mixed up with you?"

Scadler laughed at that. "Untie him," Scadler told his thugs, then he grabbed Harlan by his thinning hair and pulled his head back roughly. "You know better than to run, don't you?" he said. "You know I'll find you, and there won't be no second chance?"

Harlan nodded frantically.

Scadler sneered and let him go. "Get 'em out of here."

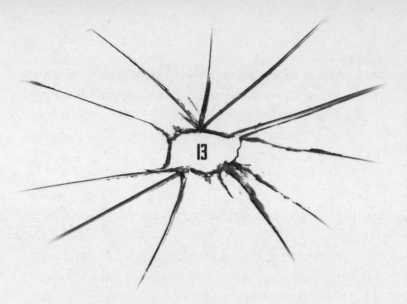

13

"Ladies and gentlemen, racers and managers, distinguished guests and members of the press, it is my great pleasure to present: the Widowmaker!"

The audience erupted in applause as Dunbery Hasp stepped back from the microphone on the stage and held out an arm, as if in invitation to come inside. Behind him, enormous screens lit up in the dark auditorium, showing camera feeds of terrifying landscapes, flashing storms, wrecked cities. Three-dimensional terrain maps showed a tangle of routes; smaller screens at the front of the stage reeled off information.

The audience, seated in semicircular rows, burst into applause. There was excited chatter and a few gasps of anticipation. Shiara, sitting between Harlan and Cassica, neither applauded nor gasped. Her eyes skipped from screen to screen, grimly calculating.

Dunbery Hasp returned to the microphone. A suit cut from bands of glittering cloth hid his withered body, and his wrinkled face was tiny behind his oversized acid-green shades. In any other world, he'd have been ridiculous. But he owned Maximum Racing, owned most of the television channels they watched, the zines they read, the music they listened to. He owned the audience, in his way. So nobody laughed.

"This year we have something quite, quite special for you," he said, in a voice dry as breeze-blown leaves scratching across the floor of some long-forgotten cabin. "As always, the Widowmaker will be made up of three stages in three different locations, raced over three days. Time bonuses and penalties will carry from stage to stage. If you're one hour slower than the leader at the end of stage one, you'll start one hour after him the next day. If you manage to get ahead of them by the end of stage two, you'll start before them in stage three. Simple, really."

He chuckled as if it were a joke. There was nobody in the audience who needed telling about time penalties, but it was necessary to have the rules confirmed. Every year they changed a little bit here and there, in response to viewer feedback.

"Each stage will have a start and a finish, but how the racers get from A to B is entirely up to them," he continued. He took out a rectangular metal object, slid it open to reveal a large red button, and held it up. "As ever, we will be providing rescue alarms for the racers, which will summon help if their car breaks down or they are too wounded to continue. Officials will, of course, only extract them if it is safe to do so. Pressing this button means instant disqualification. Once the stage has begun, they are permitted no help from anyone except their manager, or such help as they can find themselves on the way. At the end of each stage, racers and their cars will be transported to the start of the next stage, where there will be the opportunity to make repairs, switch cars and prepare for the following day."

And that, Shiara thought, was why they were going to lose. Most racers had generous sponsors that meant they could bring three different cars for three different stages, each one tuned and calibrated to suit the terrain. If they damaged their car, they could simply swap it for a new one at the end of the stage. Some racers arrived with as many as seven cars – which was the limit allowed – so they could adapt to changing race conditions.

Cassica and Shiara would have the Interceptor, and Maisie as backup: a trusty car, but hopelessly outmatched in the big leagues. They had only the barest equipment for repairs and spares. It would be a miracle if they even made it through to the end of the second stage, let alone won it.

Harlan had put them in a hole; they had no choice but to try to dig themselves out. He'd tangled them up in his debts, and worse, their success or failure might mean his fingers. That was a burden no one should have to bear, but Shiara, at least, thought they were obliged to. Angry as she was, she wouldn't be responsible for a man being maimed, whatever the circumstances. Cassica wasn't so understanding. She'd begun cutting Harlan off just like she had with Card, severing any ties of emotion or respect. If Harlan lost his fingers, she figured it was his own fault.

Shiara looked over at him, his face hidden in the dark. He hadn't wanted to come, hadn't wanted to show his injuries and his shame, but they'd made him. For all his failures, he knew this game better than they did, and they needed all the help they could get.

"Day one!" croaked Hasp, and some of the screens dimmed, drawing their attention to those which were still lit. "Crookback Bayou! A trackless swamp full of sucking bogs, treacherous locals and lethal wildlife, warped and grown to enormous size due to mutagens in the water from the Omniwar!"

There was more applause as the screens showed aerial shots of an endless expanse of tangled trees, then of the gloomy, eerie world beneath, where insects ticked and strange creatures screeched in the distance. They showed hunters standing over a huge worm as long as a truck, its mouth a sawtoothed circle, big enough to eat a grown man.

Shiara and Cassica exchanged a dismal glance. Neither of their cars were equipped for swampland. Not a good start.

"Day two!" said Hasp, and another set of screens brightened. "Lost Angeles! Once the heart of our nation, now a ruined city, half-drowned by the ocean, home to savage bands of Howlers lying in wait for unwary travellers with traps and ambushes."

Now the screens showed a panorama of shattered buildings, emerging street by street from the waves and spreading towards the mountains, before which a clump of skyscrapers leaned broken and carious against the sunset. The quake, and the tsunami that followed, put paid to the city long before the Omniwar began. Some said it helped cause it; old Merrica's economy collapsed when Lost Angeles and Frisco drowned, and things got bad after that.

"Day three!" Hasp said, as the final screens lit up. "Kniferidge Pass! A race through storm-lashed mountains. Their route will take them along the edge of the Blight Lands, where madness and poison gases lurk among the great battlefields of the Omniwar, and reality itself is not what it seems. It runs so close, in fact, that hallucinations, will-o'-the-wisps and strange tricks of perspective have been reported by our advance scouts. Our racers' nerves and sanity will be tested to the limit as they negotiate bladed rock fields, terrifying precipices and unstable terrain prone to killer landslides! They'll need an iron will to survive!"

The applause was louder this time, and over it Hasp cried: "Ladies and gentlemen, the Widowmaker!"

Now came the cheers, feverish, wolfish, and people rose from their seats to clap. Dunbery Hasp raised a hand, acknowledging their worship like some emperor of old. The auditorium lit up to show the crowd, and Shiara gazed at them in horror, at their glittering hungry eyes, their teeth bared in fearsome smiles.

They want to see blood, Shiara thought. *That's why they watch. That's why the racers are all young. It ain't nothin' to do with reactions or aggression or any of that. They just love to see pretty things die.*

Afterwards, Cassica and Shiara were dressed in white-and-blue racing leathers emblazoned with the logo of their sponsors, MaxiTruck, which neither of them had heard of. They posed for photos while Scadler looked on, dressed to the nines and grinning his gummy grin. No wonder he was happy, Cassica thought; he'd found a corporation dumb and desperate enough to pay him all the sponsorship money up front, no questions asked. By the time they realized it was all going to Scadler's pocket and not on supplies, it would be too late to get it back. A nervous-looking man in a suit, representing MaxiTruck, scurried about in Scadler's wake. Harlan was off elsewhere, doing what he could to cover the shortfall that he'd created.

"Stand closer together, girls!" the photographer urged. "Put your arms round each other. And smile! No, *really* smile!"

But Shiara never was good at faking it; she was stiff and tense where Cassica touched her. It hadn't been the same between them since Linty Maxxon. Cassica felt angry at being judged, and angrier that Shiara wouldn't talk to her about it. Cassica was prone to explosions, but once over they were forgotten. Shiara nursed her grudges, picked at them quietly like wounds, let them fester. She didn't like confrontation. Cassica thought it a kind of cowardice.

After the shoot, they were released into the after-party. It was a calmer affair than the press junket they'd attended a few weeks ago. People in smart clothes chatted in groups over drinks while a small band played folk melodies from the old times. The racers, still in their leathers, stood out from the crowd. A semicircular wall of windows let out on to a balcony overlooking the glittering city beyond.

Cassica and Shiara entered together, but their conversation was stilted and awkward, and Cassica was soon scanning the room for more entertaining company. She made eye contact with someone she vaguely recognized – a round, jolly-looking man touring the room with his sharp-faced wife – and they bustled over eagerly as if invited. It was only when they introduced themselves as Dridley and

Prua Cussens that Cassica remembered them from the press junket.

Desperate folk, Harlan had said. *Won't do us any good to be seen with them.* But now here they were.

"Lovely to meet you!" said Dridley, shaking their hands. "I must admit, you two have come quite out of nowhere!"

"Absolutely out of left field!" Prua agreed, with a shrill and slightly hysterical laugh.

"We think it's wonderful to see such grass-roots talent emerge!"

"Yes! Yes!" Prua bobbed her head like a bird.

"Well, that's very kind of you," said Cassica, a little suspicious. She took a drink from a passing waitress and sipped it.

Dridley and Prua gave each other a look, as if to say: "Shall we do it now?" Then Dridley clasped his hands together and leaned forward earnestly.

"I won't beat around the bush, ladies. Perhaps you've heard of us?"

"Sorry, we haven't," Shiara lied politely.

"Well," said Dridley. "We have something of a standing offer that we make to all the racers who enter the Widowmaker. You see, we are blessed with riches. Some might say, er, *vast* riches. And so we'd like to propose a deal. If you should win the Widowmaker, if you should win those two tickets to Olympus, we will gladly buy them from you for the sum of one billion dollars."

Cassica choked on her drink.

"Are you alright, my dear?" Prua asked, her face a picture of concern.

"Fine," Cassica wheezed.

"To be clear, the offer is for *both* tickets," said Dridley. "We won't buy them separately. I'll not go to Olympus without my wife." And he gave Prua a look of such sugary affection that Cassica wondered if she'd be able to keep her dinner down.

"Can I cut in here? Thanks," said Kyren Bane, stepping out of the crowd. He took hold of Cassica's arm, and she was surprised to find herself staring into his dark eyes. "Coming?"

She was moved as if by the force of his will. In one dizzying moment she was whisked away from the others and off through the crowd, without a thought for those left behind. Her heart beat quicker at his touch.

"Those two," he said. "They're such a pain. You know he bought his own game show just so he could host it? Totally bombed. It's pathetic. All the money in the world and they still can't get to Olympus."

"No way," she said, for want of anything better to say. "Didn't even know you could sell tickets to Olympus."

"That's 'cause no one's stupid enough to do it. Who'd want to stay down here when you could be up there?" He gave the Cussens a disparaging look over his shoulder. "Takes more than money to be a Celestial," he said.

She stole glances at him as they went. He was so perfectly dishevelled, a strung-out angel in black-and-red leathers. He was too flawless to seem real. Walking with him dazed her.

"Yeah, sorry about before," he said. "Didn't know who you were. Get a lot of girls telling me they're racers just 'cause they drive a car. But you're the real thing."

"No big deal," she heard herself say, even though she'd meant to be annoyed, make it harder for him. He shouldn't get away with stuff like that, just because he was gorgeous. But something about Kyren made her want to agree with him, and in only a moment, the matter was done.

"Anyway, you drove the hell out of that last race."

"Thanks."

"And that move you did, knocking that other chick out? Brutal." He grinned at her, and she couldn't help grinning back. "Loved it."

"You gotta do what you gotta do if you want to win."

"See, that's the kind of attitude you need if you wanna make it in this world," he said. He stopped and raised his glass to her. "To you, eh? Gonna be quite a Widowmaker."

She touched her glass to his and gave him a wicked smile. "To us."

"Uh-oh," said Sammis, as he drifted up to Shiara. "He's got her."

Shiara was embarrassed that she'd been caught staring at Cassica and Kyren across the room. She blushed, then blushed more for blushing.

"Always did have crappy taste in guys," she mumbled.

"Hey, can I introduce you to someone?"

They were joined by an older man of bearish size in his early fifties, with a wide flat face, his eyes gullied with laughter lines. She knew him immediately. Dutton Rye, a legend of Maximum Racing.

He'd never won the Widowmaker but he'd driven in six of them, and won two dozen smaller championships over his career. He was known, above all else, as Maximum Racing's great survivor. His career spanned fifteen years – a miracle in Maximum Racing – though most of it was before the age of Dunbery Hasp. He'd lived through the Slaughter Year that followed Hasp's takeover, when they let all cars carry weapons in an effort to boost ratings. One in three racers died that year in a hail of machine-gun fire, or got blown up by mines and rockets. It proved to be too much. The public loved to see a sacrifice, but not carnage on that scale. The limits of their morality had been reached, and Maximum Racing was never as lethal after that. Dutton Rye kept driving through it all.

"Shiara," said Sammis. "This is my dad." He gave her an uncertain frown. "You did know he was my dad, right?"

"I checked up on you," she said. Then, when he seemed pleased, she added hastily: "Before the last race. Tech's job, right? Know your rivals."

Flustered, she extended a hand to Dutton, who shook it. "It's an honour, sir. Used to watch old footage of you when I was little."

"Charmed," he said. "Sammis tells me you're quite a tech."

She looked at Sammis in surprise. "Did he now?"

"Well, you came third, didn't you?" Sammis said. "Drivers don't do *all* the work. I wouldn't be anywhere without a good tech."

"That's gotta be the first time I ever heard a driver say that," Shiara told him approvingly.

Dutton laughed loudly. "You're not wrong. Some of the most awful people I ever knew were drivers. Egos bigger than their engines!" He joshed Sammis, who chuckled uneasily. "Apologies, but I need to be elsewhere. Sam just wanted to introduce us quick before I went. Pleasure."

"Pleasure's mine," she said, a little bewildered. He'd wanted to introduce her to his dad? Why?

Sammis waited till his father was out of earshot, then kind-of-casually said: "Do you wanna get out of here?"

She met his eyes, saw the awkward nervous hope there. The penny dropped. Blood rushed to her face.

He interpreted her surprise as hesitation. "Just out

on the balcony, I mean," he said quickly. "It's a nice night. Too many suits in here."

"Yeah, alright," she said, suddenly painfully aware of herself. She hurried off in that direction, and Sammis trailed after.

They leaned their forearms on the balcony rail, Anchor City a million lights beneath them, and talked for a time about nothing of consequence. Shiara kept the conversation light; she was getting accustomed to the idea that Sammis liked her. It wasn't as if it was the first time a boy had taken to her, but it didn't happen often enough to take it for granted. She was less embarrassed now she knew he was interested, and he was the kind of person who put those around him at ease. Soon she was beginning to enjoy herself.

"Yeah, Dad quit soon after the Slaughter Year," Sammis was saying. "He lasted a couple more seasons – I mean, they learned their lesson, and since then only Wreckers are allowed to use weapons on other racers – but he always said it stopped being about sport and started being about money once Dunbery Hasp took over."

"So what did he do after?"

Sammis ran his hand through his hair and sighed. "Can we stop talking about my dad?"

She realized she'd been quizzing him for a quarter hour. "Sure. Sorry."

"It's . . . well, you know. Famous dad and that. He's great – I mean, couldn't ask for a better dad, but. . ."

"But you get sick of wonderin' if folks are only interested in you 'cause of him."

"Something like that."

"Don't worry. Know the feelin'. Most times people are talkin' to me it's 'cause they wanna get to Cassica."

He looked through the glass at where Cassica and Kyren stood in close conversation, bodies turned to each other, eyes linked lustfully. "Really?" he asked, and the surprise in his voice pleased her.

"You ever wonder what you're doin' this for?" she asked.

"What, you mean racing?"

"Yeah."

He gazed out over the city. "Yeah, I do, as it happens. I wonder it a lot. Guess I just don't know what else to do. I'm *good* at it. Had the best start. When you're the son of a legend, everyone assumes you'll be great too. I was racing karts when I was six. Been driving ever since."

"But?"

"But . . . I guess I never felt I had a choice, y'know? I mean, at first I *wanted* to race. Doesn't every boy wanna be like his daddy for a while? But then you grow up a bit, and you get to wondering."

A warm wind stirred her white hair against her face. She brushed it out of her eyes. "Sometimes I reckon I'm only doin' this to please Cassica," she said.

It was strange how easy it slipped out. "I ain't sure if it's her or me wants this. Certainly ain't sure I wanted it to go this far. I mean, the *Widowmaker*? Hell. I just wanna build cars, or fix 'em. Dyin' in one: that don't appeal."

"You could quit," he suggested.

"Ain't that simple."

"Why not?"

She hesitated then, wondering if she should speak of what had come about. But Sammis had the feel of someone she could trust, and she couldn't think of a good reason why not. So she told him of Harlan's deal with Scadler, and how they didn't dare pull out of the race, and how if they didn't win Scadler would cut the fingers from Harlan's left hand. By the end, Sammis's face had darkened.

"Ain't right," he said. "None of it."

"Lot about this world ain't right," said Shiara. "Speaking of which. . ." She jerked a thumb towards the window. Kyren and Cassica were leaving together, his arm around her, she laughing and pushing him away but not trying very hard.

"You wanna go stop her or something?" Sammis asked.

"You can't stop her," Shiara said. "'Sides, ain't my business what she does with him."

But there was something that soured inside her at the sight. Not that she was jealous – Kyren was plainly trouble all over, and not her type anyway.

It was how easily Cassica turned her back, like she didn't even need Shiara, like their friendship was nothing. They had things that needed fixing between them, but Cassica was walking away. It had never bothered her before when Cassica left her alone at a party, but since Linty Maxxon, things were different.

Cassica was changing, turning harder and colder. Closing her off, the way she did with Card and the way she was doing with Harlan. Shiara had come to Anchor City partly out of fear of losing her best friend, and now it felt she was losing her anyway. This damn race was turning her into someone Shiara didn't know.

"Actually, I oughta go too," said Shiara. "Sorry. This kinda party ain't really me."

Sammis almost kept the disappointment off his face. "Oh, hey, of course. I'll see you at the race, then. Best of luck, huh?"

She was about to leave, but she stopped at that. "Ain't that a funny thing to say, though? 'Best of luck.' We wish it on those we're racin' against, when what we mean is: 'Hope you blow a tyre.'"

He laughed. "You got me wrong. I mean it. I don't care if you beat me, long as you don't win."

"Oh yeah? Why's that?"

"Well." He shrugged. "Gonna be hard for me to ask you out if you're up on Olympus, isn't it?" He grinned at her. "You know, it's pretty when you blush."

159

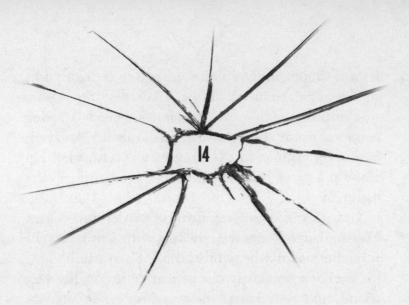

14

Kyren lounged loose-limbed behind the wheel as they tore down the expressway. Even when he was driving, he looked like he couldn't give a damn. Cassica, in the passenger seat, tried to feel as relaxed as he seemed, but her stomach was a knot and she tapped her feet nervously.

He was intimidatingly handsome. Just being next to him made her tense. This was a new feeling: usually it was the boys chasing after her, not the other way round. Usually she was in the driving seat. She wanted him too much, and it made her self-conscious, crippled her confidence.

"Some engine, huh? Listen to that!"

"Beautiful," she agreed, though she hadn't been paying attention to the car for once. In fact, she barely remembered what it looked like from the outside. After he'd led her out of her party, a concierge pulled it up to the kerb, but all her attention had been on him and she didn't even notice what the model was, only that it was black and sleek and expensive.

"All the new Banshees got this special fuel-mixing thing, gives you an extra kick when you put your foot down at high speed. Check it out."

He flicked a switch, pressed the accelerator, and the car responded eagerly. They slid past cars and trucks; bridges whipped overhead; rows of reflected lights flurried up the windscreen.

"See?" he said, over the drone of the tarmac and the hum of the engine. "We're over two twenty and you can hardly even feel it."

"Yeah. But what if you *want* to feel it?"

Kyren smiled wryly to show his approval.

"Where are we going?" she asked.

"Does it matter?"

Now it was her turn to smile. She couldn't imagine a better answer. "Guess not."

They slowed to pull off the expressway, diving down a ramp into the streets. Cassica had no idea where she was, and didn't care. It was enough to be in the belly of the city, racing past neon tangles in the yellow concrete twilight, with him next to her. She'd first seen Kyren Bane in the grubby kitchen of Gauge's diner, when he was on television looking like a Celestial and she was a waitress in a dead-end town. A month later and she was in his car. What a way she'd come. It made her giddy.

"Anderos says you got problems with your tech," Kyren said.

"How's *he* know?" Cassica was faintly disturbed.

Kyren shrugged. "He keeps his eye on stuff, I guess." He gave her a sidelong glance. "So?"

She shifted in her seat, suddenly awkward. Something in that look reminded her that he wasn't just some boy she was out with; he was a rival. And no matter how mad she was at Shiara, it still felt like a betrayal to complain about her to a stranger.

"Ain't nothing," she said at last.

"'Kay," said Kyren. She sensed disappointment in his voice, and felt like she'd failed a test of some kind.

"What about yours?" she asked in an attempt to resuscitate the conversation. "He okay?"

"Draden? Sure. He does his job."

"You guys get on?"

Kyren made a noise which she took to mean: *so-so*. "Don't really know him. Anderos put us together."

"You weren't friends before?" She knew that most teams were built that way, but it still struck her as strange, the idea of driving with someone you didn't trust down to the bone.

"Friends are for when you're off the track," said Kyren. "You don't work with 'em. Too easy for things to get complicated."

Yeah, that's the truth, thought Cassica.

"Y'know, he thinks a lot of you," Kyren said.

"Draden?"

He snorted. "Anderos. Thinks you've got what it takes. Doesn't think much of your manager, though."

"Him and me both," said Cassica, her mood curdling.

"Forget him," Kyren said. "Managers, techs, organizers, all those guys. It ain't them out there making the life-or-death decisions. Ain't them with the guts and the reactions to do what we do. Hundreds of good techs out there, but only a few great drivers. You and me, we're the talent. Everyone else makes out they're important, but they wouldn't even have jobs if not for us."

It felt like he'd read her mind, said aloud the thing she'd never dared admit to herself. Yes, damn it, yes! The drivers *were* the most important ones. More important than crew, more important than production, more important than all those other people doing jobs she wasn't aware of and didn't understand.

More important than techs.

She'd dragged Shiara to Anchor City when Shiara would have rather stayed at home, not taken the risk. They wouldn't be here if not for her. She was the one willing to do what it took to get them *both* to Olympus. And what thanks did she get? Scorn and disapproval.

It felt like a connection between them, this shared understanding. She wanted to know more about him, to see beneath the surface, and she was bold enough to push. Ahead was an intersection, showing them red lights; Kyren was slowing the Banshee when Cassica said:

"You got family?"

She saw immediately that she'd made a mistake. He didn't like that question, and the warmth went from him. "Got a daddy," he said at last.

She sought some way to repair what she'd done. "Bet he's proud of you," she suggested.

"Daddy was never proud of me for nothing," he said, and the bitterness in his voice was so thick it made her cold.

A heavy silence fell between them. *Is that what makes you want to win?* she thought.

It was as if she'd spoken aloud. He turned his head, glared at her with anger in his eyes. Like he was furious with her for exposing him, like she'd tricked him into giving himself away. For a moment, she thought he might actually hit her; but then he jammed the gearstick into a new slot, stamped on the accelerator, and she was thrown back in her seat as the Banshee roared forward.

She sucked in her breath as the intersection rushed towards them, red lights glowing a warning to stop. There was a stationary car in one lane, traffic crossing fast in both directions. But Kyren kept accelerating.

They darted past the stationary car. Headlamps lit up their faces from both sides. Horns blared and tyres screamed as they shot across four lanes of traffic. Cassica pressed her foot on an imaginary brake in the footwell, teeth gritted and hands clawed as she gripped her seat. Kyren swerved; a truck thundered towards them; there was a crash of metal . . .

. . . and then they were on the empty road with the freedom of the lanes, streetlights sweeping past like beating wings. Behind them, the intersection was a snarl of stopped traffic. Several vehicles had collided, though none of them hard.

Cassica barely had time to wonder about the people in those cars before she was thrown to the side as Kyren swerved, hauling on the handbrake. She held on as the wheels locked and the Banshee skidded hard, drawing a smoking arc of burnt rubber across the tarmac. Gawping onlookers hopped back in fright as the car slid a hundred and eighty degrees and rocked to a halt neatly against the kerb on the other side of the road.

They stared at each other, breathing hard. She didn't know whether to shout at him or laugh in dizzy relief. He had a fierce, exultant grin on his face. He'd shown her he wasn't scared of danger. He'd shown *everyone*. But Cassica saw the desperation behind his eyes, and in that moment she knew: he *was* scared, just like she was. Scared he was losing control, scared he'd got himself into something he couldn't get out of, swept along by forces he didn't understand. Scared of the Widowmaker.

She lunged across at him, seized his face, kissed him fiercely.

"Take me somewhere," she said.

And so he did.

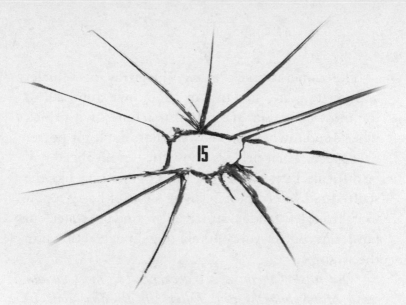

15

"It is the day, it is the time! The drivers are ready, the techs are ready, the Wreckers are ready ... and the long wait is finally over! The greatest race on Earth is about to begin! Welcome to the Widowmaker!"

Fifty vehicles in a line, engines idling in the damp heat of the bayou, watched on fifty million screens all over the planet. Around them, an enormous paddock of tents and scaffold towers, bleachers rammed with onlookers, cameras turning on masts or hovering in the air, kept aloft by whirring fans. Ahead, a sea of drooping trees, thick with vines, endless.

"They have come through fire and fury, through trials and torment; they have succeeded where their fellows have fallen. These special hundred will compete for the prize among prizes, the most precious of all things: two tickets to Olympus itself, to become Celestials, immortalized in legend!"

The cameras track along the array of vehicles waiting to start, stewing in their own fumes. For the most part, they are brutal machines, with thick wheels and towbars and cowcatchers, built for power over speed. Their drivers know the terrain ahead will be difficult. But some have risked lighter cars, like the scuffed red Interceptor bearing signs of hasty repair to its front left fender: sturdy all-rounders, faster but harder to control, more likely to get bogged down in the swamps.

"Out to stop them: the Wreckers! The most vicious band of psychopaths and killers in Pacifica will be released five minutes after the racers set off!"

A fearsome quartet of cars brood inside a bleak compound, caged in with rusty spikes and a gate adorned with skulls. They are not like the racers; some are delicate and spotless, some armoured and dirty, but each one is dark with threat.

"All of your favourites are here! Like Buzzkill!"

A car with circular bandsaws set into its flanks, hood and trunk. They whirr and spin as the driver guns the engine. He is a snarling mass of stitches behind the wheel, wearing a grimy motley of belts, buckles and blades.

"Doctor Sin and the Carnasaur!"

A crazed man in bloody scrubs and a surgeon's mask sits in the driver's seat, quivering like a plucked string, staring madly into camera. Standing in a harness, his upper body emerging from the roof of the car, is a man whose skin is tattooed with green scales like a lizard's, teeth filed sharp and narrow-packed. He is bulging with veins and muscles, stretched from within as if containing some immense pressure, and he carries a rocket launcher on his shoulder.

"The Ghost!"

A white-masked man, his features invisible, inside a grey reflective car so sleek it seems it was made to travel through the air. As the camera turns on him, his car takes on the colour of its surroundings, and suddenly it's hard to make out its outline against the background.

"And last year's champion Wrecker, with a kill count of eight in that year alone: Lady Scorpion!"

A low black car with a roof-mounted spear gun. Behind mesh windows, the Lady herself, dressed in dark leathers like a carapace. She looks ahead, patiently waiting for the moment to be unleashed, already choosing her prey.

"We have some exciting racers vying for the top prize this year! Like the son of Dutton Rye, one of Maximum Racing's all-time greats! Sammis Rye, and his tech, Tatten Breesley!"

"And ... cut to twelve!" says the producer, standing in front of a bank of tiny screens in a darkened studio, each one showing the view from a different camera. The broadcast feed switches to show Sammis in the cockpit of his racer, discussing

169

plans with a stolid, red-haired boy, who is pointing to items on a list.

"Hot favourites Kyren Bane and Draden Taxt, managed by the kingmaker of kingmakers, Anderos Cleff! These two came first in all their qualifying stages!"

Kyren knows where the camera is; he just pretends he doesn't care.

"And from the tiny town of Coppermouth way off in the Rust Bowl, two best friends who rose above their humble beginnings by building their own car to race with! Cassica Hayle and Shiara DuCal!"

In the living room of the DuCals' apartment over the auto shop, a room stuffed with Coppermouth locals explodes into cheers. Heavy pats of congratulation pound down on Blane's broad back, and he accepts them as if it were him out there and not his daughter. Creek is not there; he's in the mountains. Melly sits quietly amid that raucous lot, hands clutched together to stop them shaking, eyes glued to the television and dread in her breast.

"Latest gossip is that Kyren Bane and Cassica Hayle have become an item! Let's see if lovers can live as rivals, or if this relationship will crash and burn!"

"He did *not* just say that!" screams Beesha, as the kitchen staff of Gauge's Diner whoop and slap the countertop. Nobody is even pretending to work. Even Gauge himself has crowded in and popped a beer.

"Our Cass done good!" cries the busboy.

"That lucky sow!" Beesha shrieks. Then she cackles and punches the air. "You go, girl!"

"Over the next three days, these racers will face the most deadly test of their lives. Many will not survive. Just to make it through is an achievement most racers can only dream of."

In a humming grove in the shade of a tanglefruit tree, Card lies against a drystone wall with another girl in his arms, listening to the radio. The girl has drowsed in the sun. She's thinking of how safe she feels when she presses close to him. He's thinking of Cassica.

"The officials have given the signal! The racers are ready to begin! Just listen to those engines!"

In the silence of space, beyond the bright cloudy curve of Earth's atmosphere, Olympus waits to know who will be next to walk its halls. It hangs suspended on its vast tether, the ends of which are too distant to be seen: a space station, a monument among the stars, relic of a lost age when humanity's reach was greater than its control. Ten thousand lights speckle its dark surface, but they do nothing to warm the view. It is huge and cold and alien, and it watches.

"Three! Two! One! The Widowmaker is go!"

The vehicles pull off the line in a churning cloud of dust and fumes. Hovercams swoop down the line as they charge. The broadcast cuts from close-ups to wide shots, screaming crowds and screaming wheels. The racers separate out as they cross the open ground, faster vehicles pushing ahead. One by one they are swallowed by the trees, darting down rally trails and dirt tracks, until finally the last of them is gone.

The Widowmaker has begun.

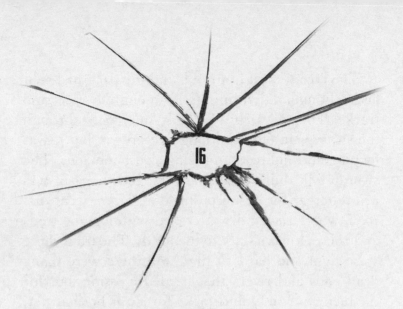

16

Mud sprayed across the Interceptor's windshield as the racer ahead of them slewed through a puddle. Cassica swung the wheel, trying to take her opponent on the inside, but the trail was too narrow and she had to brake to avoid a collision. Her wipers smeared the mud away, showing them a view of the back end of Kasey Rall's armoured Scout, brake lights glaring like a warning. It was a sight they were rapidly getting sick of.

Down the dirt paths of the Crookback Bayou they skidded and slipped, engines growling in the sweaty gloom. Gnarled trees leaned in, reaching for them: old things, bent and warped in unnatural ways, twisted and blistered by strange chemicals in the water. Moss hung from their branches in spidery curtains. The warm haze in the air softened edges, swallowed sound.

The race was an hour old, and the pack had split and split again, dividing itself among the trails and tracks. The maps showed only one route through the swamp, an old road long overgrown; but it was looping and indirect, and dangerously obvious. The swamp folk didn't like strangers, and the road was prime target for an ambush. Most racers went off-road, where the land was crazed with logging trails and routes known only to the locals. The trails there were tight and hard to find, and there were many dead ends and rivers that needed crossing, but for the lucky ones it would make for a quicker journey. Cassica and Shiara had gone that way, and had been making good progress until they caught up with Ralls and got stuck behind him.

"You got anything?" Cassica asked. A hovercam swooped overhead, tracking them; miniature cameras in their helmets provided point-of-view footage for the viewers.

"Nothin' new," said Shiara, but she checked again anyway.

A small screen bolted to the dash fed Shiara live broadcast footage, crackly and unsteady but clear enough to learn from. It was their only source of information about the race.

Right now it was showing a map of the swamp. Most of it was green and unknown, with only a few major waterways and the road marked on it. Scattered blinking dots, representing the racers, were making their way in from the bottom. Shiara made a note of their location on her own map.

A table ranked them according to distance from the finish line. It was measured as the crow flies, so it meant little when the routes were so winding. Still, Shiara was pleased to see they were seventh. She found Sammis in fifteenth, and Kyren in twentieth, but the table was shuffling about minute by minute. Next time she saw it, she expected it to be very different.

The screen switched to show footage from the road, where several racers had fallen victim to an ambush. Cassica and Shiara had been wise to take the back routes with the others. The road had been blockaded with old cars, and now the racers were frantically manoeuvring to escape as ragged frightening figures came lurching from the trees to either side: things in the shape of people, but who didn't seem like people any more. Then the picture bent and the Interceptor lost reception.

"We're doin' alright," Shiara muttered. "Better than some, anyway."

"Fork ahead!" Cassica said, perking up. She craned her neck to see past the Scout. "Which way?"

Shiara consulted her compass and map. "Go left if you can. We're drifting too far east. Don't want to hit the river."

"Ralls is going left!" Cassica protested. She was desperate to get out from behind the Scout.

"Probably his tech knows what he's doin', then," Shiara replied. She didn't know what lay ahead, but she was minded to keep going in the right direction, Ralls or no.

The fork was little more than a muddy clearing where three trails met. The way to the left was the more inviting; the trail to the right was a dark narrow tunnel through the trees, heavily overgrown. A staff stood in the ground at its centre, hung with sinister bone charms and vaguely humanoid figures fashioned with twisted twigs. The Scout smashed through it and slid off to the left, spraying mud.

Shiara took petty satisfaction in hearing Cassica tut as she followed Ralls left. *Yeah, sometimes you still got to listen to me, don't you?*

The trail widened out and the trees thinned to either side, broken up by sodden knolls. Cassica, seeing an opportunity to overtake, pushed forward again, but she had trouble keeping a steady line and the Scout pulled away from them. The Interceptor's wheels were coated in mud, and the chains they'd put on for grip were losing their effectiveness.

"We gotta get past him before the track narrows again," Cassica snarled.

She'd been on a shorter fuse than usual lately; her racer's calm seemed more fragile than before. Shiara wondered if the pressure was getting to her, or if she was distracted by Kyren. Maybe it was the way things between her and Shiara had soured.

Shiara was about to tell her to be patient, it was a long race and they wouldn't win it in the first hour; but then she saw something moving through the trees on their right. Something fast. Something *big*.

"Brakes!" she yelled, and Cassica stamped on the pedal. They were thrown against their harnesses; the Interceptor's tyres ploughed into the mud. A short way ahead of them, the Scout was smashed aside with a scream of metal as an avalanche of haunch and flank and fury charged out of the undergrowth and rammed it. It tipped over on its side and skidded along the trail until it slammed roof-first into a tree.

The Interceptor came to a shuddering halt. Shiara and Cassica stared in shock. Standing across the trail was a creature bigger than any they'd seen in their lives. It stood on all fours, twice the height of a man, a leathery monster that might once have been a reptile but had transformed over generations into something else. Its body was covered in uneven knobby protrusions, and its skull had been warped by rampant bone growth, giving it a huge lumpen forehead. Its eyes were tiny and stupid in a misshapen face; a small low mouth opened above the flapping dewlap at its throat.

It shook itself, grunting, dazed by the impact with Ralls' car. Some cool, distant part of Shiara's mind noted how the tree had smashed in the Scout's cockpit, and that Ralls and his tech had likely been killed on impact. Then shock wore off and panic flooded in, and she yelled, "Back! Back! Get us out of here!"

Cassica threw the Interceptor into reverse, its wheels chewing at the dirt. The creature raised its head at the sound of their engine, regarding them with dull interest, but it didn't pursue as the Interceptor sped backwards up the trail.

"He wants to be left alone, I reckon," said Cassica. She was twisted in her seat, one arm on the headrest, navigating through the rear window.

"Reckon so," said Shiara, watching the beast diminish in the windscreen. It lumbered over to the wreck of the Scout and began nudging it with its armoured head, curious about this strange challenger in its territory.

They reversed up the trail at speed, and when they reached the clearing where the trail forked, Cassica braked and switched gears to go forward again. The other route was tight and forbidding, but it was better than trying to get past that monster.

It was a few seconds before Shiara realized they weren't moving. She looked at Cassica, puzzled.

"We going?"

Cassica shushed her. She was still looking out of the back window. Shafts of sunlight stretched across the hazy gloom in taut blinding threads. Everything was still, and there was silence but for the Interceptor's idling engine.

Shiara felt a low, heavy thump, passing through her feet into the pit of her stomach. Then another, and another after. This was what had perturbed Cassica. The sound came faster and faster. Up the trail, the trees had begun to thrash as if tormented by a sudden wind.

The blood left her face as she put the evidence of her senses together. "Move it!" she cried.

Cassica hauled the wheel and pressed down on the accelerator as the monster burst out on the trail behind them. Shiara caught a nightmare glimpse of something like a colossal alligator, with a mouth big enough to swallow her whole, and then they plunged off down the trail and the foliage closed in behind them.

Branches whipped at the windows, assaulting them on all sides. Cassica worked the gears, one hand on the wheel, fighting the Interceptor's urge to slip. The way between the trees was so narrow that Shiara kept losing sight of it, but Cassica's reactions were fast enough to keep up. Though it felt like they were travelling at a speed close to insanity, Shiara trusted her, as she always had.

"Is it still back there?" Cassica asked, her eyes never leaving the trail.

"I can't see it," said Shiara. She wasn't sure if it had followed them or not. Hard to tell when the engine was roaring in her ears. Still, the Interceptor was surely too fast to catch on foot, whatever its size.

The trail bent left, and Cassica had to brake for the corner. Shiara checked her compass as the turn got longer and longer.

"We're doubling back on ourselves," she said.

But there was only one way to go, even if it led them in the wrong direction. Shiara's screen had found a signal again, and was now showing hovercam footage of Kasey Ralls' Scout. The beast that had rammed it was now stamping on it, rising up on its hind legs to piledrive the wreck with its forefeet. The screen switched to show the Interceptor, filmed by another hovercam which was tailing them. Watching herself live on screen was disconcerting, so Shiara looked away.

"There's another trail!" Cassica called, but before Shiara could find it, the trees ahead of them lashed into a frenzy and that enormous mutant alligator poured itself out into their path in a slithering torrent of muscle and scaled hide. It was a monster, all gaping jaws and dead-eyed reptilian purpose, encrusted in armour like the barnacled hulls of the rotting ships in Coppermouth harbour. It spoke to some deep primal fear in her, the terror of being eaten alive by wild beasts, that echoed out of the ages of history and made her weak at the sight.

Cassica, as ever, reacted first. Without missing a beat, she swerved the Interceptor down the side route she'd spotted, and they were battered again by branches. The windscreen cracked and the car jolted and rocked as they bumped wildly along.

Suddenly they broke free of the confining trees and emerged into a wide clearing partially submerged in brackish water. Grassy hillocks ran between weed-choked pools. Trees rose here and there, dominating their own little islands, twisted and magnificent in isolation.

Cassica hit the brakes. The trail ended here; beyond was a jumble of routes over strips of land that rose out of the water, some by only a few inches. Shiara saw her friend scanning the route, calculating. It was soft and soggy ground, uneven enough to give a four-wheel-drive trouble. The Interceptor wasn't made for such difficult terrain; it would likely flounder and stick. Caught between the monster behind and the swamp ahead, Shiara looked to Cassica for a decision, since she had no answers of her own.

"Hell with it," said Cassica, crunching gears. "We're going for it."

But the car, when it moved, went backwards instead of forwards.

"We're going for *what*?" Shiara cried, as they raced up the side trail in reverse.

They smashed through a mesh of branches, back out on to the trail. The rear screen filled with a wall of rippling green hide. Shiara screamed; Cassica slammed on the brakes. Shiara couldn't make out what part of the creature she was looking at; it seemed to be all around them.

The alligator let out a clattering bellow, and its tail came rushing at their flank like an oncoming truck. Shiara braced instinctively before they were smashed sideways, glass exploding inwards and scattering across her lap.

The impact knocked all reason out of her for a few seconds. She was aware of a burning sense of danger, but she couldn't make her body move, and she just stared at the dash, stunned. When she raised her head, it was as if in a dream, and everything around her seemed dull and blurred. She was aware of a rapid coughing noise and a vibration beneath her seat, but she couldn't make herself understand what it was.

Something huge moved at the periphery of her vision, as if the bayou itself was rising up. It was the teeth that focused her. The massive levered maw, looming towards them.

She screamed again, this time from the well of her guts, a place of such black terror that she thought she might lose her mind. Again, the rapid coughing, the vibration. Cassica, frantic, turning the key in the ignition, leaning into it. The Interceptor trying to start.

"Go! Go!" Shiara was too scared to be ashamed of how high and raw her voice was.

Cassica's teeth gritted. The alligator bellowed a challenge, lumbered towards them in a waddling charge.

The engine caught and roared in response. Cassica jammed the Interceptor into gear and floored the accelerator. They tore away as the alligator's immense jaws snapped closed, missing their rear end by inches.

They careered back up the trail towards the fork with the alligator thundering behind them, smashing trees aside in its rage. Both routes onwards were blocked by monsters now. Cassica would have to backtrack towards the start. It would likely lose them the race, but Shiara didn't care about that now. Forget winning; forget what Harlan had got himself into. They'd fulfilled Scadler's condition by starting the race. Just to survive would be enough.

They reached the fork. Cassica pulled on the handbrake, skidded the car in a tight right turn. Then she drove; not back towards the start as Shiara had imagined, but down the fork where the Scout had been wrecked. Where the *other* monster waited.

"What are you *doing*?" Shiara cried. But Cassica had that look on her face, that eerie determined calm, and she would neither reply nor be turned from her course. The trail widened out. On Shiara's screen, the footage was now cutting between the view from their helmet cams and the hovercam following them. Their plight was now the focus of millions.

The alligator burst out on to the trail ahead of them in a cloud of leaves, having cut through the trees to reach them. Cassica swerved around it and its teeth met in a bony clack as it snapped at the air. Now they could see the Scout, crushed halfway to scrap by the beast that had rammed it. It stopped pounding and looked up as the Interceptor approached, drawn by the sound of its engine.

Cassica hit the brakes and came to a halt. The beast stepped back from the wreck, gathered itself, lowered its armoured head to meet the challenge. Cassica waited, her eyes fixed on the beast's.

"Tell me you ain't gonna play chicken with that thing," Shiara said quietly.

Behind them, the alligator thumped into view. It slowed as it saw the beast, opened its jaws, let out a challenge. The beast's attention switched to the alligator, and it roared back.

Cassica put her foot down. The beast lowered its head and charged. The earth shook as it pounded towards them. Then, smooth as silk, Cassica swung to the right and skidded round the creature, slipping between the monster and the trees. It passed by with a sound like the end of the world, close enough to take off the paint from their fender, and a moment later they were back on the track, impossibly alive. Shiara twisted in her seat to look behind, where the two massive creatures crashed together in a snarling, shrieking tangle.

The trees closed in, the path bent, and they were gone from sight.

Shiara slumped back in her seat. Her screen was

showing footage of the titanic battle going on in their wake. Cassica was driving as if nothing had happened.

"How'd you know?" she said, when she could talk again.

"How'd I know what?"

"That it'd ignore us. That it'd fight the alligator instead."

Cassica snorted, as if she thought Shiara naive for even asking. "You see the size of those two? Think there's anything bigger than them in the bayou? They're the top dogs here." She flexed her fingers on the wheel. "The big guys don't need to pay mind to the little people. But there's only room for one at top."

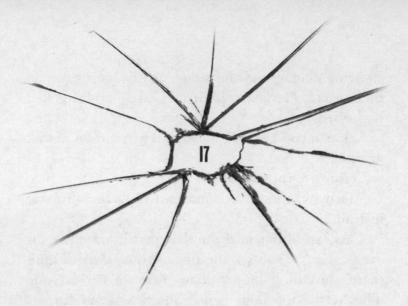

17

They were crossing a rusty iron bridge over a slow murky river when the engine began to struggle. Shiara frowned, reached to adjust the fuel feed, and saw that the screen showing the broadcast had gone blank. Cassica pumped the accelerator, the revs picked up again, and the screen blinked back to life.

It was only a temporary reprieve. Once they were off the bridge and back among the crooked trees, the engine started sputtering again, and it was clear something was wrong.

"Can't you do something about that?" Cassica said.

"Doin' what I can," said Shiara, working at the dash. "You might recall we got whacked by a damn great alligator. Reckon that might have somethin' to do with it."

Cassica tutted, though she wasn't sure if she was irritated at the Interceptor for being too fragile or

Shiara for being unable to sort it out. Maybe it was everything: Harlan, Scadler, Shiara, the lot. She was driving the wrong car for the course, and they had few parts for repair even if they made it to the next stage. A breakdown now could mean the end of the Widowmaker for them.

All she wanted to do was win. Why was everyone making it so difficult?

They sped down trails that tunnelled through the steamy twilight. Dangling ropes of moss stirred as they passed. The Interceptor's power faded every now and then, and the accelerator stopped working, but it always came back after a few seconds. Cassica hoped it would somehow fix itself, but it soon became clear it was getting worse.

"Find us a place to pull in," Shiara said.

"What? No! We gotta keep racing!"

"Engine's gonna die any minute anyway. That's if you don't crash us first 'cause the steering goes, or somesuch."

"Look, I can ride the power loss. It might hold out till the end."

"We ain't even halfway through yet! This car ain't fuelled on wishful thinkin'. Pull in!"

Cassica bit her lip in frustration. The broadcast put them in third place. Whether by luck or Shiara's instinct, they'd picked their way into the heart of the bayou without too many wrong turns.

Now this. So damn unfair.

"Look! Over there! Pull in there!"

Cassica saw a building, slumped and hulking, through the trees to their left. Ahead was a turn-off. She was tempted to defy Shiara just for the hell of it, to keep driving and hope the engine held out; but a temptation was all it was, and she turned off the trail as she was told.

The Interceptor drew to a halt in front of the building, crushing a path through waist-high weeds as it went. Cassica killed the engine, and it seemed like a defeat. For a few moments, they did nothing but sit in their seats, taking stock.

The building was mostly standing, but vines had taken hold of every part of it and the upper floor had largely collapsed. Once it had stood square and grand, surrounded by a pillared porch and a terrace above. Now its tall rectangular windows were empty frames busy with leaves and thorns.

Shiara popped her safety harness, got out, slammed the door behind her. The unexpected force of it made Cassica jump. By the time she got out, Shiara was already lifting the hood, interested only in the Interceptor.

They'd stopped in the remains of a parking lot. The concrete underfoot was tipped and cracked, shattered by the slow strength of plants. The remains of a log barrier was still visible at the boundary, black and decayed, bored hollow by woodworm.

"You need a hand?" she asked Shiara.

"Just keep lookout for a minute," Shiara replied, in that impatient way she'd taken on of late.

Cassica scanned the trees warily. The memory of the monsters was still fresh in her mind. What other wildlife might be out here? And she hadn't forgotten the warnings about the swamp folk, maddened and made strange by mutagens in the water.

The hovercam floated in the air, a whirring light in the murk, watching her with its cold blind lens. With the Interceptor's engine silent, she realized for the first time how noisy the bayou was, how it ticked and croaked and rang with crawling life. Outside the car, she felt naked and vulnerable.

She clutched herself, tapped her feet, impatient and uneasy. Now her mind was unoccupied with driving, it roamed to places she didn't want it to. To comfort herself, she thought of Kyren. That meeting at the party, and what they'd done after. A flush crept up her neck and she felt herself grow warm at the thought.

It was his eyes she remembered best, the way he looked at her, how totally *there* he was. Like nothing and no one else existed but her. Afterwards he'd been cooler, his gaze roving, his speech distracted. He hadn't lingered long, but she didn't mind that. The Widowmaker obsessed them both, and now wasn't the time for emotional tangles. It wasn't a relationship she was after: she had a race to win. But still, she wished she was there right now.

"Any joy?" she asked Shiara.

"I'd get there a lot faster if you'd stop distractin' me," Shiara replied irritably, still buried in the engine.

Cassica took the hint and shut up, but her ego had been bruised, and her mind filled with cruel and unfair things to say to Shiara in response. She tried to keep her mouth shut, but the pressure soon became too much, and she had to let it out somehow.

"Hoy," she said. "We gotta talk."

"No, we don't."

"Yes, we *do*!" Cassica snapped, slamming her hand down on the side of the car.

Shiara came up from the engine, wiping her hands on a rag, and stared at her levelly. "Go on, then."

Cassica hesitated, searching for the words. Now it came to it, she didn't know where to start. "This!" she said, waving a hand at her. "This frickin' thing you do! The silent treatment! Pretending nothing's wrong when it's plain as a dog's ass something's up! What, you want me to *guess* what it is? Is it 'cause I knocked that girl off the track? Fine, I'm sorry, but it's *done*! Is it 'cause you think I'm getting all the attention? That's not my fault: you're never there! Always wandering off or storming away or *some* damn thing! Is it Kyren? Are you jealous?"

"Huh. Yeah. Jealous," Shiara grunted sarcastically.

"So tell me what it is, then! Stop acting like a sulky frickin' child and speak up if you got a problem!"

Shiara sighed, as if an insult like that was just

what she expected from Cassica. "Forget it," she said, turning back to the engine.

"Don't *ignore* me, damn it!" Cassica shouted, and pushed her, harder than she'd meant to. Shiara staggered sideways, tripped on a lip of broken concrete and fell among the weeds.

Cassica felt dizzy, light-headed with adrenaline. She'd gone too far; she hadn't gone far enough. Shiara picked herself up again. Cassica could see she was struggling to keep her cool.

Stop being calm! she wanted to shout. *Let loose on me!*

Shiara dusted down her leathers, not meeting Cassica's gaze. Her face was red with anger. "I'll tell you the problem," she said, keeping her voice carefully even. "Problem is, you've changed. That girl with the fine hair and the make-up and the beautiful dresses, that girl who smiles all the time for the cameras, says the right thing, acts all cute and pretty when the lights are on her: that ain't the girl I knew in Coppermouth. Ever since we came to Anchor City, since that first party we went to... I mean, you just took to it like a fish to water, didn't you? All those zines you read, the shows you watched, you were studyin' up, though you didn't know it. And now you're here, and you got all the poses and all the lines down pat. But it ain't real. It ain't you. It's fake."

Cassica had expected several possible accusations, and had readied her arguments against each of them.

But she hadn't expected this. Not *real*? She wasn't *real* now? What a bizarre and ridiculous thing to say. There was only one explanation for it, and it was the one Cassica had suspected all along.

"You *are* jealous," she said. "You're mad 'cause I can handle the limelight and you're too scared."

But Shiara just shook her head in exasperation. "No, no, I *knew* you'd say that." She put her hand to her face, rubbed her temple with her fingertips, closed her eyes as if fighting off a headache. "Can you just imagine, for one moment, that the world don't revolve around you, that everybody don't want what you want and think how you think? Can you do that?" She opened her eyes and looked forlorn. "I ain't jealous of you, Cassica. I'm afraid of losin' my best friend."

Cassica had been about to launch her next assault, to hurt Shiara the way she'd been hurt herself. When she argued, she argued to win, to beat her opponent rather than making terms. But this last comment took the wind out of her sails.

"You're not losing me," she said, but it sounded limp, without conviction. "And if you are it's 'cause you won't talk to me about it."

"I'm talking now, ain't I? Look, it's just. . ." Shiara struggled visibly. "It used to be about *us*," she blurted at last. "We were *doin'* somethin'. Buildin' a car, racin' it together. It was the doin' of it that counted, not the end. Not whether we won or not. Do you get that? It was you and me."

Cassica was bewildered. "What's the point of building a car and racing it if you don't want to win? What's the point in doing anything if you don't wanna make the best you can of it? If I thought I'd settle for racing dirt tracks in the boonies my whole life, I'd never have started racing at all!"

Shiara looked wounded at that, sad and wounded, like Cassica's mom had looked that time when she baked a cake for Cassica's fifth birthday and Cassica had spat it out, because she'd recently decided she hated raisins, even though they cost more than a single mom from Coppermouth could easily afford.

Shiara sagged against the fender of the Interceptor. "You ever thought what Olympus will be like?" she said, wearily. "The glamour, the parties, the perfect people all on camera, all of the time? The most amazin' fishbowl of all, with the whole world on the outside all crowdin' to look in. That might be your dream, but it sure ain't mine."

Truth be told, Cassica hadn't thought much about what would happen after they won the Widowmaker. Going to Olympus seemed reward enough; it was beyond her to imagine the details.

"So what's your dream?" Cassica asked. "Wanna spend the rest of your life in Coppermouth? Workin' for Creek, gettin' treated like dirt, all cause your customers are so dumb they don't trust a woman with a spanner? Lookin' forward to the day when some raider from the Rust Bowl robs you and shoots you 'cause our town is such a dirt-poor dump we can't even hire a Justice or two?"

"I dream of livin' a decent life!" Shiara cried. "Doin' somethin' with my hands, somethin' *actual*, somethin' that *means* somethin'! Not bein' a performin' monkey for people to gawp at! Not bein' part of this whole damned deceit where they groom you like *this* and make you wear *that*, all so a buncha kids too young to know better will copy you instead of bein' themselves! It's a *cheat*, Cassica! They're sellin' a lie and you want to help 'em!"

"I am *not* gonna die like Momma!" Cassica shouted, and the sound of her own voice stopped her short. Not only from her mouth, but also from the car. From the screen in the car. She looked up at the hovercam, watching her with a steady eye, and she knew that they'd been live, and millions had been listening to their argument. Shiara looked up, and knew it too.

The world had heard her. All her friends and family in Coppermouth had heard her. What damage might she have done to herself and others by insulting her town and Blane's customers? She felt betrayed, violated, ashamed. Those words were meant for Shiara alone, but someone, somewhere, had made them into drama.

It must have made for great television, she thought bitterly.

I am not gonna die like Momma. She hadn't meant to say it. She didn't know where it had come from. But it was there now. It had been said. She could taste the dust in her mouth.

"Well," said Shiara, looking under the hood again. Normal service was resumed, and the argument had been shelved for another time. "Whoever designed this car don't know jack about engines. Bunch of fiddly electronic crap instead of anythin' straightforward. I can fix it, but I don't got the parts."

Cassica's heart sank; she felt some looming void yawn wide beneath her. "So that's it?"

"No, that ain't it," Shiara said. "All I need is a few bits." She jerked her thumb towards the building. "Might be there's somethin' in there I can use."

"Like what?" said Cassica.

"Air-con. Old computer. 'Most anything with a circuit board and a few wires'll do. That and ten minutes and I can route round the problem."

"You're gonna fix the car with an air-con?"

Shiara shrugged. "Ain't hardly the first time I've scavved up somethin' from junk. Built my first engine with the fan out the back of Mom's old oven."

She tossed a monkey wrench to Cassica and took a long spanner for herself out of her toolkit. "In case," she said. *In case there's somethin' in that building we don't wanna meet.* "Comin'?"

"Yeah," said Cassica, looking hatefully over her shoulder at the hovercam. "Yeah, I'm with you."

18

The porch steps creaked under their boots as they approached the entrance to the building. The doors had fallen from their hinges and split beneath the tread of years. They stepped over them, their makeshift weapons raised.

Inside, the hot gloom thickened. They found themselves in a spacious foyer, its stone floor covered in vines and rotted scraps of carpet. Dominating the room, spattered in bird droppings and greened with verdigris, was a bronze statue on a pedestal. It was a handsome smiling man in a suit, hair and jacket blowing as if in a breeze, hand raised in greeting. A carefree, happy man. The kind of man you'd want to meet in the street.

Cassica clutched the monkey wrench in both hands, listening. The foyer seemed reassuringly dead. She relaxed a little.

"Watch out for snakes," said Shiara, setting her right back on edge again.

Shiara went to investigate the reception desk, which was scattered with pieces of the ceiling. Cassica wiped the dirt from the plaque beneath the statue with a gloved hand.

"Wexley Buff," she read. "President of the United States of America. Democracy's Greatest Champion. Hero of the West. Supreme Leader of the Free World." She stood up and regarded the man on the pedestal. "Never heard of him."

"Merrica's last president," said Shiara from behind the desk.

"It says *A*-merica here. United States of *A*-merica."

"Reckon the A is silent."

"Oh."

Shiara emerged, having found nothing, and moved on. Three wide steps flanked by pillars led up from the foyer to a hall beyond. Shiara went and Cassica followed her in, casting nervous glances . The hovercam droned in behind them, shining its stark light on their backs.

The hall was darker than the foyer. Vines had choked the light from the windows, but some sifted weakly through a hole in the roof where the upper storey had fallen in. Shadows clung to the low places, and rising above them were dozens of dark figures, standing in eerie poses. Waxwork dummies, raised on platforms throughout the hall, playing out scenes from the past.

"Ah!" said Shiara, and she scampered over to a control console set against the wall. "Reckon this was for the lights and temperature and what-all." She put down her toolkit and took out a screwdriver. "Let's see if we can't get this panel off."

Cassica left her to her work and wandered over to the nearest diorama. The dummies were even more unsettling close up, faces blackened in patches and sagging, so that they seemed to have suffered terrible wounds, skulls caved in and jaws detached but grinning madly on regardless. The scene showed a child standing protectively over a fallen friend, fists raised against a group of bullies with thuggish faces. The plaque read: WEXLEY STANDS UP FOR HIS BUDDY NATE.

Next was a scene in which an adolescent Wexley Buff was posed among a smiling, perfect family, surrounded by television cameras filming them. A sitcom, Cassica realized. Later, she found him as a young man, a microphone in his hand, addressing a painted audience with enthusiasm. This time, all the cameras were on him. His clothes and hair were gaudy and weird to Cassica's eye.

"So what'd he do, anyway?" she asked.

"Don't you know *nothin'* about history?" Shiara asked. There was a clang as the panel came free.

"Always been more interested in the future, myself," Cassica muttered.

"Gramma used to go on about him all the time," Shiara said, peering inside the exposed panel. "He was the one started the Omniwar. Or leastways he was president when it started. Guess nobody's sure who shot first."

"I heard it started 'cause the weather went screwy and we started running out of food."

"Yeah, that and ten other reasons. Maybe all of 'em are true, maybe none."

Cassica moved on between the dioramas, her boots crunching on broken glass. The hovercam tracked her from above. Time was pressing on her, and every second lost was precious, yet she couldn't do a thing to speed up their return to the race. She wasn't particularly interested in Wexley Buff, but she'd go crazy if she didn't distract herself.

"So why'd they build a museum to him if he started a war?" she asked.

Shiara was hidden from sight now, her voice drifting up from the front of the hall. "It ain't a museum. They built this while he was still alive. He hadn't started it then. Used to be hundreds of places like this all over Merrica, so Gramma says. Most of 'em torn down now."

"Hundreds? What was he, the most popular guy in the world?"

"Most popular in Merrica, anyway," Shiara replied. "The way Gramma tells it – and she heard it from her *great*-gramma – is he was like their

199

equivalent of a Celestial. He was in some show as a kid and it was really big, then he was a television presenter and in movies and stuff. Then he went into politics, and everyone voted for him. They felt they'd known him all their lives, y'know. Grown up with him or something. And the other guys were these boring grey guys in suits. In the end he ran for president, won by a landslide."

A tinkle of glass near the back of the hall made Cassica turn her head sharply. Her blood ran cold.

"Now, back in the day, Gramma used to say there were all these big corporations who bought up all the small companies, and there was this one guy and he owned all the zines and the television channels and everything. Or enough of 'em that he might as well have owned 'em all. Kinda like Dunbery Hasp does now."

Cassica was hardly listening. She was searching for danger, eyes roving the aisles between the dioramas. It could have just been shifting rubble. Probably that was all it was.

"Hoy! You there?" Shiara's voice was uncomfortably loud in the silence.

"Yeah. Like Dunbery Hasp," Cassica said absently. She watched for a few seconds more, but nothing moved. Slowly she let out her breath. It was only a noise. She was just spooked and jumpy.

"Yeah." Shiara resumed her story as she worked. "So Buff, he makes good friends with this guy and pretty soon you never hear a bad word about him. Not on television or in the zines, nowhere. And people start thinkin', like, wow, he really *is* this great leader. But off in the East... Hang on a minute..." She grunted as she levered something out of the console with her screwdriver. "Off in the East, there was this other guy, Kerensky, playin' the same game. He controlled the media too, and everyone over there thought *he* was the greatest leader they'd ever had."

"Bald guy, brown beard, big black mole on his cheek?" Cassica asked.

"Dunno. Why?"

Cassica studied the action scene in front of her. Buff was surging out of his chair, delivering a punch to the jaw of another seated man, while astonished cameramen and politicians looked on.

"Did he really punch that guy out?" she asked in wonder.

"Oh, yeah. Kerensky came to Merrica on this big diplomatic visit and started shooting his mouth off. Buff decked him live on air."

"That's some fancy diplomacy," Cassica deadpanned.

"I know, right? But here's the thing. Before, he was popular. After ... hell, it was like a *cult*. That's when they built places like this. People had pictures of him in their houses. You even spoke bad about him, you got beat up, or you went to jail and *then* you got beat up."

"This Kerensky's a pretty ugly guy," said Cassica, looking closer.

"Well, he's the villain," Shiara replied. "Anyhow, understandably relations weren't so great with the other guys after Buff did that. Couple years later, Omniwar."

Cassica blew out her cheeks. "People, huh?"

"Yuh. That's why they changed everything after we got back on our feet. That's why you can't have no politicians on television, why you gotta buy special zines if you want to read about it. Used to be anyone could vote, even if they didn't know jack about it; now you gotta take a test to show you know what you're talkin' about, and keep takin' it every few years. Now they kick out and ban them politicians who promise to do stuff before the election and don't do it once they're elected, to make 'em stick to their guns and tell the truth, instead of just tellin' the people what they wanna hear. 'Cause politics ain't meant to be entertainment, and the fate of the world's too damn important to be decided on who gives the best soundbite."

Cassica heard a crunch and a snort of satisfaction. "There," Shiara said. "I'm done."

Cassica turned to head back, eager to be out of there. Behind her, a figure in one of the dioramas moved.

She spun as she heard the rush of running feet, saw a black flapping shadow racing at her. She only had time to scream before it charged into her, knocking her down among the rubble and glass. She was crushed by a body atop her, the stink of mould and rank sweat in her nose. Hands spidered for her throat. A face came into view: a terrible misshapen lump of a face, swollen and cancerous, one tiny eye glaring out from beneath an enormous brow. She screamed again at the sight of it, and then the hands clamped round her neck and she couldn't scream any more.

She tried to throw him off, to no avail. Belatedly she remembered the monkey wrench, but it was gone from her hand and she didn't know where. Her eyes bulged as she fought for breath. The swamp man's warped features filled her sight, drool sliding from his drooping mouth, a few lonely teeth brown in black gums. Behind his head, she saw a white light shining bright. She thought it must be the light that dying people spoke of, and felt a despair so great it dampened her panic.

But that wasn't the light which lured the dying, she realized, as the last of her strength slipped away. It was the light of the hovercam, zooming in on her face, showing her final moments to the world.

Then the light went out, blocked by Shiara, her spanner raised high. She brought it down on the swamp man's head. His hands went loose on Cassica's throat and air rushed in to ease her pain-scorched lungs.

She rolled on to her front, gasping, head light and

vision sparkling. Glass cut her hands. The swamp man flailed his arms as he tried to get up from his knees, wailing an idiot wail, limned by the hovercam's light. Shiara raised her spanner and brought it down on his head with a wet thud. He keeled over sideways and lay still.

Panting breaths; stillness in the hall; the whir of the hovercams' rotors.

"You alright?" Shiara said, watching the swamp man in case he should get up again.

Cassica lifted herself, felt her throat, nodded. "You kill him?" she said. It came out as a whisper.

"Not sure," said Shiara. Then she crouched and started rifling through his pockets.

"The hell you doing?" Cassica croaked. She leaned on a diorama platform and got to her knees. Her muscles had turned to water. She was afraid the swamp man would spring to life at any moment. "We gotta get out of here."

But Shiara's scavenging instinct was too strong. "Hold your horses, huh? Could be something we can use." She pulled out bone trinkets, a length of string, an old plastic mobile phone from the old times. "Could sell this," she said, dropping it in her own pocket.

"We got a race to win!" Cassica said, but the effort of it made her cough. She could smell blood. A glittering dark pool was creeping out from under the swamp man's head.

Shiara ignored her. She patted along his ribs, then threw open his trenchcoat and drew out something rectangular from his inside pocket. She opened it out, and it unfolded until it was as wide as the span of her arms. A smile grew on her face as she studied it.

A map.

She hurried over to Cassica, the map fluttering and crinkling in her arms, and showed it to her. "Look at this!" she said, alight with excitement. "Look!"

Cassica, still dizzy, was slow on the uptake. It was an old-time map of the bayou, printed on thin plastic. Shiara pointed. "Logging routes! Roads! This is what it was like before the Omniwar, see? They're overgrown now, but those trails are still there!" She pulled the map away, put a hand on Cassica's arm, eyes gleaming. "It's the way through the swamp!"

Now Cassica understood, like the drawing of a curtain to let in the morning. Strength surged back into her on a tide of new hope. Shiara lifted her, and she got to her feet.

"Let's move," she said.

Shiara had the car running again in ten minutes, good as her word. The swamp man, if he lived, never showed himself again. They raced off into the bayou, fired with new purpose.

Using the map, Shiara chose the widest trails, the most direct, those on high ground that were most likely to have survived. Shortcuts presented themselves. An hour passed, then two, and finally Shiara announced the news. According to her screen, they were in first place. Way out in first place.

Other racers ran into dead ends, lost themselves in winding back routes, fell victim to the dangers of the swamp. Shiara saw more swamp-folk ambushes, cars stuck in bogs, an armoured vehicle falling into a river when it proved too heavy for the bridge. The Carnasaur caught Babby Kay and Ronson Bleen square with a rocket and blew them sky-high. Jam Totsey took a leak against a tree, got bitten by a spider and died before the officials could respond to his rescue alarm.

But it seemed Cassica and Shiara had already endured their share of troubles, and fortune was with them. They had to backtrack once when a road proved to be flooded, but that was the worst they faced.

Their disbelief grew as the day wore on, and they drew further ahead. Suddenly the coverage was all about them. Commentators dissected Cassica's driving style and Shiara's tactics. Speculation ran wild as footage of their argument was played over and over. Personal details. Finally, when Card appeared on the screen to talk about his relationship with Cassica, Shiara turned it off in disgust.

They escaped the bayou in the late afternoon, with the sun still burning in a sky banded with greens and purples. The finish line was flanked with stands and surrounded by scaffold, and behind it was a huge paddock like a miniature town, similar to the one they'd set off from. They drove towards it on a clear road, and the cheers of the crowd got louder and louder until it seemed they could hear nothing else.

19

"You're going great, girls! Real great!" Harlan called as he came hurrying across the asphalt.

It must have been the tenth time he'd said it since they finished the first stage of the Widowmaker. Almost like he couldn't believe it himself. By now, as the sun touched the ocean behind the rotted tips of submerged tower blocks, Cassica and Shiara were tired of it.

They stood in a compound in the hills overlooking the city: Lost Angeles, all broken and overgrown and laid out before them. Scaffolding sliced up the ruddy yellow light, casting spiderwebs of shadow; garages and tents surrounded them; fenced areas divided racers and press, VIPs and spectators. Another place, another media carnival; in three days it would be gone, and leave only debris behind.

The journey from the bayou in Pacifica's drowned

south had taken three hours. They were still waving to the crowds at the finish line when their car was taken away by teamsters and the contents of their garage – Maisie and all – were packed up in trucks for transport to the next stage. Cassica, Shiara and an overly excited Harlan had travelled with them, in a convoy of camera-laden jeeps and other vehicles.

They rested and talked tactics on the way, in the back of their own bus, while their injuries were treated by medics. Cassica's throat was still purple where the swamp man's fingers had gripped, but they'd given her an anaesthetic spray to kill the pain, and a stylish neckscarf to cover up.

Eventually news came in of other racers finishing. Five cars hadn't made it: ten people dead or out of the race. Kyren came in third, Sammis sixth. But thanks to their map, even their closest competitor was two hours behind them. A two-hour head start on the rest of the pack.

That was when Harlan started to believe he might get to keep his fingers.

Shiara kept a close eye on the teamsters as they backed Maisie out of the truck and drove her into the garage area. She was itching to get going. A two-hour advantage was all well and good, but she'd need every minute of time if she was going to get the Interceptor into shape by tomorrow. Harlan's fevered optimism only annoyed her; if not for him, they could have simply switched to a new car for the second stage. But

Maisie, for all the fondness Shiara bore her, was just not fast enough for the Widowmaker.

Harlan seemed disappointed by their lack of response to his encouragement. He squeezed the fingers of his left hand with his right – a habit he'd picked up over the last few days – and tried again. "I got good news!" he said. "The sponsors are going crazy! They're so keen, I reckon I can pre-sell an endorsement contract, get you a deal to advertise some products after the Widowmaker's done! Moolah, see? With a handshake advance I can get us the money by tomorrow, we can bring in a new car and—"

"We don't need it tomorrow, we need it now," Shiara said. "I gotta fix up that Interceptor and I got only the barest of kit to do it with. Can't even take the parts out of Maisie, since the damned thing's so newfangled, most of 'em won't fit."

"You can do it," said Cassica. "You always could spin gold out of junk."

Shiara was reluctantly pleased by that. Their differences lay unresolved, but Cassica's faith touched her. "Well, I'm gonna see what I can do," she muttered grudgingly.

Harlan flapped in the background. Once, they'd hung on his every word; now, they barely managed to be polite. "I've got a meeting with Dunbery Hasp himself!" he declared, desperately. "The big cheese wants to see me tonight! That means you caught his eye! Good things are gonna come from this, just you wait!"

But they didn't trust him any more, and no assurances would change that. They only had themselves to rely on.

"I gotta get workin' on that car," Shiara said. "Gonna take me all night if I'm lucky."

"Need a hand?" Cassica asked.

"No, no, no!" Harlan cried. "The sponsors! The world's press is here, girls, and they want to talk to you! Listen, even if you don't win, play your cards right and there'll be chat shows, game shows, reality television... I can practically *guarantee* you a diaper advert right now!"

Shiara gave Cassica a weary look. "You go," she said.

"You sure?"

"It's your thing, not mine. I'll get started on the car. You just make sure to come when you're done, okay?"

Cassica held her gaze for long enough to ensure that Shiara wasn't playing the martyr. Then she nodded. "I'll be as quick as I can."

Harlan led her off towards the press area, where newsies waited to fall on her like wolves. Shiara stood alone for a time, gathering herself, her shadow long on the asphalt. Then she headed off to the garage, where her work awaited her.

*

211

Cassica followed Harlan in a strange daze. She was both hyper-alert and not quite there. Everything was sharp and clear, sights and sounds and smells as fresh as if she were experiencing them for the first time. Yet she felt out of control, as if everything were sliding beneath her feet, carrying her in a steadily accelerating landslide towards some jumbled and frightening end.

She closed her eyes, saw the swamp man's warped face in shadow, lit from behind by the hovercam's light. She smelt the mouldy stink of him, felt his hands at her throat.

Her eyes snapped open and her heart lurched as if starting from sleep. Just for an instant, she'd felt herself falling into the silent black, and jerked back from the precipice.

Shiara seemed unfazed by their encounter with the swamp man. She thought nothing of the fact that she might have killed someone. To her, it wasn't even a person, only a thing that was attacking her friend. There was no question of guilt or shock. Cassica wished she could be like that, to roll with the punches the way Shiara did, but she just couldn't.

She knew what dying felt like now, and it leaked out all over her thoughts. How could anything possibly ever be the same?

Harlan was babbling at her shoulder, but she didn't listen. Ahead, the newsies thronged behind a gate. The other racers were still on their way from the bayou; the press had Cassica to themselves for now. Her feet carried her towards them. It seemed a fool's dream to turn back.

Hours passed in a blur that felt like minutes. A parade of faces, smiling at her. She smiled back and answered their questions, the same questions over and over. She said words that meant nothing and offended no one. Shiara had been right: she'd been trained, though she didn't know it. No hint of the real Cassica showed through as she chatted and smiled and said what she ought to. Even when they asked her about being strangled by the swamp man, she gave them a fiction. If there were words to describe it, she didn't know them.

And then, as she was pushing her way from one camera to another, Kyren came out of the crowd, took her arm and pulled her aside. So quick was he, so sure, that she was snatched out from under Harlan's nose. By the time anyone realized she was gone, she was already out of sight.

Behind a stage, he pressed up against her, his body close and his forehead touching hers. The heat coming off him woke her up, made her breathing heavy.

"Look at you," he said.

"Look at me," she agreed.

"You killed it out there. I gotta watch out for you."

"Maybe you do."

He kissed her, hard, and it was like dark fireworks behind her eyes.

"Let's get out of here," he said, quick and eager.

"I've got interviews."

"Who cares? So have I."

Who cares? It seemed so obvious to her then. What did it matter? What did anything matter? She was alive. She was winning. Nobody could command her.

Her fierce smile was answer enough for him. They hurried away, and thought of nothing but each other after that.

Shiara was sweaty, angry and deep in the guts of the Interceptor when she heard the door to the garage squeak.

"And where in hell have *you* been?" she cried as she turned on the newcomer.

Sammis Rye wore an expression of amused innocence. "Hey, sorry. Took a wrong turn in the swamp."

Her anger went out, smothered by embarrassment. "Thought you were someone else." She noticed he was holding a pair of steaming mugs.

"I figured that." He looked around the garage. A toolkit yawned beside the opened shell of the car, its contents scattered about. The air reeked of oil and burnt solder. "You missing your driver?"

"Driver, manager... I'm alone here!" She tossed her spanner to the ground with a clang. "Cassica was meant to come help when she was done interviewin', but it looks like she's got better things to do. I ain't askin' much, just a little frickin' support now and then! Reckon it's only me doin' anythin' to help us win this race, and I'm the only one who don't want to win it!"

"You don't want to win?" A line creased Sammis's brow. "Sure doing a bad job of losing, though."

Shiara laughed. She hadn't meant to confess that – exasperation had driven her to it – but it was a relief to say it aloud.

He held up one of the mugs. "Coffee?"

"You bring that for me?"

"Thought you could use it. I got with milk or without."

"Long as there's caffeine." She wiped down her hands on her overalls and walked over. Past time for a break anyway, and his thoughtfulness surprised her. She didn't know what she'd done to deserve it.

They leaned up against a worktop together and regarded the Interceptor.

"Croc did that?" he asked, indicating the massive dent in the flank.

"It was a big croc," she replied. "More like an alligator, actually."

"There's a difference?"

She gave him a look. "You *are* a Greenbelt boy, aren't you?"

"Can't help it if I come from a place where not everything wants to kill you."

"Well, lucky you." She sipped her coffee, then said:

"Glad you made it through." It sounded awkward to her ears.

"Me too," he replied. "So what's the story with you and your driver? It's all over the television."

Shiara sighed. Of course it was. She checked the room for cameras, but if they were there, she couldn't see them.

"I think it's just you and me," said Sammis, catching her thought. "Can't promise, though."

She sighed, wondering whether she should say anything. But she wanted to unburden herself, and Cassica had abandoned her. Why not him?

"Ah, I dunno," she said at last. "You ever feel like you spend too much time doin' what other people want, and not enough doin' what *you* want?"

"Story of my life," Sammis said.

"Riskin' my damn neck and I don't even *want* to go to Olympus," she said.

"Well, that's good to hear. Me either."

"You serious?"

"You said it yourself: I'm a Greenbelt boy. Hills and lakes, trees and sky. What would I do up in space?" His tone was light, and she wasn't sure if he was taking her seriously.

"What about your partner?"

"Haven't asked him. What about yours?"

"She's my best friend. It's her dream, winnin' the Widowmaker. I ain't gonna be responsible for ruinin' it."

"And I don't want to disappoint my daddy. But what if you *do* win?"

"Maybe I'll sell my ticket."

"Oh, you been talkin' to the Cussens? You know they'll only buy two tickets together, right? So either you go with Cassica, or she has to stay."

"So I'll sell it to someone else."

"Nobody sells a ticket to Olympus," he scoffed. "Never been done. A few people made out they'd sell it if they won – rebel types, you know the sort – but when it comes to it, they all cave. I mean, it's *Olympus*, right?"

"Well, maybe I'll be the first." She looked him over. "What if *you* win? You gonna go to Olympus the way your daddy never did? Leave everyone behind and go live among the stars?"

"Nah," said Sammis with a grin. "I'll sell it."

She hit him on the arm, and he spilled his coffee and laughed. "Hey, watch it! Hot!"

"Ain't we a pair?" Shiara mused fondly, sipping her drink and smiling.

He bumped her with his shoulder, a playful nudge that made her melt. "Reckon we are," he said.

They shared a companionable silence, full of possibilities. Then Sammis motioned at the Interceptor. "You gonna get her runnin' in time, you think?"

Shiara shook her head. "Not without a miracle. I don't got the parts and I can't make 'em with what I got."

"What do you need?"

"Head gasket, stabilizer links, new windows – though that's the least of my worries. I scavved the safety limiter off Maisie 'cause the Interceptor's was shot, but most of her stuff I can't use. Couple of new shocks, flywheel—"

"Make a list."

"What for?"

"I'm the son of Dutton Rye. We were fightin' off sponsors before I even got on the track. I got enough spares to build ten cars."

"You're gonna give me your spares?" She gawked in amazement.

"I'd give you a car if it wasn't against the rules. I've got six."

She just stared at him. "You do know we're meant to be rivals, right?"

He shrugged. "Make a list," he said again. "I'll get 'em sent over. One thing, though: there's a price."

Ah. Here it was. The catch. Shiara's face hardened with suspicion. "What price?"

"You gotta let me help you fix her."

That wasn't what she expected. "You wanna, er, help?"

He spread out his hands. "I'm no tech, but I can do my bit. Hand you spanners and such."

She searched his face for a trick, found none. He rolled his eyes. "Just say yes," he told her.

"Yes?" she ventured.

"So make a list!"

They worked into the small hours, and though Cassica never arrived, Shiara didn't care. She was enjoying herself too much. The threat of tomorrow was forgotten; she fixed the Interceptor just for the challenge of fixing it. Sammis kept her company, chattering and joking as he handed her tools and held things in place. She laughed more than she had in days.

At times, it felt like it used to in her father's auto shop, when she and Cassica spent long nights tinkering with Maisie; but then she was touched with guilt, as if she were betraying her friend by sharing such moments with another.

She waited for Sammis to reveal himself, to drop the front and take off his mask. Surely he wasn't actually like this? This honest and decent and funny, this kind, this *right*?

But down in her belly, she didn't believe he was faking, and it made her loose and warm and a little giddy. More than anything, she just couldn't believe her luck.

When Harlan arrived, it came as a rude interruption. He threw the door open so that it clattered against the wall, and tottered in. One look told Shiara he was drunk. He focused puzzled eyes on Sammis, then found Shiara.

"Oh," he said, in a tone of surprised disapproval.

"Having fun?" Shiara asked him poisonously.

"Meetin' with clients, you gotta drink," he said, stumbling in. "Need to talk to you. *Alone*." This last was directed at Sammis.

Sammis forestalled Shiara's protest. "Reckon we're about done here anyway," he said. He gave her a wink. "See you tomorrow."

"Today," she corrected him.

He checked his watch. "You're right. I need my beauty sleep." He nodded at Harlan as he passed. "Mr Massini."

Harlan didn't reply, just watched him with boozy suspicion as he left. Shiara crossed her arms angrily. His intrusion had burst her bubble.

"You let a rival get his hands on your car?" Harlan asked, appalled.

"If it weren't for him, this car wouldn't be runnin' at all," Shiara replied scornfully. "Don't need to remind you who got us in *that* situation."

It took a moment for that to compute. Harlan decided not to argue further. "Anyway, forget all that. I got something to show you." He blundered over, tugging out a map from his pocket, which he laid on the worktop next to her. She didn't recognize it at first; it was like no map she'd ever seen. Then she realized what it was: an aerial photo of Lost Angeles.

"Taken only yesterday," Harlan proudly declared. "Forget all them old out-of-date maps the others are

using. This one's fresh, up to the minute! And look!"
He traced along a red line that had been drawn on
it like the solution to a maze. A route through the
city. "You think the powers that be gonna plan a
race without knowin' what the Howlers are up to
in there? Trust me, they know every hideout, every
ambush, every base. And this. . ." He stabbed the map
with his finger. "This is the safe route through."

Shiara studied it. It didn't seem possible that they'd
be handed such a break a second time. "How did you
get this?"

"Old Harlan ain't so useless after all, is he?"
Harlan crowed. "You made quite an impression with
your run through the bayou. The people are cheering
for you now. And what makes the people happy
makes the big cheeses happy." He leered, and a wave
of whisky came on his breath. "Somebody up there
wants you to win."

"Dunbery Hasp? Did he give you this?"

Harlan just tapped the side of his nose. "You
been given a leg up, girl. Just you be sure to take it.
Memorize that route. Burn it. Come the mornin',
there'll be cameras. Don't let 'em see."

Shiara couldn't take her eyes from the map. "They
want us to win? Ain't this cheatin', though?"

"It's the game," Harlan said impatiently. "And if
you ain't playin' it, someone else is."

"So it *is* cheatin', then."

"It's the game," Harlan said again, and just for a

moment she caught something dangerous in his eyes, something desperate and hard. She remembered his fingers. "It ain't how you win, it's that you win at all."

"Yeah," said Shiara, dispirited. "Seems that's what everyone thinks around here."

"Study that map," he told her. "Tomorrow..." Something caught in his throat and she was shocked to see tears in his eyes. "Tomorrow we'll show 'em all."

He turned away and hurried out. Shiara watched him go. Just for an instant, she'd glimpsed something, some drunken emotion that slipped through his guard. And in that instant he'd seemed small, pathetic and terrified. Terrified that he was relying on two young girls to prevent himself being maimed. Terrified of what was to come if they failed.

She sighed, spat on the ground. For Cassica. For Harlan. For everyone else's sake, she'd do it. So she bent over the map and began.

20

They drove along the lonely eerie highways of a weed-strangled city. Cracked asphalt blurred beneath their wheels; the echoing roar of their engine sent black birds scattering skyward. Broken trucks lay across the road like felled beasts and wrecks clogged the rotted streets to either side.

They felt like the only living people in the world.

Cassica's focus was total. She drove with a fierce calm in her eyes, and didn't say a word. They had a two-hour lead on the other racers, and the Wreckers couldn't start until at least half the pack had set off. They were way out ahead on their own, and thanks to Harlan's map they'd progressed deep into Lost Angeles without seeing a single Howler. The worst they'd encountered was a few shots from a rogue sniper, but they'd been far away and the shots had missed.

Others hadn't been so lucky. The second stage of the Widowmaker was a little over four hours old now, and most of the other racers had made their way through the outskirts. The Howlers were waiting in number out there, with barricades and explosives. They didn't tolerate any invaders in their territory, and their love of violence and chaos was notorious. They dropped rubble from above and blocked in racers with armoured vehicles, they swarmed out of alleys to attack trapped cars, they popped up from hidey-holes with belt-fed machine guns. Already two pairs of racers had been killed, one car riddled with bullets and the other crushed by a building toppled with dynamite. Another car had broken down and the racers had used their rescue alarm to summon help, disqualifying themselves. Shiara hoped they were found by the race officials before the Howlers got them. There was no telling what they might do to prisoners.

She'd felt guilty for taking that map when Harlan offered it. Now, not so much. Winning wasn't so important to her, but survival most certainly was.

Cassica skidded round a burned-out car that lay slumped in their path. Given their lead, she could have afforded to take things a little easy, but that wouldn't be Cassica. She drove with more urgency and aggression than ever, jaw tight, stare hard.

"Take the slip road left," Shiara told her. Cassica didn't question Shiara's directions, or wonder why she was so confident in her route. She just drove.

Shiara hadn't told Cassica about the map. Maybe she would have, if Cassica had been around to tell. But Cassica didn't come back to the garage all night, and she wasn't in their quarters when Shiara went to bed to snatch a couple of hours' sleep. Shiara had been forced to oversee the morning preparations on her own, while Harlan ran about in a flap looking for Cassica. She appeared at last a few minutes before they were due to set off, walking casually across the tarmac to where Shiara sat fuming in the car.

Cassica got in, settled herself and adjusted the neckscarf that disguised her bruised throat. Then she looked over at Shiara and asked: "We ready?"

We ready? That was all. No apology. No explanation. No word of thanks.

And Shiara just said: "Yeah."

All that work she'd done to get the Interceptor back up to scratch. The way Sammis had saved them with his spare parts. How Harlan had cut them a deal and acquired a map to get them through Lost Angeles safely. Cassica didn't know about any of it, didn't ask, didn't care. She'd been off doing who knew what (but then, Shiara *did* know what) while everyone else broke their backs to make it possible for her to continue her challenge for the Widowmaker title. And then, when all the work was done, she sauntered back, expecting everything to be in place, everything set up, like a bunch of damned fairies had waved their wands in the night and made their busted-up car all better.

Shiara was so angry she wanted to slap her; but there was a long way between wanting and doing in Shiara's world. So she gave her driver directions, and she kept an eye on the gauges, and she watched out for Howlers. Beyond that, they didn't speak.

She looked for news of Sammis among the trailing pack, a worm of concern gnawing at her gut. Maybe she should have told him about the map? But no, that was naive, that would have been stupid. She liked him, for sure, but she didn't trust him that far based on a few sweet hours in his company.

Still, it would have been nice to daydream a little, to remember how kind he'd been, what a time they'd had fixing the car. But she was too mad at Cassica, too busy with the race.

They came off the highway and into gridded streets that sprawled away into the sea. Flaking buildings rose around them; rubble lay on the sidewalks. The roads of Lost Angeles were covered in slippery weeds, and its walls were bedraggled with creepers. Nature had had its way with the city once the people left. Now those who remained scavenged among the debris in the shadow of the Howlers, or moved in roving gangs for protection.

Cassica and Shiara had spotted evidence of recently used shelters, seen darting silhouettes in upper windows and a battered car driving quickly away from them. The scavs were like mice, eager to stay out of sight. If the Howlers caught them, they'd be dead meat.

Shiara's eye was caught by the screen again. The sound was off – they found the commentary distracting – but the announcers were leaning in excitedly, and she could tell something major had just happened. The scene cut to a hovercam view of a yellow-and-red Hyena, driving down a narrow road, weaving through the wrecks. The caption at the bottom of the screen told Shiara what she already knew. SAMMIS RYE AND TATTEN BREESLEY.

A little smile grew on her lips as the screen switched to an interior camera, showing Sammis driving, his tech pointing out a route to him. That broad, easy face already felt strangely familiar to her. Those were eyes you could come home to.

Then there was a bright flash, and her smile dropped away. For a moment, everything on the screen was shaking, Sammis hauling desperately on the wheel: then the camera cut to black.

The hovercam took up the story, replaying the incident from the outside. Shiara watched, ice gathering at her core, as the Hyena hit a buried mine. Even with the sound off she felt the dusty thump of the explosion. The car skidded and rolled, bouncing down the road, leaving pieces of itself behind as it went.

"Which way?" Cassica asked, eyes still on the road.

Shiara just watched the screen. The Hyena rocked to a halt on what was left of its wheels. The passenger door had been blown clean off. Tatten slumped in his harness, blackened and bloody and dead. Beyond him, Sammis was motionless in his seat.

A childish voice of protest clamoured in her head. *No! It ain't fair! It ain't! He didn't even wanna be there!*

"Which *way*?" Cassica demanded, irritable and impatient.

"Take a right," Shiara murmured.

Cassica did so. After a moment, she looked back at Shiara. "You okay?"

Her voice buzzed in Shiara's ear like a mosquito, tinny and faint. "There's been a crash," she said quietly, feeling numb. "Bad one."

"Good," said Cassica. "One less rival to worry about."

Shiara felt something twist like a knife inside her. Rage seeped from the wound, creeping through her body, touching her skin with angry heat. She gritted her teeth, trying to keep it in, but it was unstoppable.

"Is that all we are to you?" she said, her voice thick. "Rivals? Supportin' cast? Background players in the inspirin' story of Cassica Hayle's rise to fame?"

Cassica gazed at her like she was mad. "What in hell are you talking about?"

"You just don't care, do you? You don't care what happens as long as you get to win! You don't care who lives or who dies or who—"

"Where's all *this* coming from?" Cassica cried. "You're angry 'cause I don't shed some fake tears over a couple of dead racers? This is the Widowmaker, dumb-ass! Did you think no one was gonna die?"

Shiara wasn't even listening. It all came spewing out of her, like some long-dammed river that had burst. "We're frickin' *people*, okay? Everyone who does your hair, who sets up the lights so you look good, who fixes your damn car while you go runnin' off with—"

"Oh, *that's* what it's about, is it? I *knew* you were jealous!"

"It's about respect!" Shiara almost screamed. "It's about the way you only think of you! We're *equals*, don't you get that? You, me, and every other racer and tech out there! All the ground crew that make it possible, and the management and the television folk and all those people that do their jobs day after day just so you can stand up in front of a camera and be worshipped! Do you get that? I mean, really? Do you understand that the whole world doesn't exist to service your needs? I'm not your *follower*, I'm not your *servant*! You wouldn't be *nothin'* without me!"

"I nearly died!" Cassica screamed back, before Shiara had even finished. "Not one day past some hell-damned horror had his stinking hands round my throat and I felt it coming, I felt *death* coming, Shiara, and I looked right into that pit before you got him off me. I nearly died! So excuse me if I ain't at my most considerate today! Excuse me if I thought I deserved a bit of personal time when I'd just narrowly avoided my own frickin' extinction from this earth!"

They were full-out now. Finally this was the fight Cassica had wanted. But in the fury of the clash, Cassica had taken her attention from the road, and that was why neither of them spotted the truck rolling out in front of them until it had already blocked the road.

Cassica instinctively stamped on the brakes the moment she saw it. The Interceptor's wheels screeched and smoked as they were thrown against their harnesses. Through the shuddering windscreen Shiara saw a figure rise up on the rooftop of a nearby building, carrying something on his shoulder.

A rocket launcher.

There was a flash, and a rocket flew towards them. Shiara didn't see where it hit, but she felt the Interceptor slammed by a terrific force, felt it lift up off the ground, flying, flipping, and all she could hear was her own scream as the tarmac rushed towards them and the car came down again.

When her senses returned, they came slowly, as if from some great distance. The sharp smell of leaked oil. The dull ache of muscles that would later bruise. Upon opening her eyes, she found the Interceptor's cockpit jumbled. Everything was out of place, every straight line bent, the dash punched in and broken glass on the dented roof above her.

It was the glass that told her she was upside down before her body did. Glass shouldn't fall upward.

Cassica was in the seat next to her, hanging in her harness, puffy eyes opening, now narrow, now wide as realization came. She cast about in alarm, found Shiara; then she looked beyond her, and her face loosened in horror. Shiara turned her head painfully and saw what Cassica had seen through the crushed window of the Interceptor.

Howlers. Men and women more animal than human. They came running between the wrecks, wearing shredded leathers and buckles and oil painted on their faces.

Cassica and Shiara thrashed in their harnesses, fighting to get free. Cassica managed to release herself and fell on to the roof of the car, but Shiara's straps held her fast. She couldn't find the buckle, and when she did, she couldn't make it work. Panic made her clumsy. She glanced fearfully at the Howlers – so close now, knives glinting in the punishing sunlight – and then Cassica was there, yanking at her harness. But even with her help, the straps stayed tight.

Cassica let go. She backed away, shuffling on her knees in the cramped cockpit of the upside-down car. Shiara saw in her eyes what she was thinking, and a hopeless emptiness filled her.

"Don't leave me," she whispered.

Tears glittered in Cassica's eyes. She held Shiara's gaze for a heartbeat. Then she scrambled backwards, out through the driver's side window. Shiara saw her booted feet running, and she was gone.

The last thing she heard before unconsciousness took her was the happy screams of the Howlers as they gave chase. The last thought in her head was the hope that she'd never wake again.

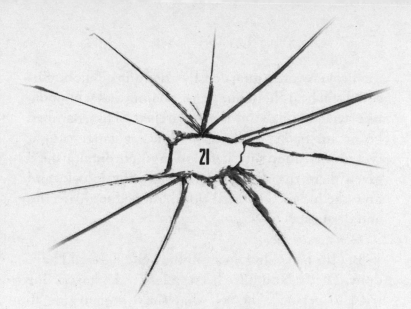

21

The hovercam whirred in the air, its steady glass eye trained on Cassica. Reflected in its lens, she was no longer the beautiful idol that the cream of Pacifica's sports newsies had once clamoured to interview. She sat huddled in the corner of a long-abandoned call centre, among fallen ceiling tiles and smashed desks and cubicles. Her driving leathers were scarred, her hair dirty and messy, her eyes swollen, mascara smudged with tears. Her neckscarf had been lost and her neck was yellow and purple in places. By her side was a long metal table leg that was her best attempt at a weapon.

She was staring at an object in her hand, turning it over and over. A small rectangular metal case, opened to reveal a single red button. Her rescue alarm.

It had taken over an hour to lose them in the hot shadowed alleys, the corroded department stores, the broken yards guarded by chain-link fences. She could still hear them out there, wailing and whooping like wild animals as they searched. That damned hovercam hadn't helped: it almost got her caught twice when they saw it following her. Finally she'd given them the slip inside an old office block, and now she hid on the third floor, listened to their cries and despaired.

Don't leave me.

But she had. There was nothing else she could have done. They'd both have been caught if she stayed. She tried to persuade herself that she'd been trying to draw the Howlers away, but it was a lie. She'd been running for her life, running to save herself.

"You couldn't help her," she muttered. She looked up at the hovercam as she realized she'd said it aloud. It just hung there, watching. The whole world watched with it. Discussing her. Judging her.

They didn't know. They didn't know the fear that took her, seeing those monsters run shrieking towards the car. They didn't know what it was like to have someone's hands on your throat, to abandon yourself to death. They didn't know what that did to your head. They didn't know how it felt to remember your best friend's face as she was left to her fate.

Don't leave me.

They didn't know. Nobody knew. She wanted to die. Better than being this helpless. Better than living on, knowing she'd abandoned Shiara to those creatures of madness. The thought of what they might do made such horror well up inside that she retched on it.

Don't leave me.

Through tear-blurred eyes she stared at the rescue alarm in her hand. Shiara had one too; all the racers did. Surely she'd pressed it already? Surely troops and medics had already flown in to save her?

No. She'd heard no 'coptors. And anyway, she knew the rules. Rescue teams would only extract a racer if it was safe. They wouldn't risk their lives busting into a Howler nest. Wherever Shiara had gone, wherever they'd taken her, there was no help coming.

They'd come for Cassica, though. She just had to get up on the roof. One press of the button and they'd pick her up, take her away from all this. One press of the button and her race would be over.

The race? The race is already over, Cassica. Your car's totalled. Your tech's gone. It's done.

She swallowed against a dry throat. She'd never been so alone, or so adrift. Times like these, when she was all turmoil inside and so high-strung she couldn't think straight, she needed someone to talk her down. Someone like—

"Shiara," she whispered hoarsely.

A landslide of memories swept over her: childhood adventures in Coppermouth; laughing themselves sick at some stupid joke; talking long into the night in their bedroom over the auto shop; crying over boys; fixing up Maisie; and driving, driving on highways and dirt roads and racetracks with the hot air of the badlands in their faces. They'd never felt so free as in those moments; nothing ever felt so right.

Shiara was Cassica's home, more than her real home ever was, or the DuCals' flat over the auto shop where she'd gone after Momma died. Shiara was the safe place she came back to after her wildness took her roaming. Shiara was the one who tempered her fire, who made her see reason when she didn't want to, who picked up the pieces when she broke. Shiara, who always had her back.

You wouldn't be nothin' without me, Shiara had spat at her earlier. And she'd been right.

Cassica snapped the case closed on her rescue alarm and shoved it back in her pocket. She got to her feet, picking up the metal table leg as she did so. It was heavy and had square edges. She looked up at the hovercam.

"Hoy," she said to it, and beckoned. "Over here."

The hovercam moved closer, whirring as it focused. Capturing her face in close-up for the viewers, her grief, her determination. She looked deep into the darkness of the lens, and there at the heart of it, she saw nothing but a point of empty white light.

She swung the table leg hard, knocking the

machine to the floor. It still buzzed with life, rotors whirring as it laboured to rise, a huge wounded insect. She hit it again, and with increasing viciousness she kept hitting it, until it was still, and the light in the lens had died.

When she was done, she stood over it, panting. Finally she straightened, brushed her hair back from her face, then pulled her helmet off and let it drop to the floor. The small round eye of her helmet cam was left staring uselessly at the wall. She let out a sigh as if a great weight had been taken from her.

Shiara. Taken, condemned to torment and death, and a legion of maniacs in between.

"I'm coming," said Cassica to the empty building, and she set off back towards the Interceptor.

22

Cassica crouched behind a burnt-out car, heart thumping hard, breaths shallow and rapid like a frightened bird's. The metal table leg, her makeshift weapon, gave her no comfort. In the cockpit she was fearless, but not outside. The terror of discovery was such that she wasn't sure she'd be able to move when the time came.

Ahead of her, a high wall surrounded the forecourt of a drab, crumbling building. It was a dull anvil of a place, low and wide with dark square windows in regular rows along its length. Once it had been an administrative headquarters, or perhaps a hospital, built from grey stone in the days before they made everything out of glass and steel. Now the Howlers had it.

It hadn't been hard to follow their trail from the ambush point once she'd established that Shiara had been taken from the wrecked Interceptor. Howler gangs were not known for their stealth, and it was a mere two blocks to their base. The way was marked with graffiti, littered with fresh trash, and the road had been conspicuously cleared of vehicles so that they cluttered the sidewalks instead.

Cassica had used the vehicles for cover, her senses straining as she crept along, shrinking whenever she heard a shriek echoing through the streets. Once she was forced to hide as a car, bristling with spikes and decorated with skulls, sped by. Soon after, she had to detour through a rusty playground to avoid a pair of Howlers engaged in a snarling argument in a language she didn't recognize.

Now she'd reached the hideout, and when she did, she found the entrance open and apparently unguarded.

It was worse than if there *had* been guards. The threat of the unseen, the suspicion of a trap kept her paralysed. The original gate was gone, and all that was left was a gap in the wall. Through it, she could see cars and small trucks haphazardly parked all over the weedy forecourt. The occasional Howler wandered about in a skatch-addled daze, but there seemed to be no organized defence at all. Perhaps they believed they had nothing to fear, or perhaps they were too fractious and wild for discipline.

Cassica watched and waited until she dared watch

and wait no longer. When she was sure there were no Howlers in sight, she took a few panting breaths to psych herself up, then broke cover and ran to the gate.

She stopped at the corner and peered round, gripping the table leg tight in both hands. Parked on the other side of the wall was a bus, its flank plated with welded iron. That was how they sealed their base: they merely drove it forward a dozen yards to barricade the entrance when needed. Beyond, in the forecourt, she counted three Howlers. Two were listless, drifting; the other was walking purposefully towards the building.

Her skin crawled. Surely, if she moved, they'd see her? And surely someone would see her if she didn't.

Fear of what was behind drove her onwards. She scampered into the forecourt and scrambled under the bus.

Pressed flat in the dirt, she listened to the pulse in her ears. Where were the screams, the cries of the hunters as they sighted prey? They didn't come. After a time, she dared to crawl along the length of the bus to its rear. She looked out, but all she saw from this low angle were parked cars.

Bunching up her courage like a fist, she told herself to move. She slithered out, belly to the ground, then got to her feet and ran in a crouch. She took shelter behind a flatbed truck, putting it between her and the Howlers.

Again, no screams of outrage, no hunting calls. She

240

swallowed against the pain in her throat and ran again.

In this way, she skirted the edge of the forecourt and made her way close to the building. As she neared, she was surprised by a sudden shriek, and the shock almost made her shriek herself; but it wasn't meant for her – it was just the random cry of the deranged.

She searched frantically for its source. One of them was nearby, lurching and staggering past on the other side of the car she hid behind. She spotted him through the grubby windows: a horrible, ragged shred of a man, ropes of tangled hair hanging over his eyes. He moaned and twitched, caught in a web of dreams and nightmares from which he'd never wake.

Cassica had seen Howlers a few times when she was younger. They sometimes ventured out of the Rust Bowl when they needed repairs at Blane's auto shop. She'd thought them unpredictable, edgy and dangerous; but in fact they were the least wild, junior members of the gang sent to deal with the outside world. Skatch was a kind of moonshine brewed from the roots of the skatch bush, a mutant plant that grew in the wastelands left after the Omniwar. It provoked wild and vivid visions, but it ate away at the mind until, with time, fantasy replaced reality. Long-term users were left on a see-saw teetering between bliss and rage. The Howlers embraced the chaos, choosing short lives of violence and delirious joy over the grind of daily living, but in the end they all lost their minds.

She hunkered down and let him pass, listening to his shuffling footsteps as he moved away. When she felt it was safe, she lifted her head and looked again. He was heading off; the danger had abated for now.

Through the window, she caught sight of something inside the car. Hanging from the ignition was a preserved human finger, dry and brown like biltong. At first she was disgusted, but then she realized it was hanging from a key ring. There was a key in the ignition.

She ran her gaze over the vehicle she hid behind. Until now, it had been merely cover. Now it was a car, armoured with riveted metal sheets, its windows protected by grids. Filthy but sturdy-looking, and the tyres were full.

A treacherous thought came to her. *Get in. Drive. You had a two-hour lead. You could still be a contender. You could still win the race. If you get in now.*

She caught herself. No. The plan was to rescue Shiara, sneak them both out to safety, and press the rescue alarm to get them picked up. No more risks. The race was over. Shiara was what was important.

But just in case, she quietly opened the car door and pulled the key from its slot. Grimacing, she slid it from its grotesque key ring and put it in a pocket of her driving leathers.

Just in case.

An open fire door let her inside. She found

herself in hot, sunlit corridors littered with flaked plaster, tattered plastic bags and empty soda cans. The building smelt of rodent droppings, sweat and neglect. She passed broken skatch bottles, a battered shoe, an old bloodstain so large its donor couldn't have survived it. The squeals and mutters of the Howlers rang from the walls, deeper within.

She snuck onward, clutching the table leg, ready to use it if need be. She wasn't convinced of its worth.

"Hello?"

The voice came from down the corridor. A man's voice, a *sane* voice, though it sounded oddly flat and dead.

"Hello? Are you there?"

Her heart jumped. Could he *hear* her?

"Hello? Come in!"

She cringed. He was making so much noise. Come in *where*? Up ahead, there was an open doorway on her left. The voice seemed to issue from there.

"Come in, come in."

A crackle of static, and something in the way he said it, made her realize: the voice was coming from a speaker. A walkie-talkie or a ham radio. She let out a shaky breath. So she hadn't been seen after all.

And yet there was the voice on the radio. Maybe she could talk to him. Maybe she could call for help.

She moved quietly down the corridor. The voice would draw Howlers, perhaps, but it drew her too. A voice from outside this madness. Comforting and somehow familiar.

She was almost at the doorway when the voice came again. "Is anybody ther—"

"I'm here."

The new voice froze her in her tracks. She pressed up against the wall, eyes wide. She wanted to flee, but she didn't dare. There was someone in the room. Another moment and she would have stepped into the doorway.

"Where've you been?" demanded the voice on the radio.

"I been here," came the lazy reply. The Howler's voice was deep and smoky, a voice for starting bar brawls.

"You found the other girl yet?"

"They out there lookin', man. Most everyone out there lookin'," said the Howler. "So how 'bout you gimme a clue where she's at?"

"I told you, she smashed the damn hovercam and she's not wearing her helmet. We don't *know* where she is!"

Disbelief and dread settled on Cassica like a numbing shroud. It wasn't possible. Someone was *helping* the Howlers. Someone had set them up.

This wasn't sport. This was murder.

"What you care anyway, man?" the Howler asked. "She out of the race. You said yourself you made it so their rescue alarms don' work. So why don' you leave her to us?"

Cassica felt sick. Their alarms. Their way out. One way or another, they'd been sabotaged. They were trapped here.

"It's imperative that neither of them make it out. The man doesn't want anyone talking about this. There's too much at stake!"

"Yeah, yeah."

"I got here four crates of the best skatch in Pacifica. You want it, you be sure you get *both* those girls."

The man on the radio was nervous, talking rapidly. Did she know that voice? It was hard to tell — the speaker made his voice dull and buzzy — but there was something in the rhythm of his words. . .

"What have you done with the one you caught?" he asked.

"You don' wanna say her name no more?"

A hateful silence on the other end. Then: "Shiara. Where's Shiara?"

"She down in the basement. Might need her as a lure if we can't root the other out. Stake her out in the street, do this 'n' that till she sings. See if her friend stays hidin' when they can hear her screamin' down the block."

The basement! That was the spur to move her. She crept off, back the way she came, towards a junction in the corridor that would let her take another route round. All she had to do was find some stairs down, find Shiara, get her out. That was as far ahead as she could imagine now. After that, she didn't know.

As she made her way on silent feet, the unseen men kept talking. She heard their final exchange just as she reached the corner.

"Alright," said the man on the radio. "I'll call back in an hour or so. You better have news."

"Don' worry, Harlan. I'll be here."

Cassica stopped, looked back over her shoulder. Bleak-eyed and aghast. The name dropped on her like a stone; the weight of his betrayal made her weak.

Harlan.

Their own manager. The man whose fingers they were trying to save. The man who got them in such a mess in the first place.

Harlan.

She gritted her teeth against the tears of rage and frustration, then turned the corner and was gone.

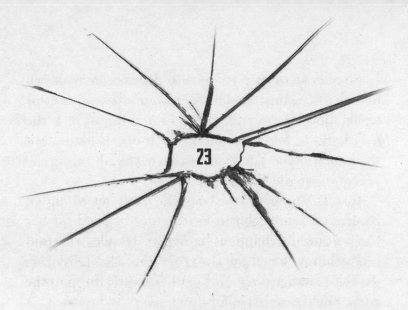

23

Shiara had fixed all kinds of machines in her day, from washing machines to petrol generators. She'd mastered the complex interplay of parts that made up combustion engines, brake systems, nitrous oxide injection arrays. All that, and yet the thing that was going to get her killed was a simple pin-and-tumbler lock on a pair of handcuffs.

She knelt on the floor of a concrete room, wrists shackled to a heavy iron radiator, her body aching in a dozen places. Broken furniture and a mouldy bedroll lay among the dust and fallen plaster. Near the doorway, leaning back in his chair, was a Howler, a shaggy heap of a man with an oil-stained face. Next to him a shotgun leaned against the wall, and nearby, a recently emptied bottle of skatch. The Howler's eyes were on the ceiling, where his delirium showed him fascinating things invisible to Shiara.

She took advantage of his distraction to work her wrists against the cuffs, to test the radiator for weak spots. She searched for something to pick the lock with. In her heart she knew it was hopeless, but she hoped anyway. The alternative was admitting she was going to die.

Just thinking it, she felt the cold thrashing of panic, and wanted to scream.

It couldn't happen to her. It was beyond imagination. Somehow she'd get free. She'd dislocate the bones in her wrist and get her hands through the cuffs. She'd save herself. Somehow.

The thought that someone else might save her never entered her head. She didn't expect help from the Maximum Racing officials – she'd seen how they treated their racers – and as for Cassica, not a chance. It had always been Shiara who'd been there for Cassica, not the other way round.

She couldn't find it in her heart to be angry at Cassica for running out on her. Rather, it was resignation she felt. No sense both of them dying; leaving had been the smart thing to do. Perhaps, her whole life, she'd been waiting for the moment when Cassica would abandon her for good. Cassica was too fast for her, too flighty, too full of fierce life. Some part of Shiara wanted to be like her, but since she couldn't, being near her was the next best thing. It couldn't last, though. It was inevitable that Cassica would move on in the end, find someone new to protect her from herself.

At least, that was what she'd always thought. But then, through the doorway, Shiara saw her.

She came creeping into sight in the corridor, nervous like some tatty fox. She peered into the room, eyes widening as they found Shiara's. And in that moment Shiara felt a connection re-established, like the closing of a circuit breaker. Life and joy and the possibility of a future surged into her. She couldn't believe she'd ever doubted her friend.

Cassica opened her mouth to speak; Shiara shook her head frantically. She gestured with her eyes at the Howler sitting just inside the door, out of Cassica's sight. Cassica dithered in the doorway, unsure of how to proceed. She was holding a length of metal as a weapon, but Shiara didn't trust her to put down a Howler that big.

The Howler lost interest in whatever he saw on the ceiling. His head lolled forward and he fixed his bleary attention on Shiara. A grin stretched his lips.

"Gonna enjoy killin' you," he said, voice drowsy with skatch. "Kill you slow."

Suddenly, an idea came to her. A plan, half thought through. "Yeah?" she said. "Come here and try it."

The Howler was surprised and confused by the tone in her voice. She faked as much aggression as she could, shook the manacles noisily. "Come and have a go, see what happens," she snarled.

He lifted himself up from his seat, staring at her like she was some curious errant puppy, yapping at him.

"I said come on!" She swung a hopeless kick at him from the floor, though he was far out of reach.

The anger in her voice sparked anger in him. He lumbered over to her, his grin replaced with gritted teeth, joy turned to fury. She writhed away from him as he grabbed at her clumsily, trying to hold her down. She kicked away a clutching hand; he recoiled from her, kicked her in response, slamming a boot into her thigh. She gasped in agony as her leg went dead.

"Get off her!"

Cassica's order drew the Howler up short. He swung around and saw Cassica holding the shotgun he'd left by the doorway. She held it uncertainly, pointed at his chest.

"Take off her handcuffs," Cassica said. But there was a tremble in her voice.

The Howler lunged at her. Startled, Cassica squeezed the trigger. The shotgun bellowed. Shiara flinched away and closed her eyes as hot blood spattered her cheek.

When she opened them again, Cassica was standing there shocked, and the Howler was on the ground, dead.

"He just ran at me," Cassica said weakly.

"Get the keys off him!" Shiara told her. The sound of the shotgun would bring the Howlers running. Already she could hear their shrieks rising in volume. "The keys!" she snapped, when the first time didn't penetrate.

Cassica moved then. She dropped to her knees and dug in the Howler's pockets, averting her eyes from his face and the wound in his chest, until she found the keys. As soon as Shiara was out of the handcuffs, she got to her feet and pulled Cassica up with her.

"They're comin'. You got a way out?"

Cassica stared at her blankly for a moment before something clicked. She pulled out a car key from her pocket and held it up.

Shiara slapped her on the shoulder. "Smart thinkin'. Lead on."

The yammering and wailing of the Howlers echoed in their ears as they fled through the building. The alarm had been raised, and booted feet pounded the corridors. It was hard to tell if there were a dozen or five times that: the racket they kicked up made them sound like a horde. Cassica and Shiara darted past dim rooms with stained mattresses laid amid the debris. Twice they changed direction when they heard someone coming the other way. But whether there were few Howlers or many, they made it outside without being seen.

The forecourt wavered like a mirage in the oppressive heat of the day. Howlers were out there, stirred up by the clamour, cavorting like demons in the scorching yellow sunlight. They ran crazily between the cars and trucks, waving their knives. Shiara reckoned most of them didn't even know the reason why they were excited; like a pack of animals, any alarm was trigger enough.

"Which one?" she asked Cassica. Shiara was the calm one now. Cassica needed her strength; she knew it by the wild look in her friend's eyes.

Cassica pointed to the car. Mercifully, it was on the edge of the forecourt, near to them. They scampered towards it, and reached it unseen. Shiara pulled open the door.

"You drive," she said, because that was how it had always been. Cassica drove; Shiara did the rest. And together, only together, it worked.

Cassica clambered over to the driver's seat, keeping low, and threw the shotgun in the back. Shiara slipped in after, shutting the door behind her.

Cassica put the key in the ignition. Just as she was about to turn it, Shiara stopped her hand.

"Thanks," said Shiara, because she had to say it. Because if all this went wrong, she wanted her friend to know. And though that word was pitifully inadequate, though it said nothing of the pride and gratitude she felt towards Cassica, the relief and joy of seeing her, she had no better word to give.

Cassica held her gaze, and Shiara knew she'd understood. "Yeah," she said. "Sorry."

It was an apology more profound than any she'd ever given, deeper and wider in its pain and regret than two quick syllables could ever express. An apology for everything: for how she'd been, how she was, what she'd done.

That was how it was between them. One word, and all was forgiven.

Shiara let go of her hand. Cassica faced forward. She turned the key, and the car coughed, chattered and died.

"You've got to be frickin' kidding me," Cassica said.

Across the forecourt, painted faces swivelled towards them. The Howlers had heard the engine. One screeched and pointed; another ran off towards the bus by the gate.

Cassica tried the engine again. It stuttered and refused to turn over. Shiara clambered over into the back seat as the Howlers came racing towards them. She picked up the shotgun, smashed out a window with the butt and aimed into the forecourt. She'd grown up with four brothers: she knew how to fire a gun.

A Howler had climbed into the driver's seat of the bus now. Shiara saw his intention. He was going to drive the bus forward, block the gate, seal them in.

Move, she willed the car.

She saw flashes of shrieking shadowed shapes between the cars and trucks, rushing closer. She aimed, ready on the trigger, blood pulsing against the backs of her eyes. They wouldn't take her alive again. Either of them.

A Howler came screaming at them.

The car's engine caught and roared. Cassica wrenched it into gear and it lurched forward just as Shiara squeezed the trigger. Her shot went wide; the Howler hit the back of the car and spun away. Tyres smoking, they accelerated, Cassica hunched over the wheel as they raced across the crowded forecourt. They heard gunshots, and ducked as bullets pinged off the car's armoured flanks.

Through the windscreen, Shiara could see they were approaching the gate. The bus had come to life, coughing black smoke; now it lurched forward to cut off their escape, and as they raced towards the narrowing gap Shiara thought they couldn't possibly get through in time.

They flashed across the front of the bus. Shiara saw its dirty grille looming in the side windows, terrifyingly close, and smelt the stink of oil as it thundered closer. But it was a fraction of a second too slow to ram them; instead it clipped them on the back fender as they shot past, throwing Shiara against the front seat, where she struck her head. The car swerved with the impact, but Cassica turned into the slide, found a straight line, and they were away.

After the tumbling chaos of escape came an incredible peace. They were on the road. Cassica was driving. All was as it should be.

Shiara looked back, amazed at their survival. The bus had blocked the gate, preventing the other

Howlers from following. She slumped down in her seat.

"Nice drivin'," she said.

Cassica got them a few blocks away from the Howlers' lair before she spoke again. She was bloody and haggard, and on the edge of cracking. Yesterday she'd been almost strangled to death. Today she'd shot someone.

"They were waiting for us," she said. "They'd been tipped off."

"The map," said Shiara.

"What map?"

"Harlan gave me a map, said it was a safe route. I shoulda told you, but . . . y'know."

"Harlan," said Cassica, her voice dull. "I heard him on the radio. He was talking to the Howlers. It was him."

Shiara felt cold and numb. She ought to feel angry, but what was the point? The odds had been stacked against them from the start. She'd wanted to win on merit, beat their opponents fair and square, but she'd taken that map from Harlan in the end. It didn't matter that it was a trap: she'd thought it was genuine. She'd cheated. Perhaps they deserved their betrayal.

She'd wanted to show the world what she could do, that she wasn't just some girl working in her daddy's auto shop. But winning the Widowmaker was a childish dream, and always had been. She realized that now.

"How much time you think we lost?" Shiara asked, fanning the last ember of vain hope.

"Too much."

The defeat in Cassica's voice was enough for her. It was over. Both of them knew it. The best they could hope for now was to get out of the city in one piece.

"Hoy," said Shiara. "Least we're alive, right?"

"Yeah," said Cassica flatly, as she took the slip road on to the freeway. "Least there's that."

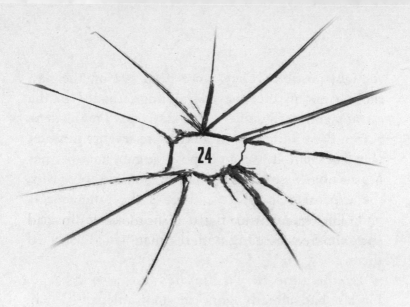

24

"Where's Harlan?" Cassica demanded as she stormed into the hotel bar. "Where's Harlan Massini?"

Her voice was loud in the softly lit room, silencing the murmurs of conversation. She swept the occupants with her eyes, reckless with rage. Men conspired in dim booths; women stared at her from their stools at the bar, drinks balanced in their hands. The barman, young and pox-marked with a flowing moustache, slid along the bar to her.

"Can I help you, miss?"

His patronizing sneer infuriated her. She snatched a bottle off the counter, smashed it against the bar. Alcohol sloshed along the counter; a woman nearby yelped in shock as she was pelted with bits of glass.

"Where's Harlan Massini?" Cassica snarled.

In the few hours since they'd rolled over the finish line, Cassica had reached a pitch of anger she'd never thought possible. They were dead last on the day, though not in the overall rankings, thanks to the advantage they'd built up on day one. The leaders, Kyren Bane and Draden Taxt, were seventy minutes ahead of them. It was an impossible gap, since neither Maisie nor the stolen Howler car could compete with the expensive sponsored vehicles the other racers had. The Widowmaker was lost to Cassica; instead she sought a reckoning with the man who'd betrayed them.

By the time they'd finished the second stage, Harlan had already gone on to Rattlepan Gulch, where the last leg of the Widowmaker would begin. They followed, riding with the teamsters who were transporting their cars and gear. It turned out to be a bleak, hardscrabble town at the foot of a mountain, with the Blight Lands so close you could feel the weirdness in the air. Only the desperate would pitch up so close to the heart of insanity, the dread land where few dared to venture and fewer still came back from; and this place seemed desperate indeed.

Cassica set out to find Harlan as soon as they arrived. Shiara, infuriatingly, showed little interest in confrontation. She said she'd rather be done with the whole damn mess; yelling at Harlan would do them no good. But Cassica wasn't the sort to let that kind of thing go, so she went alone.

Once-empty streets heaved with activity as spectators got drunk and crew made preparations for the morning. Every bar she visited sent her to another, increasing her rage each time, until finally she found a man who swore he'd been drinking with Harlan not a half-hour before.

Here. In this hotel bar. And yet still there was no sign of him.

She stood there, mad-eyed, a broken bottle in her hand. The barman was no longer patronizing: now he stared at her like she was a maniac. She had a sense that she'd gone too far, but she didn't care. She wanted Harlan.

"He ain't here," said a voice behind her, a slow drawl familiar enough to make her skin creep. She looked over her shoulder and saw a lanky man unfolding himself from a shadowed booth where he'd been drinking alone. His hangdog face was unshaven, jaw greasy with sweat, and he wore a battered porkpie hat. He walked over to her with a gangly lope.

The man who'd had her kidnapped, who'd stolen their sponsorship money, who'd threatened to take Harlan's fingers. Scadler.

He tossed some coins on the bar. "For the inconvenience," he told the barman. Then he snatched a bottle from the bar. "And this," he said. "Gimme another glass too."

The barman did as he was told, keeping his eye on Cassica.

"Where is he?" Cassica asked Scadler.

"He's gone. Hidin' out, I shouldn't wonder. Man came in a few minutes ago, told him you were in town and gunnin' for him. Don't reckon him for a feller big on courage." He motioned towards the booth with the bottle in his hand. "Shall we?"

"I'm not going anywhere with you."

"Might be I can explain a few things," he said. "Put down the broken bottle, though, huh?"

There was something in his manner that defused her anger. It would get her nowhere with him. And at least he was offering something. She put the remains of the bottle on the counter and went to the booth.

Scadler sat opposite her, put the new shot glass down next to the one on the table, and filled both with whisky.

"I don't want that," Cassica told him.

He shrugged, downed one, then downed the other and gave her that gummy, vile grin of his.

"Your problem," he said, as he filled a glass again, "is you don't know your place."

Cassica watched him carefully, the folds of his face made deep by the downlights, and waited for more.

"You know how much money they got swillin' around in a sport like Maximum Racin'? I'll tell you: it's a lot. And you know where all that money starts out? People in their livin' rooms, in bars all over the world, watchin' their televisions. All the advertisin', the sponsors, the clothes they put on you and the way you get your hair done, the only point of any of it is to keep people watchin' those adverts, buyin' them clothes, copyin' that style. Widowmaker's the biggest television event in the world. The opportunity to tell millions of people how they ought to spend their money. Somethin' that big, that's too important to leave to chance. Too important to let a couple girls from the boonies mess things up."

"We weren't messing *anything* up! We were trying to win!"

"That *is* messing things up. The outcome of this race got decided long before you joined it." He wagged a knowing finger at her. "You two, you're the plucky outsiders, poor kids done good, meant to bravely fail so we can all say how well you done. But you two as Celestials? Nah."

"Why not?" she cried.

"Your tech's chubby and surly. She couldn't be more dislikable if she tried. And you? You got the looks, but you got a frickin' temper. All that stuff you said yesterday, how your hometown was a dump and people out there were dumb, that didn't win you no friends. You backwater girls are supposed to be wholesome."

Cassica began to boil inside. "Who says?"

"The *viewers* say," Scadler told her, with a wicked glint in his eye. He was enjoying putting her through the mangle of his truth. "You gotta be what they want you to be, or they'll switch over. And Dunbery Hasp, he knows how to give the people what they want."

"What do they want?" She knew the answer before she even asked the question.

"Kyren Bane." He sank his whisky, smacked his lips. "Draden Taxt."

Cassica wanted to grind that glass into his face. "You're lying. You don't know."

He studied his glass as if reading wisdom in the reflections of light through its angles. "Two boys, perfectly machined for purpose," he said. "Bad boys who'll do what it takes to be famous. Dangerous, so Molly can safely dream of danger. Rebels, so Bobbi-Jo thinks she's a rebel too, and maybe she'll make Daddy angry. They're already plottin' next month's *Celestial Hour*, y'know. Already worked out which little starlet Kyren's gonna get with. Their managers have cut deals, sold 'em to each other, see? Cause they know it'll make headlines, and headlines are the secret to staying on Olympus. Keep the viewers watching. Give 'em what they want."

"That ain't what *I* want!"

"Ain't it?" He sighed and put down his glass. "I know your kind," he said scornfully. "You want the bad boys, but you don't know what bad is."

Cassica's head was going light as the rage seeped out of her, leaving her empty. She felt used and cheap and disgusted with herself. She wanted to argue that she was better than that, but she couldn't any more. Hadn't she bought the image of Kyren Bane from the moment she saw him on television? Hadn't she given herself to him, become the groupie cliché, even though he was an arrogant ass to her the first time they met? All that affected cool: did he even *know* he was fake, manufactured, designed by others?

Did *she*?

"It ain't that way," she said weakly. "It ain't."

Scadler poured himself another shot, talking with the languid rhythm of a man drunk and in love with his own ideas. "It's all fixed. The world's fixed. They make it look fair so's you'll keep playin' the game, but it ain't. All that's important is that it seems to be." He raised his glass to her. "An' they call *me* a criminal."

It was all too much. To be told that all their endeavour, all their dreams meant nothing, that it was a fool's chase from the off. They didn't fit the story. They weren't wanted. And yet after what Harlan did, how could she disbelieve it?

"He told me he had a meeting with Dunbery Hasp," she said.

"Uh-huh," said Scadler. "That bit of luck you had in the swamp got you so far out in front the bigwigs started sweatin'. So Hasp had a word with Harlan. Gave him a map and told him to make sure you didn't win. In return, Hasp would put him in line to manage some *real* contenders next time. That, and he'd get me off his back."

"How do you know all that?"

Anger passed across Scadler's face. "'Cause Hasp

had a word with me too. Some folk you just don't say no to." He downed another shot and gasped as it burned down his throat. "But I'll tell you somethin': I'll be rootin' for you when you race tomorrow. 'Cause if by some miracle you should win, that deal would be off – and Harlan wouldn't have no one to protect him from me then." He gave her a look, long and steady. "An' I wouldn't just stop at his fingers this time."

Cassica felt a chill. In that gaze she saw a man who'd killed without mercy and without thought, and would again. Kyren's posturing and sulkiness seemed ridiculous, weighed against that stare.

You want the bad boys, but you don't know what bad is.

She'd had enough of this. Enough of it all. Her dream of winning the Widowmaker had turned into something dirty and tawdry that she didn't even recognize. Harlan had cheated her of satisfaction by hiding from her, too cowardly to face a teenage girl. The godfather of Maximum Racing had tried to have her killed. And the boy she'd been chasing had been promised to someone else before they'd even met. He'd never been for Cassica: he was just passing the time. She was humiliated at how naive she'd been. The thought of seeing him again made her want to curl up and die.

Everyone was in it together. The only one who'd given it to her straight was this vicious thug, annoyed at being robbed of his bloody prize.

"We ain't racing tomorrow," she said. "We're done."

"Ah, that's a shame. A real shame. Well, can't say I'm surprised. You seem a smart girl." He touched the tip of his hat. "I think I've done about all the preachin' I'm goin' to for one night. You take care now, Cassica Hayle. Go on home."

Go on home. It seemed like the best idea she could imagine right then. So she got to her feet, thanked Scadler for his honesty and wished him a good night. Then she walked out of the bar, and the whole way she didn't raise her eyes from the floor.

Sammis Rye lay on a surgeon's table, surrounded by doctors and nurses, his bruised face hidden by a breather mask and his body sprouting tubes. The bleeping rhythm of his heart punctuated the murmured instructions from the man with the knife. Blood slipped in runnels over skin stained yellow with iodine.

Shiara watched through a window, her arms folded tightly. Next to her stood Dutton Rye, pale with worry. They wouldn't even have let her in, if he hadn't seen her and insisted she be allowed.

"He liked you," Dutton told her. "Thought a lot of you."

She knew that, but hearing it from his father made it worse.

After the crash, Sammis had regained consciousness long enough to activate his rescue alarm, otherwise they'd have left him there. As it was, he was lucky to have made it back. His tech hadn't been so fortunate.

"He's bleedin' on the inside," Dutton said. "They gotta try to stabilize him."

He spoke in the taut clipped manner of a man battening down his grief. Shiara knew that feeling. She hadn't dared think of Sammis since the crash. She wasn't even sure she wanted to be here now. If he was to die, she preferred to remember him as the boy who'd helped her fix her car, the boy with the easy smile who'd won her over with his kindness.

"They say he might not walk again if he lives," Dutton said.

Shiara wanted to comfort him, but she wasn't good at comforting strangers, so she kept quiet.

"I didn't even want him to be a racer," he said. "I knew how dangerous it was. I knew what might happen. But it seemed like what he wanted."

"He did it to make you proud," she told him.

He turned away from her then, and she could tell by his breath he was crying.

"Is that you?" said Melly, tears in her voice. "Is that really you, my darlin'?"

Shiara fought back tears herself as she watched her mom on the grainy monitor before her. Melly

266

seemed shrunken, smaller and frailer than Shiara remembered, dwarfed by her husband, who sat with one meaty arm around her.

"It's me, Mom," Shiara said. She wanted to say more, but it didn't feel right. There was a camera filming her from behind the monitor, and another cameraman next to her to catch a different angle. Lighting techs and a producer crowded the trailer where she sat in the midst of a makeshift studio.

The world was watching her, hungry for emotion.

"My little girl, my little girl!" Melly was crying openly now. Blane patted her ineffectually. "We thought you were gone! When the cameras went out, we thought . . . oh!" She turned into Blane's chest and wept.

"We're all mighty relieved here," said Blane. He masked his feelings with a brusque, let's-get-on-with-it tone. He was as awkward as she in front of cameras. "How'd you do it?"

"Cassica got me out," said Shiara. She glanced off-camera at the producer, who was making encouraging gestures. "I'm gonna do an interview about it at eight, tell the whole story." The producer kept gesturing. "With Tandy MacKail, only on Channel 3," she added finally.

It made her feel greasy, but such was the deal she made, and she honoured her deals. In return, she got this: the chance to see her parents. To see how she'd wrung them out with worry and care.

"They say you're gonna quit the race," Blane said. "How you ain't got a car left that's fast enough to make up the time."

"Uh-huh," said Shiara.

"Y'know, the Wreckers pick off the ones at the back. You don't wanna be laggin'."

"I know, Daddy."

Melly raised her head, sniffling. "Come home, baby," she said. "You done enough now. You come home."

"We're all real proud o' you here," said Blane. "You and Cassica. Even after all that stuff she said about Coppermouth."

Shiara gave a brief laugh. She'd forgotten that. "She didn't mean it, Daddy. You know Cassica."

"Come home," said Melly again.

The cicadas were calling in the floodlit night when Shiara made her way to the garage. There she found Cassica sitting inside Maisie, her hands on the wheel.

"Remember her?" she asked as Shiara came over. She patted the dash and touched the seat, as if familiarizing herself anew. "Don't it seem like for ever since we took her out?"

Shiara climbed in the passenger seat next to her friend. She rarely heard Cassica reminisce.

"Remember that time we were racing the Mooncliff rally? We were in, like, seventh place or something, and then—"

"Somethin' happened," said Shiara, nodding. They never did figure out what it was, only that suddenly—

"We were in the *zone*," said Cassica, her eyes distant as she saw it all again. "Just for a minute it was like everything fell into place, like the whole world shifted to suit us. Like we were just *meant* to win, and nothing or nobody could stop it. And we flew. Past one, past two. Seventh to first in thirty seconds, and we took that race." She came back to the present, and she was smiling. "That was something."

"That was somethin'," Shiara agreed.

Cassica laid a hand on Shiara's wrist. "It's enough, you know," she said, brave and sad all together. "You, me and Maisie. Coppermouth. It's enough."

Shiara felt something bite down inside her, something that threatened to start a flood. Simple as that, they could go home, and this would all be over. The only thing she had to do was nothing.

But Cassica was her friend. Her *best* friend. And she'd had a dream. So Shiara reached into her pocket and pulled out a map, which she flattened on the dash.

Cassica frowned. It showed the third stage of the Widowmaker, a crescent-shaped cluster of mountains with Kniferidge Pass at the heart of it.

"I think we can win it," Shiara said.

Cassica shook her head. "No, Shiara. There's no point."

"We can win it," she insisted.

"They won't let us!"

"We can win it if we go through the Blight Lands."

Shiara pointed at the map. On its eastern edge was an empty space, the only hint of the vast desert that sprawled beyond the mountains. "Everyone's gonna drive up towards the Kniferidge Pass, right? Because that's the route. But there ain't no reason we gotta *take* that route. Long as we get from A to B, anything goes." She drew a line with her finger. "They're gonna be drivin' in a crescent, pickin' their way through all kinda difficult terrain." Then she drew a new line, a straight line from one horn of the crescent to the other. "Not us."

Cassica was speechless for a moment. "You know ... you know it's the frickin' *Blight Lands* you're talking about? The kind of place even Howlers ain't crazy enough to go? There's things in the Blight Lands left over from the Omniwar, things that don't even have names any more, just waitin' to kill us! People go nuts just from being in that place! Hell, you can choke from breathin' a patch of poison air!"

"We can win it," Shiara told her again.

"Yeah, and we could die!"

"Pretty sure that's been the case every time we got in the cockpit together."

"And what would we go in?"

"Maisie," said Shiara, slapping the dash. "We gonna

take Maisie. Anyone can get us through, she can."

Cassica was confused, and it was beginning to make her angry. "Look, what you trying to do here, Shiara? I'd figured on going home. I thought this was over, and I'd made my peace with that. I almost got you killed for this damn dream of mine. Now you wanna go on?"

"I do," said Shiara. "I wanna beat 'em."

"Beat *who*?" Cassica cried in exasperation.

"Everyone who said we couldn't. Them that tried to get us killed. Them that made it so Sammis got hurt so bad, and Linty Maxxon, and all o' them who died. I wanna do it just to show 'em they don't get to decide."

Cassica studied her doubtfully, trying to decide if Shiara was only doing this for her sake, or if she really meant it. But Shiara meant it, alright. She'd rarely been so certain of anything.

"You know they'll send the Wreckers after us," said Cassica. "Soon as they realize what we're up to, they'll do anything they can to stop it."

"Let 'em," said Shiara. "Us two and Maisie can take the best they can throw at us. Plus I hear television and radio don't work in the Blight Lands. Wreckers can't track so well without their bosses tellin' 'em where the racers are."

Cassica put her hands on the wheel, flexed her fingers, faced forward. All her life she'd relied on Shiara's sane, sensible advice to steer her when she had no answers for herself. Now Shiara used those same relentless, plodding arguments to push her to a level of recklessness even Cassica would normally balk at.

But Shiara was taking a stand. And she needed Cassica by her side.

"Alright," said Cassica. A smile spread across her lips. "Alright. Let's do it. You and me."

"You and me," said Shiara. "Let's get to work."

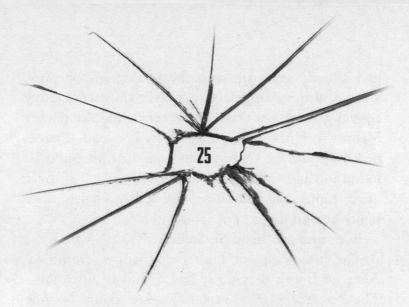

25

The broadcasters didn't pay much attention to Cassica and Shiara in the build-up to the Widowmaker's final stage. The commentators made noises about how plucky they were for continuing in their home-made racer – the gutsy, never-say-die spirit of the boondocks – but everyone knew they couldn't win, so the focus was mostly on those like Kyren Bane, who could.

An hour and a half into the race, twenty minutes after Maisie set off, things were different.

"We've stirred 'em up now!" said Shiara, as she watched the footage on the screen they'd attached to Maisie's dash. Commentators were going bug-eyed. Experts spluttered their amazement. People wondered: could it actually be done?

Cassica and Shiara were heading into the Blight Lands.

All the other racers – those who counted, anyway –

had already gone up into the mountains by now. They couldn't change course even if they were crazy enough to want to. Those few racers who started after Maisie were not inclined to follow her lead. They'd heard the stories. Only madness and death could be found in the Blight Lands. Most who went in there never came out, and those that did often left their sanity behind them.

But some got through. Some.

The broadcast got fainter and more scrambled. After an hour's driving it had dissolved into static. The hovercam that was following them became confused by the charged atmosphere and gradually fell behind until it was out of sight.

"Guess we're on our own now," said Shiara.

"Yeah."

And it was a lonely place they found themselves; lonely and strange. They cut a straight line over the hardpan, mountains rearing to their left, a thin trail of dust drifting skyward in their wake. The sun seethed in an acid sky, and felt more foreign than Cassica had ever known it, as if they were driving in the glare of an alien star.

The desert spread out before them, dry and rocky and cracked, broken with outcrops that thrust up like stone thorns. A blasted land, hostile to soft life. Crooked plants, black and twisted, clawed at the earth. Those in flower showed long fleshy cups, wet throats that oozed poison.

"The hell they do to this place?" Cassica said. The sense of doom and desolation was so strong it had begun to seep into her, causing a deep unease.

"This area got it bad in the Omniwar," said Shiara. Her voice sounded wrong to Cassica: tinny and flat. "Stuff got let loose you can't imagine. Stuff that messed with the laws of physics. Make you crazy just thinkin' about it." She tucked a strand of white hair under her helmet. "You should see the other guys, though. Way I hear it, their whole country's like this."

They drove for an hour without seeing another living creature, navigating by the mountains. The land rose around them in towering red mesas and wind-carved formations that looked eerily like giants and monsters. The ghostly wail of distant singstones came to them on a hot breeze, and the air began to smell acrid and eggy.

"Has the sun even moved?" Cassica asked.

"Course it has. It must have."

"Could swear it hasn't."

A drop of sweat crawled down Cassica's scalp. It was hard to convince herself it wasn't some creeping insect trapped beneath her helmet. The singstones' lament was making her edgy.

"When you think they'll catch us?" she asked.

"The Wreckers? Dunno. We were so far back in the pack, they all set off ahead of us. They're a lot faster than we are, but they gotta double back, come

275

down the mountain, chase us down on the flats. That's if they can find us without the producers tellin' 'em where we are."

"Might be they won't send anyone," said Cassica hopefully. "Might be they'll gamble we won't make it through. I mean, even if the Wreckers catch us, they won't get it on camera. Pretty boring for the viewers, right?" Since they weren't receiving signals, she assumed the cameras in the car and on our helmets weren't broadcasting either. "Might be they'll leave us alone."

Shiara said nothing, but her face was grim. She wasn't remotely convinced of that.

The ground began to lift ahead of them and they started a long climb up a shallow incline towards the crest of a rise.

"I heard they got flesh-eating gas here," Shiara said suddenly.

"What?"

"Invisible gas. Clouds of it that stay close to the ground, blowin' about with the wind. You drive through it and it just eats you to the bone."

Cassica was horrified. "Why in hell you just tell me that?"

"Dunno," said Shiara. "Was thinkin' about it, is all."

"Well, keep it to yourself next time!"

But it was too late: the thought was there, and doubt swarmed in. Why hadn't they encountered anything yet? The Blight Lands had such a terrible reputation, but they'd travelled so far unopposed. Had they already brushed past death unaware? Was it waiting for them just ahead, impossible to detect?

In the footwell next to Shiara was the shotgun she'd killed the Howler with. It was illegal to use weapons against other racers and Wreckers, although locals and wildlife were fair game. Perhaps they should have been carrying some from the start, but their meagre funds had been needed elsewhere, and they'd never thought they'd need them, never thought they'd have to step out of their car. Time had taught them otherwise, so they brought the shotgun for protection; but it wouldn't protect against gas.

How would it begin? A tingling on the skin, then a pain like sunburn, deepening to agony till her whole body was aflame with it? Cassica looked down at her hands and for an instant she saw them rotting away before her eyes. It gave her such a jolt of terror that she jerked the wheel and they swerved.

"Whoa! Hoy!" Shiara cried as she was thrown against her harness.

Shut up! Why don't you shut up? Cassica clenched her jaw. Damn, she was irritable! What was wrong with her? She was about to say something when she spotted movement up on the top of a mesa to their right, and her heart jumped. "You see that?"

"See what?"

"There!" She pointed. "I saw someone!"

"You did?" There was nothing there now.

"Looked like . . . I think it was one of them swamp folk."

A flash in her mind: hands on her throat; that deformed face close to hers; the vile damp smell of him.

"One of *them*? Out here?" Shiara sounded doubtful.

"Maybe a Howler, then!" Cassica snapped.

Shiara scanned the tops of the mesas. "Might've been a Howler," she said, a note of worry creeping into her voice.

"There!" A scramble of movement; dark figures running along the ridge. A different mesa this time. "Howlers! I definitely saw 'em that time!"

"I don't see 'em." Shiara was fidgeting in her seat. Cassica knew the thought of Howlers scared her badly. Those hours she'd spent chained to the radiator, waiting to die, must have chewed at her soul the way the swamp man chewed at Cassica's. "You think they're after us? Think they've set an ambush?"

"Frickin' Howlers," Cassica muttered hatefully.

"Wait, the screen's back on," Shiara said.

"What are they saying?" Cassica kept an eye out for more Howlers, fingers drumming restlessly on the wheel. She remembered the rocket launcher that took out their Interceptor yesterday, and stayed tense, ready for anything. "Shiara? What's happening?"

"It's Mom," said Shiara softly.

"*Melly?* You serious?"

"She's tellin' us we gotta come home. There's somethin' bad ahead. We gotta turn back."

Cassica looked over at the screen, then at Shiara, whose eyes had become wide and childlike. A cold feeling crept into her.

"Shiara," she said. "Shiara, there ain't nothing but static on that screen."

Shiara stared at her like she'd been slapped. "What you talkin' about? She's right there! She's sayin' we oughta turn back."

"I'm telling you, she ain't."

Shiara was becoming hysterical, her voice rising higher and higher. "We gotta turn back! Mom says! We gotta turn back!"

"We ain't doing that," Cassica told her firmly.

Shiara shut up. Then her eyes narrowed, and her face became suspicious and shrewd, and she lunged across the cockpit and seized the wheel. Cassica was flung sideways by the sudden turn, but she wrenched the wheel back before it could tip them. Shiara popped her harness and threw herself at Cassica, wrestling her hands away, teeth gritted and face red. Cassica's kicking foot found the brake, and Maisie screeched as her wheels locked and she skidded to a halt in a cloud of dust. Shiara was thrown on top of Cassica, crushing her down, and though Cassica fought, she couldn't get out from under her.

She's gonna strangle me.

The thought sent her into a frenzy. Somehow she got free of her harness, and she shoved and thumped at her attacker while Shiara tried to hold her down. Grunting, panting, desperate, Cassica pushed the heel of her palm against Shiara's cheek, forcing her head back ...

... and Shiara's face crumbled beneath her hand.

The horror of that sight almost toppled her sanity. Where there had been flesh and bone there was only a powdery dust, the red dust of the Rust Bowl. As Cassica flailed and shrieked, cracks ran outward across Shiara's face and neck, chunks of her breaking away like a sandcastle on the edge of an incoming tide.

The dust was everywhere: in her lungs, in her eyes, in her nostrils. Shiara fell apart in front of her, replaced by something else: a terrifying, groaning thing of red dust, something that slid and collapsed and reformed again, a monster with sharp glinting eyes that loomed from the choking murk to paw at her.

Momma.

She screamed in raw wild panic. Somehow she got a knee between them and shoved the creature away. It reared back, and she grabbed for the shotgun in Shiara's footwell and pulled it to her. The creature saw the danger and grabbed it, mitten hands sloughing dust, and they fought for the weapon between them.

But the creature was strong. Cassica was losing the battle. And when she did, it would smother her, force its dry arm down her throat, throttle her with dust the way it happened to Momma. Then Cassica would be dust too, nothing more than powder to be blown away on the wind and forgotten. It would be like she'd never existed at all.

With one last cry of abject, senseless denial, she butted her forehead into the creature's face. The dust gave before the blow, bursting in a cloud, and she hit something solid and heard a crack of bone. The monster reared away with a howl and Cassica pushed it across the cockpit with her boot, launching herself backwards. Her elbow hit the door release and it fell open behind her, dumping her heavily on the hard desert ground, her legs tangled in her harness and the shotgun clutched to her chest.

The impact stunned her. She found herself looking up at the sun, which was somehow directly overhead, when a few minutes ago it had been nowhere near zenith.

Then she felt the weight of the creature on her legs, which were still up on the seat. She tried to pull away but she couldn't. Awkwardly she turned the shotgun so her finger was on the trigger, barrel aimed up towards the door, just as the creature billowed forth, eyes glowing in rage.

Right into her sights.

Something wet spotted her face, her lips, making

her flinch. Before she could stop herself, she'd tasted it. Salty, metallic.

Blood. The thing was *bleeding*.

But creatures made of dust couldn't bleed.

A sense of wrongness filled her. Some quiet alarm, previously unheard, now shrilled loud in her mind. How could it be so heavy, made of dust as it was? What did she hit when she headbutted it? How could it bleed?

Her finger hovered on the trigger. *This place, this place*. Some vital knowledge tickled at the edge of her consciousness, something she remembered, something about the Blight Lands and the stories they told, the way it twisted your mind if you let it. This dust creature didn't add up. How could it *be*?

It raised itself up to lunge down upon her, screeching as it did so.

Kill it kill it kill it!

A gust of wind blew past them, and it seemed that the dust drew back a little, and behind its features she saw another face, one she'd known and loved all her life.

"Shiara!"

But the finger on the trigger was driven by fear. It twitched, and with a deafening boom the shotgun fired.

The roar of the weapon echoed into the silence, and with it, the illusion was dispelled. With a shivering hiss the dust fell away from Shiara, and

Cassica looked up into the eyes of her friend. Shiara, half her face ribboned with blood from a cut over her eye, stared blankly at the shotgun in Cassica's hands.

It was pointed at the sky. Jerked away at the last instant.

"I thought you were a Howler," Shiara whispered.

"I thought..." Cassica began, but she couldn't finish.

Shiara climbed out and helped Cassica untangle her legs from the harness. Cassica got to her feet. Neither knew what to say. They felt scoured out and bleached by what had just occurred. The realization that she'd almost killed her best friend made Cassica's legs weak.

She didn't know what had caused their hallucinations, whether it was gas or the insidious effect of the landscape itself, but it seemed they'd overcome them, at least for the moment. Now she understood what they'd taken on when they decided to tackle the Blight Lands. This place had seen the worst of humanity's madness, and had become mad itself. Reality itself was uncertain here.

They'd come to a halt near the crest of a rise. Cassica walked unsteadily towards it. Any direction was good, as long as it was away from the thing she'd nearly done. The sun glared down balefully as she went.

She got to the top of the rise, and the land fell away. From where she stood, she could see for miles. She gazed numbly over what was ahead.

A vast plain lay before her. The land was scarred with glassy wounds where beams from space had melted the earth. Crazed, unnatural mineral structures gathered at their edges, where stone had surged and fused and transformed in the wake of those deadly rays. Scattered between was a field of debris incredible in scope, a junkyard bigger than she'd ever seen. Vehicles smashed to shrapnel, flying machines torn to bits, gun emplacements sunk into the ground where it had turned to liquid.

Around them, a hundred thousand battle mechs, the legendary soldiers of the Omniwar, scattered like tinfoil shreds under the sun. Some with tracks like tanks, some with missile launchers for hands, some with faces, some without. Slumped here and there, Titans lay like rusted islands, great beetle-like mobile fortresses that once thundered across the face of the world like the legends of the first civilizations come to life.

A heat haze wavered over that hellish gravesite, and the air had a sinister tinge. All that destruction awed her. In the tangle it was impossible to know which were the enemy and which were not. In the end, it didn't matter. They'd both lost.

"Hoy!"

She heard her friend's voice and turned away gratefully. Shiara was shading her eyes and looking to the south. Cassica followed her gaze.

A cloud of dust. Vehicles, approaching fast up the rise behind them.

The Wreckers. No one else would be insane enough to follow them here. She wondered briefly if they were real or another hallucination.

"How many they send?" Cassica called.

Shiara let her hand fall away from her eyes. "All of 'em," she replied. "They sent all of 'em."

26

Pedal to the metal, engine screaming, sitting behind the wheel of a car she knew like an old friend; a car she knew exactly. This *is racing,* Cassica thought.

Piles of jagged metal shot past to their left and right. Half-buried faces peered out at her with dead mechanical eyes. She swerved past vehicles bigger than the biggest truck she'd ever seen, bristling with cannons, backs broken, hollowed out by smoke. Dust from the parched earth clouded the air behind them.

Hard on their heels came the Wreckers.

"He's lining up for a shot!" Shiara cried. She was twisted round in her seat, trying to keep their pursuer in sight. Cassica glanced in her mirror, caught a glimpse of what she was seeing.

Dr Sin hunched over the steering wheel of a dirt-smeared white racer, its hood and flanks daubed with dried gore in a mockery of medical crosses. His eyes were bloodshot and staring, face concealed by a surgeon's mask. Standing in a harness, his upper torso protruding through the sunroof, was the Carnasaur. Veins wrapped his swollen muscles like creepers; his skin was tattooed with yellow-green scales; his fanged mouth split in a hungry grin. Reptile eyes narrowed as he aimed down the sights of his rocket launcher, fighting to steady himself as the car jerked him about.

"Tell me when," said Cassica.

"He's gonna fire!" There was an edge of panic in her voice, but Shiara had never had Cassica's calm in a race.

"Tell me when," Cassica said again. She had her hands full weaving through the maze of wreckage. Somewhere to her left, she saw another car flash between the downed fractions of a crashed aircraft. Buzzsaw, getting ahead of them.

"Now!"

She was turning even as Shiara formed the word. Maisie lurched to the right, and the rocket hissed past. There was a flash and a detonation that shook them both in their seats. Somehow Cassica kept them from crashing as they skidded away from the bloom of oily flame, daggers of shrapnel thumping into Maisie's flanks.

"Yeah!" Shiara screamed at the back window, wild with relief. "Yeah! Try again, why don't ya?"

"Shiara," said Cassica, her voice level and firm. "Stay in the game. I need you."

Shiara sobered at that, got back in her seat, swallowed and nodded and turned her attention to the dash. It was hard to keep their heads in this place, where the sun seemed hateful and the iron ghosts of murdered history glared from all sides, loathing these intruders in their graveyard. But they'd need to be better than they'd ever been if they hoped to live out the hour.

They broke out from among the wrecks into a wide clear patch, where the ground glittered with petals of half-buried alloys and the air quivered with the merciless heat. Robbed of cover, they lit out in a straight line for the far side, keen to hide themselves again. In a flat race, they'd be easy pickings.

Buzzsaw emerged into the clearing at the same time. The circular saws that ran round the edge of his car spun and whined as he angled towards them. Dr Sin hung back, to allow the Carnasaur time to slot in a new rocket. Of Lady Scorpion and the Ghost, they saw no sign; but they likely wouldn't see the Ghost till it was too late anyway.

Cassica's thumb hovered over the turbo button. "Not yet," Shiara told her.

"We can't outrun him if we don't!"

"If we turbo, he'll do the same. And I'll wager his are better. Save 'em. They're runnin' hot anyway."

"So what?"

"So I used Maisie's safety limiter to repair the Interceptor, and I must've knocked off the calibration

288

when I did it. The turbos ain't venting heat as fast as they should." She said it angrily, but it was directed inward, at herself. "There's no cut-off any more. Push the turbos too hard, we'll explode. So when I say cut 'em, you cut 'em."

Cassica cursed under her breath.

"We didn't get a chance to run her out with the new alterations," Shiara said, by way of an excuse.

Cassica hated being leashed. But Shiara's tone stopped her snapping at her, as she might have done before. Shiara had done the best she could with the time she had, and she'd hardly slept for two nights. Cassica swallowed down the anger. This wasn't about her.

"You did a good job," she said. "We'll work with it." She looked up over at Buzzsaw, closing in from the left. "Gimme alternatives."

"We could . . . wait, what's *that*?"

All at once, thin tendrils came bursting from the ground, tearing free of the dry earth in powdery puffs, coiling and curling like a nest of snakes. They were all around them, all over the clearing, lashing the air, whipping this way and that.

Wire. Long strands of sharp wire, barbed with hooks and nightmarishly alive.

Cassica didn't wait for Shiara's say-so this time. She thumbed the turbos and held on.

The whole clearing writhed. Wires tore free from the baked soil, pulling themselves up like ripcords, rolling and reaching out with blind fury. Cassica drove Maisie towards the edge as hard as she could, desperate to escape the trap, dodging here and there as new tangles unspooled in her path.

Wires snatched at Maisie, trying to throttle her driveshaft and slash her wheels; but their attacks were sluggish, and they snapped away as soon as they got a grip. Whatever unnatural technology this was, it had been too long dormant under the earth, and its purpose had been dulled. Cassica fought to stay clear of the wires, defeating them with speed: under full turbo, Maisie was too quick to get a hold on.

The Wreckers, too, were caught in the wires. Buzzsaw's blades cut them away with ease, but Dr Sin had no such protection, and he hadn't been quick enough on his turbos. He skidded and slid as the wires took hold of his axles in clumps, and though they were torn out they slowed him enough for more to take hold, and more and more, until his blood-daubed car was dragged to a halt in a cloud of dust. Then the wire took them, wrapping car and Carnasaur, baling them up like hay, winding thicker and thicker until the tendrils became unbreakably strong. The wire tightened suddenly, and both the car and its occupants were pulled down into the earth with atrocious force, breaking as they went.

Now Cassica knew why there was no junk left on this patch of ground.

They reached the edge of the clearing, leaving

the wires behind them, a sea of insidious movement swiping at the air. And somewhere in that clouded haze they left Dr Sin and the Carnasaur too.

Shiara sucked air in through her teeth. "Turbos," she reminded Cassica, one eye on the temperature gauge. Cassica let the speed off as they plunged back into the field of wreckage.

They'd hoped that escaping the clearing would bring them some respite, but there was none to be had. Tripping the wire trap had caused some kind of alarm to spread. For the first time, they'd been noticed, and the graveyard was waking up.

Crushed mechs jerked into life, pawing at them from beneath a heap of fallen comrades. Coloured lights scampered across the dashboards of long-dormant vehicles, blinking fitfully as ancient systems booted up. Metal shrieked as enormous machines mobilized rusted joints and broken limbs, attempting to rise and slough away the smashed warriors that covered them.

"Oh, hell," Shiara muttered.

A rapid popping sound came to them from somewhere ahead. Cassica looked in time to see a broken mech on its back atop a heap of junk, a rectangular rack of tiny rockets mounted on its shoulder and tilted towards the sky. The last of the rockets were just popping off, straggling into the air like weak fireworks before turning nose-downward and falling.

Falling towards Maisie.

"Incoming!" Shiara cried, and Cassica threw them into a sequence of evasive manoeuvres as the world began to detonate around them. Each of the tiny rockets carried a payload far out of proportion to its size, and they exploded on contact with the ground. Maisie careered between the explosions, pummelled by concussion and showered with shrapnel.

Cassica couldn't even see the rockets coming down in the chaos: it was more luck than skill that got them through. She emerged breathless, exhilarated, bright-eyed. There was a wild joy in being abandoned to instinct and chance, and coming out alive.

"On the left!" she heard Shiara shout through the ringing in her ears.

She swerved as Buzzsaw swung in towards them. Sparks flew from Maisie's fender as the Wrecker's spin saws touched metal. Cassica saw a mad patchwork face through the window, criss-crossed with stitches, teeth gritted in a snarl; then the cars came apart, and she darted away.

The whole plain was astir now, as the message spread through the remnants of those once-mighty warriors. They marshalled the last dregs of stored power to inspire centuries-dead mechanisms back to life. Smashed mechs moved what parts remained to them, flexing stiffened arms, struggling to free themselves. They aimed weapons, some of which were empty and some carrying ammo that had decayed past the point of usefulness.

But some were still loaded and ready, even after centuries in the desert. Targeting systems, damaged but functional, groped after the intruders as they sped past.

The mechs opened fire.

Cassica slewed between islands of junk as the air filled with the din of weaponry. Bullets pocked the earth, raising little plumes of dust. Mechs blew themselves up trying to fire rockets from dust-clogged tubes. Listing turrets spat transparent globes that burst in sprays of acid, eating through metal and earth alike.

Cassica held her nerve. Here, with destruction raining down around them, future and past had ceased to exist. She was a creature of reaction, dodging attacks she could barely see, evading obstacles that sprang from the dust-clouded air without warning. Shiara jumped and shrieked and flinched at every impact, but Cassica was the eye of the storm, the still heart of the maelstrom.

To their left, through the crossfire, she saw Buzzsaw again. He was laughing like a maniac, the veins of his neck stark, eyes bulging. He caught her gaze and looked over at her, and just for a moment she saw fear on his face, as if he sensed what was coming, a premonition of the end.

Somewhere, a turret turned and a railgun

screamed. A spear of metal hit his car faster than the speed of sound, and he was driven into a trench in the earth with a brutal squeal of ripped metal.

"We gotta get out of the firin' line!" Shiara yelled. "Head for the glass canyons!"

"Those kind of ideas are why I keep you around," Cassica said, with a grim twitch of a smile.

Shards of crystal and melted stone towered over the junk to their right. The formations stood along the rim of an enormous scar in the earth, left by space weaponry of unimaginable power. Nothing had survived in those canyons. And that meant there were no mechs there.

She swerved, and a green ray raked the earth where they'd been, boiling the cracked soil into spume. Darting through the wreckage, chased by artillery, she raced towards the scar.

The land broke up beneath Maisie's wheels as she neared. It was smooth and reflective in spots. What mechs had been here had been melted into piles of cold slag; nothing stirred. As they drew closer to the scar, the assault on them lessened, and the explosions and gunfire diminished behind them.

The way became cluttered with columns of fused rock and clusters of giant crystals veined with strange colours. Cassica let off the speed a little, no longer trusting her wheels, which were slipping on patches of slick metallic ground.

Still, it was better than before. Somewhere distant,

the mechs were still firing at something: the other Wreckers, no doubt. Cassica hoped their aim was good.

She turned and drove alongside the scar. To her right was a slope of melted rock, scattered with strange fists of bubbled stone and great mineral spikes. At the bottom was a yawning chasm where the planet itself had been cut deep enough to bleed.

"We can ride along this edge; should take us near the limits of the battlefield," Shiara said.

Cassica's forehead creased in a frown. Something was nagging her, some sound on the edge of her hearing. So hard to rely on her senses in the Blight Lands; they tricked and deceived. She'd almost killed her best friend, until she learned to see beneath the way things seemed.

But her instincts clamoured. Something was wrong. Something.

She looked to her left. The junk and wreckage there made jagged shadowed mountains. The heat haze was terrible in this area; the air wavered and blurred so much, it was hard to focus her eyes.

And yet she could hear…

Another engine.

Her brain pulled the picture together just in time. The same process that made old men's faces from gnarled trees, animals from clouds, showed her the shape of the distortion and let her see what was invisible a moment before.

A car with a masked man inside, swerving towards them.

The Ghost.

She hit the brakes an instant before the Ghost sideswiped them, hard. Shiara screamed as Maisie's windshield exploded, throwing glass in their faces. Cassica swerved, eyes squeezed shut, and she felt Maisie's wheels lose traction on her right side. Then they were tipping, and even as Cassica fought with the wheel a pit opened in her stomach and she knew she'd lost control.

Maisie slid sideways down the slope, wheels spinning uselessly, seeking a grip. Shiara scrambled at the dash, as if there was some adjustment she could make that would stop their progress towards the chasm at the bottom. Cassica pulled the handbrake – stop the wheels, give them a chance to get some bite – but Maisie kept slipping.

Ahead and downslope was a knob of rock, knuckled and smooth; they'd pass behind it if they continued in their current direction. Cassica's foot hovered over the accelerator. Shiara was making incoherant noises of fear, but Cassica shut her out. She was waiting with keen patience for the moment when her instinct would tell her to go. When it did, she popped the handbrake and pressed gently on the accelerator, resisting the urge to floor it.

Maisie's wheels spun, half gripped, pushed against the ground, slipped, caught again and shoved. She surged forward, changing the angle of the slide so they were heading towards the knob of rock instead of past it. Shiara cringed away and covered herself as it loomed in Maisie's side windows. They hit it with an impact that threw them against their harnesses, jerked them like dolls.

Cassica raised her head. Shiara peeped out from between her arms. They'd stopped.

Shiara breathed out a long and elaborate curse that would have had them banned from the airwaves if anyone had been there to record it.

"Maisie alright?" Cassica asked.

Shiara looked out through her window. "Reckon so," she said, with a tone of faint surprise.

"Course she is," said Cassica. "You built her."

Then she slipped Maisie into gear and drove away.

27

The way back up the slope was slow, and Maisie slipped alarmingly and often, but with steady determination they crawled over the lip of the great crystalline scar in the earth and back on to level ground.

"How are we still alive?" Shiara asked in disbelief.

"Boondock girls," said Cassica. "We're like roaches. Can't get rid of us."

She put her foot down, and Maisie responded, none the worse for wear after her crash. Cassica exchanged a glance with Shiara; it was all she needed to show her approval of Shiara's engineering job. Shiara grinned back at her.

"You reckon they think they got us?" Shiara asked.

"Reckon so," said Cassica. "And no television feed to tell 'em different."

"So let's get out of here," said Shiara. "Stick close to the chasm where there ain't no guns, we can—"

"Uh-uh. With the Ghost still running about? It's open ground past the battlefield: you think we'll see him coming next time?"

"So what are we gonna do?"

"He thinks we're gone. We got the advantage now," said Cassica. Her gaze hardened. "We're gonna take him out."

She saw the hesitation on Shiara's face. "This ain't like before, Cassica," she said. "Ain't like when I brained that freak that was tryin' to kill you, or when you did that Howler. That was self-defence."

"*This* is self-defence," said Cassica. "We don't deal with him now, he's gonna keep after us till we're dead."

Shiara was unconvinced. She was thinking of Linty Maxxon, Cassica could tell. But sometimes she needed Cassica to make the hard choices so she didn't have to; sometimes Shiara needed that push. In days gone by, Cassica would have done it anyway, with or without Shiara's okay. But she needed her on board with this now. If they were in this together, they made their choices together, and took responsibility together.

"This ain't no movie," Cassica said, more gently. "In real life, you give the bad guys a second chance, they're gonna kill you. That ain't doing the right thing, it's being stupid. He's a professional killer. It's him or us."

"You're right," Shiara said at last.

"We doin' this, then?"

Shiara nodded, more firmly. "Do it."

Cassica pressed on the turbos, pushing them to reckless speeds. The Ghost probably had the same idea as Shiara: he'd travel along the narrow alley of safer ground between the scar and the junk graveyard, where there were no mechs to shoot at him. After that, he'd have a short, straight run to the edge of the battlefield.

But if he thought Cassica and Shiara were dead, there was no reason to rush and risk a crash. They'd lost time on him, but the turbos would eat that up. And Cassica was determined to catch him.

"Turbos," Shiara reminded her, watching the temperature.

"Few seconds more."

Shiara gave her those seconds, then said, "Kill 'em."

It didn't seem nearly enough. Cassica clicked her tongue in annoyance, but she did what she was told.

The scar was pinching closed to their right. Cassica listened to the gunfire and spotted explosions up ahead. There they'd find the Ghost.

"Least he's sucking up their ammo for us," Shiara said with cautious optimism.

Cassica laughed. She was beginning to feel invincible. The shock of the crash had jolted something loose inside her, detaching her from care. She'd scraped by death so many times this past month that its threat seemed hollow now.

They were going to win. She believed that now. It couldn't be otherwise. It was fated.

They peeled away from the scar and headed back into the battlefield, past the scattered remnants of the mechanical dead. Immediately they began to draw fire, but it wasn't as intense as before; Shiara's hope hadn't been misplaced.

Cassica threaded her way through projectiles and obstacles, leaving explosions in her wake. It seemed as if nothing could touch her. She felt at one with Maisie, the two of them in perfect sync. It was like a ride on a ghost train she'd taken once at a travelling carnival, like they were on rails that would take them through the terror, and all the noise and fury was just the bluster of harmless things. Metal soldiers from the distant past reached out, wheeled monsters stirred and groaned, old barrels coughed their deadly payloads; but she was in the zone, and nothing could touch her.

It was Shiara that spotted the Ghost. She sprang forward in her seat and pointed. Cassica saw a grey movement through the dust. His car was blank and smooth without its camouflage engaged. The Ghost could only enter stealth mode for a few minutes at a time – it took too much power to use for long periods – and it was probably of limited use against the mechs' targeting systems anyway.

"You're mine," she muttered, and gave chase.

The Ghost had his hands full keeping himself

alive. With the bulk of the artillery focused on him, he didn't see Cassica darting through the wrecks behind him, closing the gap steadily.

"Use the bumper," said Shiara. "Anythin' else, you'll hurt Maisie worse than him."

"Just gonna give him a little love tap," said Cassica. She glanced at the temperature gauge for the turbos.

"You're good," said Shiara. "Do it."

They surged forward, roaring up behind the Ghost. At the last moment he heard them over the explosions, tried to swerve away; but Cassica had counted on that, and had guessed which way he'd go.

Maisie clipped his fender, jolting them hard in their seats. The Ghost's back end skidded out, and his momentum took care of the rest. The car tipped on to its side and ploughed several dozen metres through the dirt before crashing into the flank of an armoured transport.

Cassica got control of Maisie again, riding out the impact, and sped past as a half-dozen mechs aimed their cannons at the Ghost's now-stationary car. There was a shriek of weaponry and a blast of flame.

"Guess he's a real ghost now," Cassica said. Shiara gave her a look but said nothing.

They swerved round the blasted husk of a tank with many turrets, and Cassica's heart jumped as she came face to towering face with a Titan, the most colossal of the ancient war mechs: an armoured monster, vast and insectile. It was slumped and part-buried, but as she drove into view, one huge mechanical eye fixed on her, glowing green in its depths.

She was made small by its regard; her sense of invulnerability wavered. She quailed under the gaze of a half-dead god from the old times.

Then she was past it, and beyond there was only the empty plain, the scorched expanse of the Blight Lands stretching out under an envenomed sky.

"We made it?" Shiara asked, as they raced away from the battlefield and the Titan that lay at its edge.

"We made it," Cassica said. "But so did she."

In the cracked pane of her rear-view mirror, Lady Scorpion slid into view.

Her car was a dirty black. Mounted on the roof was her stinger, a cannon holding a metal spear that carried a thousand volts. Cassica saw again the moment from last year's Widowmaker, Chabley Pott in the Devil's Basin, Lady Scorpion nailing him. Saw again the charred bodies inside the flaming wreck.

They said it took an hour for the stinger to recharge after she used it. If she missed, you had the chance to get away. It was just that she never missed.

Cassica reached for the turbos. Shiara stopped her. She gestured at the plain ahead of them. "Where we gonna go?"

Lady Scorpion's car swelled in their mirrors. She

wasn't using her turbos. She didn't need to: her car was already far faster. Like Shiara said, there was no escape here. It would all come down to one shot.

"What's the range on her stinger?"

"Twenty metres," Shiara replied. She'd twisted in her seat and was looking behind.

"Count it."

"She's at seventy metres," said Shiara. "Roughly."

Cassica looked in her mirror. Behind the Lady, the battlefield of junked warriors was diminishing behind them, the fallen Titan like a mountain in the foreground.

It was still watching them with that enormous green eye. It had moved its head, dragging its beetle-like bulk through the dirt to keep them in sight. From its heat-scarred carapace, a conical device that resembled an elongated satellite dish had emerged, and was turning towards them.

"Sixty."

She narrowed her eyes. What *was* that? Some kind of weapon?

"Fifty. Get ready to dodge."

Wait for the moment. Dodge the stinger. Had that been what Chabley Pott thought, just before he died? Nobody dodged the Stinger. But everybody tried.

"Forty." Shiara was getting increasingly frantic. "Oh, hell, I might have been wrong about the range. I think she's gonna fire!"

Cassica ignored her.

"Thirty! Start dodgin'!"

But it was the Titan Cassica was watching, not Lady Scorpion. The device on its back was tracking them now. She fancied, with the strange delirium of the Blight Lands, that she could see it calculating trajectories and plotting angles.

"Maybe you *can't* dodge the stinger," said Cassica.

"So what are we gonna do, if we ain't gonna dodge?"

"We're gonna outrun her."

"I just told you, we can't outrun her here!" Shiara shrieked. "Twenty-five!"

"You don't need to be the fastest," said Cassica. "You just gotta be the last one in the race."

A bolt of green energy spat silently from the device on the Titan's back, aimed at them. The Titan's last, defiant stab at the intruders that had disturbed its rest. The bolt arced through the sky, a second sun, rising into the air and then falling down towards them, growing in intensity and size as it came. Shiara saw it, and her pupils shrank.

"If I dodge, she'll dodge," said Cassica.

"Twenty," Shiara whispered.

The stinger rotated atop the Lady's car, aiming for their fuel tank. Cassica could see her through the windshield now, a dark shape in the shadows of the car. The green sun above them grew brighter, but she didn't see it. She was focused entirely on the kill.

Yet still she didn't fire. Her target couldn't escape, and wasn't even attempting to dodge. She moved in closer, to be sure of her shot.

"Fifteen."

And now the brightness in the sky was impossible to ignore, a light that flared so fiercely it was blinding. Lady Scorpion looked up, and in that moment when she was distracted, Cassica hit the turbos.

Maisie roared forward. Lady Scorpion screamed, not knowing why, knowing only that she'd been beaten somehow. The bolt fell upon her like a meteor, dissolving Lady Scorpion, her car and a good chunk of the ground beneath her into a sparkling quantum froth.

Cassica let off the turbos, and watched in her rear-view mirror as the cloud of glimmering motes drifted into the sky, winking out of existence one by one. Then she turned her gaze forward, and put her foot down.

28

With the graveyard behind them, they began to believe they'd faced the worst the Blight Lands had to offer. The next few hours were easy riding over flat hardpan, between long mesas of tawny rock that divided the emptiness. The mood in the car lightened. Even the oppressive sun didn't seem so dreadful any more.

They talked of Coppermouth as they drove, of the hazy days of childhood: camp-outs and cookouts, wild escapades when all had seemed bright and new. They remembered friends and enemies, people they'd fought with, loved or mocked. Home seemed so far away now, and those they'd left behind had been diminished by distance. Old grudges became petty, great triumphs made small by what they'd achieved by leaving. Still they spoke fondly of their shared history.

They talked of batty Miss Elly; Jann, who could

roll cigarettes one-handed and always knew what to say to make you feel good; Ab and Chell, who'd been a couple for ever but who'd cheated on each other with everyone in town; Boba, who'd looked after his three sisters single-handed after the dust lung got his folks, but who was always ready for a punch-up; Kinty, who hung out when she felt like it but spent most of her time with her dogs.

"It ain't never gonna be the same, you know," said Shiara. "Win or lose, them times are past. We always gonna be the girls who left."

Cassica didn't say anything to that. She didn't want to think about the future. Just to win would be enough. Just to throw it in the faces of the people who'd sold them out. Fame, fortune, Olympus: once they'd been things she'd dearly wished for, but she understood them better now. In the end, all she wanted was to be the best.

No, she corrected herself silently, and glanced at her friend in the passenger seat. All she wanted was to be on the best *team*.

"Hoy! Signal's comin' back!" exclaimed Shiara. She leaned close to the screen, trying to make out shapes in the static. "Must be we're gettin' close to the edge of the Blight Lands!"

She unfolded a map and held it open against the gritty wind blowing through the smashed windshield. "Let's see ... sun's over there ... that mountain must be there ... mesa to the north. . ." She stabbed a finger at the map. "Bear left a little. We ain't far." Possibilities sparkled in her eyes. "We're gonna make it!"

"Reckon we might," said Cassica, with less enthusiasm. After what they'd just been through, making it wasn't enough. The question was, were they in the lead? There was no telling how long they'd been out here. Time was elastic in the Blight Lands, and Maisie didn't have the speed of her rivals. Even their ridiculously audacious shortcut may not have been enough.

"Turn up the sound," she told Shiara. "I wanna hear."

Phantom voices came through the crackling. She couldn't make out the words, but she could tell they were excited. She kept her attention on the plain before her. Now wasn't the time to hit a pothole and break an axle.

Shortly afterwards, she spotted three black specks in the sky, rising above a mesa that loomed before them and blocked out the horizon. They grew as they approached.

"Hovercams," said Shiara, who had the better eyesight. "Looks like we're back on the grid."

"Let 'em watch," said Cassica.

"I wish I could be there when Harlan sees us up on that screen. Or Hasp, or Cleff, or any of that whole corrupt bunch of weasels. Love to see their faces."

As they neared the mesa, the wavy commentators

on the screen found their voices, fading in and out of the static buzz. "... *incredible scenes as ... finish line ... assica Hayle and Shia ... yren Bane and Draden Taxt!*"

Cassica looked over at the screen. "What'd he say about Kyren?"

Shiara shushed her. The commentators' voices stabilized as they kept talking.

"*You know, I think we all thought Bane and Taxt had this whole thing sewn up! And no one, I mean* no one, *thought we'd see our plucky boondock girls again. But now it seems we're in for the closest finish in years! Let me repeat for anyone who's just tuned in: Hayle and DuCal have come out of the Blight Lands in one piece and ahead of the pack! But Kyren Bane is coming down off the mountain and into the final sprint even as we speak! This could go to the wire! Don't you dare change channel!*"

"Where is he?" Cassica cried, looking about. She felt something sinking inside her. There was no sign of Kyren anywhere.

Then they rounded the mesa, and they saw.

The finish line was closer than they'd imagined, a mere few miles away; it had been obscured by the mesa till now. Enormous stands rose from the dead earth, packed with cheering spectators watching huge screens. Beneath a pile of scaffold and lights, a makeshift town waited to celebrate the end of the year's greatest sporting spectacle.

To their left, the crescent-shaped row of mountains which the other racers had been following petered out. There, where the mountain trail met the plain, a rising cloud of dust could be seen, and at its head was a black-and-red car.

Kyren Bane.

She hit her turbos. So did he.

The ground blurred beneath Maisie as she tore towards the finish line. Kyren was some distance behind them, but it wasn't enough distance for Cassica's liking. All they had left was a straight sprint, car versus car, his path converging with theirs. A home-made racer built with spit and ingenuity, against a vehicle built of the best components money could buy.

But she wouldn't be beaten. Not by him, and not by those who backed him.

Shiara turned the volume off to silence the commentators. "Here's how it's gonna go," she said, over the noise of the wind blasting around them. "No way we can turbo all the way to the end. We don't got the fuel, even if we didn't explode first. So you cut them when I say and *exactly* when I say, and we'll let 'em cool a little, and then we ought to have enough for another burn before the finish. It'll work out better than just one big burn. You get me?"

Cassica nodded, her jaw tight.

"You trust me?" Shiara prompted her.

"Always did," said Cassica. Even when she didn't understand the calculations, the tactics, the things her friend did to help them win.

"Good. Cut 'em!"

It took her by surprise. So soon? But she could hardly refuse now. She let them go.

"You better know what you're doing," she said. Kyren was still burning turbos behind them, eating up the distance.

"I know the specs on his car," she said. "Unless he manages it right, he'll overheat. The safety limiter gonna kill his turbos before he can overtake us. But we'll get *two* burns. It'll be close, but we can beat him."

"What if he *does* manage it right?"

"Kyren don't strike me as the sort that listens to his tech when he's got the finish line in his sights," Shiara said pointedly, giving her a hard look.

"I said I trusted you, didn't I?" said Cassica. "I'll be good." But damn, was it difficult to put her faith in patience and mathematics right now, when all she wanted to do was go, go, go!

They sped over the cracked earth, raising dust behind them, the thunder of Maisie's engine in their ears. Cassica's foot was pressed to the floor. She leaned forward, fierce with determination. Shiara worked at the dash, making minute adjustments, optimizing Maisie for the sprint. The tiniest advantage could make the difference.

Kyren came closer and closer. And then:

"His turbos have cut!" Cassica cried.

"Told you. Automatic safety. He's overhot."

Cassica watched him nervously in her mirrors.

Overhot or not, he was still gaining. And the finish line wasn't approaching fast enough.

"We've got one more burn. He hasn't," Shiara reassured her. She eyed the temperature gauge. "His turbos won't cool in time."

"Will *ours?*" Cassica was ready to scream with the pressure. He was too close, he was going to overtake, he was going to win!

"Thirty seconds or so," Shiara said.

Then Kyren fired his turbos again. Cassica's eyes narrowed in anger.

"I thought you said—"

"I know! He's taken the safety off! He's—"

But she didn't hear the rest, because she'd pressed the turbos herself.

One last burn. One last surge to the finish. *Come on, Maisie! You can do it!*

The wind roared around her, and Maisie roared with it. Still she imagined she could hear the cheers from the stands. They were near enough now to pick out individual people in the mass.

A scaffold arch, hung with adverts, straddled the finish line. MaxCo, TessaCorp, Foo and Blick's, Chomson's Chews and more: the keepers of the gate, beyond which lay a life of unimaginable fame, for whoever got there first.

"We're too hot!" Shiara said.

"He's still burning his turbos!" Cassica cried. "So we are too!"

She glanced in her mirrors. They were close enough to see his face now. His beautiful face, stern and flawless like a statue of a gladiator from ancient days. She'd fallen for those looks once. But now she saw him for something else: an opponent, an enemy, inhuman. He existed only to steal the victory that should be hers, the victory she'd earned through blood and sacrifice.

"You only got a few seconds' more burn," Shiara told her.

"That ain't enough!"

"It's enough if you don't wanna blow us both to hell!"

"Damn it, you know they set these gauges too high to be extra safe! We got more time!"

How could he still be turboing, still eating up the distance between them? It seemed impossible that his car could sustain it.

"I built this car!" Shiara yelled. "She ain't gonna take it!"

"She'll take it," Cassica replied. The finish line wasn't far now, the end was upon them, and it was too cruel to have it snatched away like this, too unbearably cruel. Shiara was always too sensible, too unadventurous; it was Cassica's job to push her where she didn't dare to go.

"You're gonna kill us!" Shiara screamed over the howl of the wind, her white hair flapping where it had escaped her helmet. The temperature gauge was into the red and climbing.

"We ain't giving up now!" Cassica shouted into the maelstrom. Because she couldn't give up, because she *needed* to win, because she couldn't let Kyren beat her, and Harlan and Hasp and all the rest.

"It's not worth it!" Shiara shrieked. "It don't *matter* if we win! It just don't *matter* enough!"

"The hell do you mean, it's not worth it?" Cassica cried, because that was just about the most insane thing she'd ever heard right then. "It's *everything*!"

Shiara reached over and grabbed her by the front of her racing leathers, forcing Cassica to look away from the finish line and into her eyes. There were tears running down her face, tears of fright and desperation, and in her eyes was an animal fear like Cassica had never seen before. The look of someone falling from a tall building, plunging to their death.

"Not to me," she said. "It ain't everything to me."

And there was something in those words, in her expression, that frightened Cassica, quenched the madness inside her. She saw then the risk she was taking, not just her life but Shiara's, a risk she didn't have a right to take.

And for what? What happened if she won?

She didn't really know.

So she took her thumb from the turbo button.

Maisie began to slow immediately, pushed back by wind resistance. Shiara hit a switch to activate emergency cooling, drawing more power from the engines, slowing them further. The needle on the temperature gauge hovered where it was, almost at the top of the meter . . . and then slowly it began to swing back towards blue, and safety.

"Thank you," Shiara whispered.

Kyren shot past them on their left. Cassica heard his whoop of celebration as he overtook them, turbos blazing. She saw the savage joy of victory, the righteous gleam of the entitled in his eye. He was someone who always expected to win, who believed he deserved to, because no one in his life had ever shown him otherwise. And now, neither would she.

The crowd went crazy as he raced away ahead of them. Cassica fell back into her seat, smothered by a numbing sense of resignation as Maisie dropped back to cruising speed and the needle on the temperature gauge crept out of the danger zone.

There was nothing she could do, no way to claw back the lead. They'd fallen at the final hurdle. They'd lost. The game had gone to the men who rigged it, the men who prized money over fair competition, appearances over talent, sponsors over souls. Perhaps, against such relentless disregard for decency, they'd never had a chance at all.

But they'd tried. And they came damn close.

She watched the black-and-red car tearing towards the finishing line, carrying victory away with it. In her mind, she heard Kyren's whoop of triumph again as he took first place, a position apparently assigned to him by destiny.

Kyren Bane and Draden Taxt were a hundred metres from the finish line when their car exploded.

The crowd were shocked into silence. Cassica and Shiara stared, breath stilled in their lungs. The car flipped and spun, a blackened metal chassis trailing flame and smoke, bouncing heavily over the hardpan. One instant it had been a machine of precision engineering and elegance, and the boys inside had lived and thought and fought. Then, in a heartbeat, they were gone.

The blazing chassis crashed to a halt just short of the finish. A flaming wheel rolled away. Cassica drove past the wreck in a daze of horror.

He'd taken off the safety, pushed the turbos too hard. That could have been Maisie. It could have been them.

When they crossed the finish line, she was barely aware of it. She slowed and stopped without thought, body operated by her subconscious.

"Hoy!" She felt Shiara pushing her on the shoulder. Her friend's face was lit with excitement. "Hoy! We made it! We won! You hear me? We frickin' *won*!"

Cassica didn't feel present. It was as if she'd been disconnected from her own body, like she was watching herself on television. She popped her harness, pushed open the door and got out.

The barrage of noise came to her gradually, as if someone were steadily turning up the volume in her ears. She stood by the side of her racer with the hot sun warming her dirt-caked cheeks and looked about with an expression of vague confusion.

The stands were going wild. People cheered and yelled and punched the air. It didn't quite connect. What did it all have to do with her?

Emergency vehicles sped past, heading for the wreck of Kyren's car, sirens wailing. On one of the enormous screens, she saw a face that she recognized. Harlan, the man who'd been their manager once, standing in a VIP box. He was slack-jawed with horror, skin shining with sweat, staring into space. With him were Dunbery Hasp and Anderos Cleff; they'd all been watching the event together. All on the same side, since Harlan sold his racers out.

But now Hasp and Cleff gave Harlan a look of anger and disgust. They were cheated of their winner, and their money and their arrangements and all they'd put in place had come crashing down around them. They walked away, out of the frame, leaving Harlan abandoned.

Their departure revealed another man, standing in the background, picking his nails with the point of a knife. His eyes were on Harlan, now unprotected.

Scadler grinned his horse grin.

"Cassica!" It was Shiara again, now at her side. Through the cloud of shock she focused on her friend, and it brought her back a little. "You there? Can't you hear 'em?" She gestured to the crowd.

They shouted their approval. She raised her fist, and they roared again.

"Take a turn, why don'tcha?" Shiara said. She took Cassica's arm and raised it high, and the cheers became ecstatic.

"Put your hands together for this year's champions!" the tannoy urged the spectators. *"Widowmaker winners, instant legends and soon to be Celestials! Those brave girls from the backcountry! Cassica Hayle and Shiara DuCal!"*

And slowly, as she stood there with Shiara holding her arm up, it began to sink in.

"Did we do it?" she asked, tears pricking at her eyes.

"We did it," said Shiara. "Both of us."

And the cheers went on and on and on, until Cassica's heart seemed ready to burst.

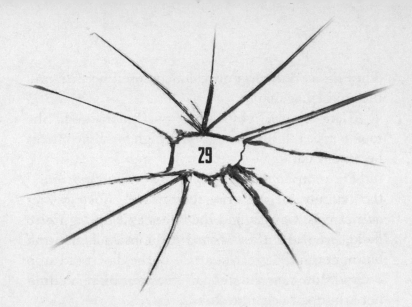

29

"Cassica Hayle, Shiara DuCal ... your chariot approaches!"

They stood side by side on a stage, their heads tipped back to the sky. Behind them, penned behind fences, a sea of hushed faces filled the boulevard. A red-carpet walkway cut through the centre of the crowd. They'd passed along that way, through the cheering throng. They'd accepted congratulations and given their thanks. But here was the moment the crowd had been waiting for.

The space elevator was descending. A ring of light could be seen against the red dusk, slipping down the cable from the unimaginable heights of space, coming to lift them up to a life among the stars.

Anchor City seemed to hold its breath. Neon advertisements glowed acid colours against the dusk. People had gathered on the rooftops of nearby buildings. The streets were choked for several blocks in all directions.

Shiara felt the eyes of the world upon them. She saw them on the enormous screens that showed them to the crowd. They'd been styled and dressed by the most famous designers in the world, who'd paid handsomely for the privilege of hiring their bodies as a canvas. Cassica had the bones and the figure to make even the most absurd fashions look natural, but not even the greatest artists of the day could stop Shiara feeling ridiculous. She squirmed and sweated under the hot lights, and wished it was over.

Did Cassica feel what she felt? The crawling terror in the pit of her stomach? Was she having second thoughts, as Shiara was? She wanted her friend to turn to her then, to tell her they didn't have to go through with it. But it seemed like it had all gone too far to turn back now.

"Cassica," said the interviewer, Jenty Gane, a television presenter all hair and teeth whom Shiara had never heard of till today. "Can you tell us a little bit about what you're feeling right now?"

"Well, Jenty, I guess first and foremost I'm really just excited to be here," Cassica began, in that voice she used for interviews, the one that sounded like she was an overenthusiastic teacher trying to gee up a room of bored children. She said some inoffensive and meaningless things, exactly what the crowd expected to hear. They cheered at pretty much everything. Shiara tuned her out and let her get on with it.

Some of the screens, mounted on scaffold frames around the boulevard, were showing the best parts from their races. Their encounter with the mutant beasts in Crookback Bayou. The Howler attack in Lost Angeles. Taking out Slick with the magnet trap on the Anchor City qualifier. Driving over a rock bridge with singstones falling all around them in Ragrattle Caves.

The Linty Maxxon crash. That one still made her stomach knot. Linty was alive, but minor brain damage meant she'd have to relearn certain motor skills. She'd never drive again, and one side of her face would always droop.

Notable by their absence were the parts where Cassica rescued Shiara from the Howler lair, and the whole final day in the Blight Lands. There had been no cameras on them then, during their most desperate moments, when four Wreckers had met their end. Dunbery Hasp was seething about that. It was the worst crime in broadcasting to miss the best bits.

But those parts nobody saw were more vivid than the others, more real to Shiara. Only she and Cassica had experienced those times; they hadn't been shared with anyone else. A bond of memories, unrecorded except in their minds. That was more special to her than a thousand replays.

Other screens showed the crowd, faces turned upwards in adoration. Faces she didn't know. Cassica basked in the love of strangers, but it meant nothing to Shiara. They were in love with an idea, a story told to them through their zines and televisions: a simple tale of rags to riches, two poor girls from the Pacifica badlands who overcame great odds to win fame and fortune, a place in the heavens and a place in their hearts. It made them happy; it made them believe that life was safe and understandable and controllable. It made them believe that they could do it too.

The truth, as ever, was murkier. People had got hurt on their way to the top. People had died. The game was fixed so businessmen could make money. The powers that be, who were praising and congratulating them now, had cheated and plotted against them.

But the crowd didn't want the truth. They wanted the story.

Up there on the stage, in the company of millions, Shiara had never felt so alone.

She'd had one brief video-link conversation with her family since they won the Widowmaker, and that, as ever, was broadcast to the world. Mom cried; stout Daddy held it together. Everyone back home was so proud of her. They all wanted to see her again, but they knew they probably wouldn't be able to, except on *Celestial Hour*. They couldn't leave the auto shop to come see her; it'd likely be robbed and ruined by the time they returned. Shiara promised she'd visit them soon, but she could tell they didn't believe her. Once you were on Olympus, people seldom came back down. There wasn't much call to visit Earth when you were living a life of pampered luxury in space.

Talk had turned to news of home. There were rumours of a harsh winter with high winds blowing off the Rust Bowl. It'd be a bad time for dust lung. A ship had beached in the harbour a few days back; it was silted up so high that even light fishing vessels were having a hard time getting through. They might have to close the docks entirely. Meanwhile, the town council were trying to get a Justice appointed to deal with all the dangerous scavs that came south with the bad weather, like they did every year. They all knew what the chances were of *that* happening.

Grim news, but grim news didn't faze the folks of Coppermouth. Melly, who'd apparently forgotten they were being broadcast to the world, launched into an anecdote about a plague of cats that was driving Mrs Jebbit spare. Then she told Shiara about Mimzy Muckle's wedding, which the whole town turned out for, and how her brothers had too much moonshine and got into a fight with the groom, and how by the morning it was all forgotten.

Shiara smiled through the tears in her eyes. That was home. She missed it badly.

The bright ring slid down the cable of the space elevator. Now they could see there were long rows of lights running the length of the cable, lighting in sequence to mark the elevator's location. The crowd hushed as the lights reached the base of the enormous cable, and the elevator settled to Earth without a sound.

A warm breeze blew through the darkening city streets, brushing past them. Shiara reached out and took Cassica's hand. She was frightened. Cassica gripped her fingers, and she knew Cassica was too. That thought reassured her.

"Cassica and Shiara," Jenty Gane stage-whispered into his mic. "Olympus awaits!"

The doors of the elevator slid slowly open. They watched in awe as the gate to a new world opened before them. Within, a cavern of lights, empty but for one thing: a small black oblong about four feet high, standing on its end just inside the doors. It was tiny in comparison to the gateway, but it seemed so solid, so *present*, that it loomed larger than its size.

Shiara stared at it. Her mouth was dry.

"And now," Jenty cried, "to present our winners with their tickets to Olympus: the father of Maximum Racing, Dunbery Hasp!"

A cheer went up as Hasp emerged from backstage and approached them. He was wearing a uniform not unlike an old-time bellboy, his trademark glasses dwarfing his ancient face. He raised his hand in acknowledgement of the crowd, then turned to Cassica and Shiara. Jenty Gane stepped back respectfully.

Shiara had never been this close to the man who owned Maximum Racing before. He smelt sour and dry, with a hint of something antiseptic. He held in his thin veined hands two gold oblongs the size of playing cards, inscribed with strange patterns that looked almost mystical. The language of the days before the Omniwar.

She steeled herself to meet his gaze. By winning, by beating Kyren Bane to Olympus, they'd cost him untold amounts of money in broken contracts and failed deals. All the plans he'd put in place to fashion a new Celestial for the people had fallen apart. She expected anger, resentment, the promise of revenge. And the wrath of Dunbery Hasp wasn't to be taken lightly.

Instead, as he handed her the ticket, she saw nothing. He didn't care. Even the millions he'd lost had hardly scratched the surface of his fortune. Kyren's death was a minor inconvenience for his underlings to deal with. There'd be another year, another race. The machine rumbled on, too huge to be stopped, and their triumph was insignificant in the big scheme of things.

Shiara felt herself flush. She wanted to hit him, this man who'd tried to have them killed. She wanted to hit him so he'd feel something.

But he was just an old man.

"Many congratulations," he said to them. The ticket was cool and weighty in her palm. "You're both worthy winners." Then he stepped back from them and swept an arm towards the elevator. "Olympus awaits!"

Jenty Gane took up his mic. "All that's left is for our champions to enter the elevator, insert their tickets in the special slots to either side of the obelisk, and they will be on their way to Olympus. Cassica, Shiara ... are you ready?"

The cheer from the crowd was so loud it was like a push in the back, urging them onwards to their destiny. They exchanged a glance. They stood there on the threshold of a life of indulgence and ease up above the atmosphere. *Are we really gonna do this?*

She saw determination in Cassica's eyes, and took it for her own. She nodded, and it was decided.

Cassica reached out and snatched the microphone from the surprised Jenty. "Hoy! Dridley! Prua! Get out here!"

The crowd muttered in surprise as a middle-aged man and woman came out from backstage, one almost skipping with delight, the other sheepish and nervous. He was round and jolly, she angular and thin. They were dressed as if for an expensive dinner.

Jenty looked lost. A frown of anger drew a line between Dunbery Hasp's eyes. This wasn't how the ascension was supposed to go.

"Ladies and gentlemen, meet the Cussens!" said Cassica to the crowd. A ripple of uncertain applause passed down the boulevard. Dridley bowed theatrically. His bald pate was shining with sweat and he couldn't stop grinning.

Cassica took Shiara's ticket from her and held them both up. "Mr Hasp," she said into the mic, for all to hear. "We'd like to thank you for this amazing opportunity to go to Olympus. But we've had a talk, Shiara and I, and we just don't think it's for us. So we figured we'd give it to someone who really wants it." She turned to the crowd. "Everyone, meet your two newest Celestials: Dridley and Prua Cussens!"

The crowd was silent. Only a few lonely whoops rang out, dying quickly. Dridley's face fell a little, and Prua looked pained. They glanced nervously at Dunbery Hasp, whose face had darkened with rage. He was being humiliated in front of the world, his most extravagant gift given away like a carnival ticket.

Yeah, now you care, thought Shiara with bitter satisfaction.

Cassica tossed the mic to the floor with an amplified thump and a squeal of feedback. She handed the tickets to the Cussens. Dridley clutched her hands gratefully in his.

"I can't tell you how much this means to us," he breathed. "The money's in an account for you, every cent of it. One billion dollars, like we agreed. Thank you! Thank you both!"

"Get going, before they work out how to stop you," Cassica said. "Go on."

He glanced again at Hasp, worry crossing his face, then took his wife's hand and made for the elevator. In the covered wings of the stage, Cassica could see executives gabbling into walkie-talkies. Was this legal? Was there anything in the rules against it? How could they stop this happening? Nobody had ever done it before. Nobody had given their tickets to someone else. Nobody *ever* said no to Olympus!

"Do something!" Hasp spluttered at them, pointing a withered hand towards the elevator. But there was nothing they could do; not with the eyes of the world upon them. Cheating behind the scenes was one thing, but if their viewers ever suspected the game wasn't fair, it was all over. And there was nothing that said Cassica and Shiara couldn't do whatever they wanted with their tickets.

Security guards waited helplessly for the order to storm the stage. But Hasp's men dithered too long. The Cussens slid the tickets into the slots on the black obelisk, and the doors to the space elevator began to rumble shut. After that, nobody dared cross the threshold. Dridley Cussens gave a cheery wave to the crowd, then he seized his wife and kissed her. The gates boomed shut, and the ring of lights began to ascend, carrying them up into the dark.

"They ain't gonna last a year up there before they

get voted out," said Shiara.

"Not our problem," said Cassica.

The crowd were stunned, unsure of what they'd seen. Was the elevator really leaving? Was it all a trick? Where was their celebration? They wanted to see their heroes ascend into legend, not these nobodies who they'd never heard of. They'd been cheated of their triumph.

Shiara began to feel uncomfortable. The security guards were watching them in angry confusion. Hasp had stormed offstage. Jenty Gane, awkward now that things had gone off-script, picked up the mic and attempted to get things back on track.

"Well ... er ... how about that, folks?" he said, his voice echoing in the silence. "We certainly haven't seen *that* before. One thing's for sure, this Widowmaker is just full of surprises!"

Nobody responded.

Cassica motioned to Shiara. They couldn't stay on the stage any longer. They didn't dare go backstage – they'd just made a lot of enemies there – so they walked down the steps at the front of the stage, and along the red carpet that ran down a fenced-off aisle which divided the crowd.

Shiara felt her throat becoming tight with nerves as they walked. She felt vulnerable in her stupid designer dress. The people to either side stared at them, not knowing what to make of them now. They hadn't acted the way they were supposed to.

They hadn't followed the story. What were their fans supposed to think? Some looked bewildered, some hurt and betrayed. Shiara began to wonder if they'd made a terrible mistake. She hadn't wanted to be famous, but she hadn't wanted to be hated either.

Then, to her surprise, she saw a face she knew. A weathered, seamed old face, but one that still held a shadow of the handsome man he'd been. A man who'd loomed large over her childhood in Coppermouth. A man who drank fazz.

She halted. Rutterby LaKeyne, the fallen Celestial she'd once bought a coffee in a cheap diner. He was here, standing up against the metal barriers that fenced off the red carpet, dressed in a shabby old suit and gazing at her with the confident steady stare of a man who'd once known what it was like to be treated as a god.

For a long moment, they just looked at each other. Then he began to clap his hands. Slowly at first, a heavy slap of his palms, ringing out into the silence. Then faster, louder, putting his arms into it. The people around him were uncertain at first, but his clapping was relentless and it infected them, and one by one they started clapping too. Out into the crowd it spread, a rising wave of sound; and when the others saw what was happening on their screens, they joined in as well. As the clapping got louder, cheers broke out.

Jenty Gane caught the mood, and seized the

advantage. "Viewers, friends and guests, I give you the girls who looked up to Olympus and said 'No!' Cassica Hayle and Shiara DuCal!"

The crowd went crazy. Shiara and Cassica were pummelled with the sound of their joy. It was overwhelming, incredible, fantastic. The adoration of millions, won on their own terms. Won for being themselves, not what they were expected to be.

Spontaneously, Shiara hugged her friend, who'd given up her dreams of Olympus for Shiara's sake. Because they wanted to stay together; because they were a team. She'd never felt so lucky or so happy. The crowd roared its approval as they watched them embrace on their screens.

"You wanna get out of here?" Cassica said.

"Sure," said Shiara. She cast a grateful smile over Cassica's shoulder at Rutterby LaKeyne, who acknowledged it with a nod. "Let's go home."

30

Music pulsed and meat sizzled on the grill: haunch of goat, snake fillet, chicken wings searing to the breakbeat in the warm evening. Wielding the tongs was Blane, belly pressing against his T-shirt and flames reflected in his shades, the grinning master of the barbecue.

The party had been going on since morning up on the Point. It was Pacifica Day, the day of their nation's founding, and the folks of Coppermouth knew how to cut loose when they got the chance. Overstimulated children, made hyperactive by sugar and fazz, screamed and chased each other round the tables. Grannies cackled drunkenly together in plastic chairs. The older kids flirted as best they could while their parents cracked each other up with out-of-date jokes and got up unsteadily to dance whenever a song they knew came on the radio.

This Pacifica Day, there were newcomers to the party. Men and women whom the people of Coppermouth made a fuss of. They were never without a plate of food, a glass of fazz or something stronger; but they were careful not to overindulge. They had a job to do, after all, and they were still in uniform. As Coppermouth's first official Justices for thirty years or more, they were as keen to make a good impression as the townsfolk were.

There was new bunting strung between the poles, and coloured lights which were turned on as the sky reddened and dusk approached. The crowd on the Point thinned out a little as people made their way back to town for the parade, but plenty stayed who were not interested or were too drunk to bother moving.

Cassica and Shiara leaned against the metal safety barrier that ran round the cliff edge, and looked down on to the town. The main street was all lit up and strung with lamps in preparation. In the harbour, five dredging vessels rested at anchor. They were quiet today, their crews ashore, but in the morning they'd resume their work of sucking up silt from the harbour.

Already the docks had been reopened to medium-size vessels. In six months they'd have cleared the channel enough that barges would be able to make their way from Division Lake up the Copper River again. Plans were in place to fix up the docks and restore the main street in preparation for the trade and passengers they'd bring. The whole town was abuzz with talk of it. Grandparents told stories of how things used to be when Coppermouth was thriving, and people began to imagine how it might be again.

"Ain't so bad, is it?" Shiara said contentedly.

"No," said Cassica. "Ain't so bad at all."

She'd never thought she'd find herself back here. Once, this place had been a trap to her. But she'd been out in the world since then, and knew she could do so again if she wanted. She was no longer afraid of home, now it had no power to hold her. She chose to stay; that was the difference.

This whole thing was Shiara's idea, of course. She was always the planner, always the one Cassica relied on to help her do what was right. She was the one who suggested they sell the tickets and use the money to fix up Coppermouth.

"You gotta help them who helped you get where you are," she said. "And no matter where we go, Coppermouth's always gonna be where we're from."

At the time, Cassica hadn't really got what she was saying. She'd agreed because it was what Shiara wanted, and because she didn't have any better ideas. She knew her friend would have withered on Olympus, and she didn't want to go without her. She was sick of Anchor City and that whole corrupt scene. Home seemed a good idea, at least for a while.

But now they'd been back a few months, now they'd started to see the effects of Shiara's plan, Cassica understood. Coppermouth was a different place these days. People wore hope on their faces; she heard it in their talk. That was a gift Cassica and Shiara had given them, and it provided her with a deep sense of well-being, more profound and long-lasting than any victory on the racetrack. It made her happy.

Sometimes she thought of what might have been, how she could have been a Celestial. But she knew now that it was an illusion she hungered for, and she didn't think on it long. Real life was good enough.

Shiara's plan had gone further than dredging the harbour and installing Justices to protect the townsfolk from the highway gangs. A new water processing plant was on its way, so the kids wouldn't have to drink fazz every day. One of the old warehouses was being converted into a small hospital, with doctors and specialist equipment to treat respiratory diseases. Coppermouth was one of the worst places in Pacifica for dust lung, but soon they'd have the best survival rate too.

The dust had been the one thing that Cassica had really balked at. She didn't want to come home to a town that might kill her in thirty years. She didn't want to end up like her momma.

Shiara, as ever, had an answer. They hired engineers, geologists, environmentalists. They looked into this and that. In the end, they planted a forest up on the ridge: a whole new forest, a barrier miles thick, populated by hardy trees that could survive the harsh conditions. They were only saplings now, but in fifteen years they'd be catching almost seventy per cent of the killing dust that blew off the Rust Bowl towards Coppermouth. In thirty years, they'd be catching almost all of it.

Even that wasn't enough for Cassica; she needed something that would work right now. So they installed, at great expense, a system of magnetic poles along the ridge, which drew the invisible metal-eating nanobots from the air as they blew past and fried them with electricity. Without the nanobots, the dust was only dust. It wasn't the perfect defence, but it would do until the trees grew.

Thirty years, they said. In thirty years dust lung would be just a memory in Coppermouth.

Once, Cassica had dreamed of writing herself into legend. But legends like Rutterby LaKeyne were soon replaced, and no matter how bright they burned, they faded fast as soon as they were out of sight. What they'd done here, this was something better. Children would survive that wouldn't have otherwise. The elderly would live long enough to know their grandkids. Coppermouth would grow and prosper, and its people would prosper with it, generation after generation. Families would spread into the future that wouldn't have even started if Cassica and Shiara had gone to Olympus.

In time, they'd be forgotten, and their names would slip from history. By then, it wouldn't matter. Even if the distant descendants of Coppermouth never knew or cared who Cassica Hayle and Shiara DuCal were, they'd remember them by every breath in their lungs.

Cassica and Shiara watched *Celestial Hour* now and then. Dridley and Prua Cussens were proving surprisingly popular, though only as figures of fun. Still, as long as the viewers' eyes were upon them, it didn't matter why. Perhaps they'd make it on Olympus after all. Shiara liked that thought. "Everyone tryin' to give the people what they want all the time, and nobody knows what the hell it is!"

Of Harlan, they never heard another thing. They didn't know what that meant, and didn't much care.

Life at the auto shop had continued pretty much as before, after they got back. Blane refused to accept a cent from his fantastically rich daughter, being a man who liked to earn what he had. The only difference was that nowadays people didn't mind having their cars worked on by a girl. This particular girl, at least. The world wouldn't shift its attitudes overnight, but if a few minds got changed because of their success, that was a start as far as Shiara was concerned. And if one day she decided she wanted to take over the family business and run it herself, that was fine by everybody, including Creek, who'd rather be in the mountains anyway.

They left Maisie just as she was, in the corner of the auto shop where she'd always been. Shiara hadn't even touched her. They'd been too busy to drive her since their return, and they'd never be let near Maximum Racing again after what they'd done to Dunbery Hasp. Some private collectors offered vast sums of money to take her off their hands, but they refused. They could afford to be sentimental. Maybe someday they'd go racing again, but Cassica was surprised to find she really didn't miss it all that much. Perhaps she didn't need it like she once had.

"Parade's startin' soon," Shiara said distantly.

"You got time," said Cassica.

They made themselves plates of food and sat at a table while the party swirled around them. Shiara picked at hers without appetite.

"You're fretting," said Cassica through a mouthful of chicken.

Shiara shrugged.

"He's coming, don't worry."

"How'd you know?"

"Cause he'd be a fool if he didn't," she said. She pointed over Shiara's shoulder with a half-eaten chicken leg. "Besides, I see him over there."

Shiara jerked around in her seat. At the edge of the party, just by the road, Sammis Rye was standing by his car, searching the crowd. She raised a hand; he saw her and raised his own in greeting.

"I'm just gonna—"

Cassica waved her off. "Go see your boy. I got chicken."

"You gonna be alright without me?"

Cassica gave her a look.

"I'll catch you later, alright?" Shiara said.

Cassica pulled Shiara's plate towards her and winked. "I'll be here."

She watched her friend make her way over to Sammis. They kissed as they met, then got into the car and drove off, taking the road down to the town, where the parade would soon begin. Cassica smiled to herself and quietly ate her meal.

As they left, they passed beneath a billboard, lovingly restored and lit up against the gathering night. On it, pristine and new, a man out of legend raised a bottle to the town below, eternally young and eternally handsome.

In Coppermouth, at least, Rutterby LaKeyne was still drinking fazz.

ACKNOWLEDGEMENTS

This book, like any book, is the work of many hands, but I'd like to extend special thanks to Cressida Godding, for technical advice on race cars and the science of driving really, really fast. Any inaccuracies are likely due to the author's tendency to pick dramatic licence over precision.

ABOUT THE AUTHOR

Chris Wooding is the author of eighteen books that have been translated into twenty languages. His books have won the Nestlé Smarties Silver Award and the Bram Stoker Award, among others, and have been shortlisted for the Arthur C. Clarke Award and the CILIP Carnegie Medal. He also writes for TV and film, and his first graphic novel was published in 2012.

chriswooding.com